ELECTRIC
BLUE
Love

REBECCA JENSHAK

Rebecca Jenshak ♥

Copyright

Rebecca Jenshak
www.rebeccajenshak.com
Cover Design by Jena Brignola
Editing by JaVa Editing
Formatting by Love Affair With Fiction

Paperback ISBN: 978-0-9997820-2-6
Ebook ISBN: 978-0-9997820-3-3

PLAYLIST

Electric by Alina Baraz featuring Khalid
She Talks to Angels by The Black Crowes
Say It Ain't So by Weezer
Glycerine by Bush
Call Out My Name by The Weekend
I Can't Make You Love Me (cover) by Adele
Fast Car (cover) by Justin Beiber
You are the Reason by Calum Scott
Every Rose Has Its Thorns by Guns N' Roses
Love Lies by Khalid with Normani
I Like Me Better by Lauv
The Chain (cover) by Harry Styles
Zombies (cover) by Bad Wolves
Forever Blue by Chris Isaak
The Middle by Zedd, Maren Morris & Grey
Champagne Supernova (cover) by The Pretty Reckless
Everywhere by Fleetwood Mac
Stay (cover) by Thirty Seconds to Mars
Mine by Bazzi

SYNOPSIS

Court

Here's a thing I learned a long time ago... guys and girls don't think about relationships the same way. Especially in college. So, when I caught the girl sitting next to me on the plane reading a magazine article on how to get out of the friend zone, I did something I never do – I got involved.

One look into her electric blue eyes and the darkness inside of me faded.
Light and hope radiated from her like a neon sign.

Guys like me know how to get the girl, but we rarely get to keep them.

Bianca

Girls like me fade into the background. Nice, quiet, smart girls who don't wear trendy clothes. My friendship with Court started as an opportunity to get inside the male mind, but it turned into so much more.

His touch sent current coursing through my veins.
His kiss jolted my heart.

But here is something I learned a long time ago you can't force people to love you back. No matter how much you long for them.

"There is the heat of Love, the pulsing rush of Longing, the lover's whisper, irresistible – magic to make the sanest man go mad."
Homer, The Iliad.

PROLOGUE

Bianca

V OLTAGE, A NOUN. The difference in electric potential between two points.

I loved electricity. It fascinated me as a child – a magic force that could be felt, but not seen. Instead of jumping back and gasping in surprise when I accidentally zapped myself turning off the TV, like I'd seen others do, I reveled in it – giggling and shuffling my feet on the carpet, desperately wanting to recreate it.

As I'd gotten older, I obsessed over the other type of electrical shock. The kind that happened between two people that were meant to be together. While a cliché notion to some, I held out hope that electric potential could exist between two people the same way it could between two points. I sought it out – waiting for the other person who could set my potential in motion.

Maybe part of me wanted to believe in the same way I believed in voltage. It made the idea of navigating love and relationships so much simpler… waiting for the touch of my perfect match that would send shock waves to my very core. And how great would that feel to have this jolt to the heart, so you'd know *this* person would be worth whatever struggles or problems that stood in your way. A spark that would leave no doubts.

So, I sat in wait – tension coiled and ready to be transferred to the other point. To the person that would love me in an electric way.

I loved electricity, but I hadn't learned all there was to learn about it yet and my naivety made me stupid. In electricity and love. While I had been sitting in wait – hoping to find that perfect person whose touch sent a shock through my body, I had lost sight of a crucial part of voltage.

Current.

Because while voltage exists without current, current does not exist without voltage. I equated love with electric potential and the two points were me and my perfect match. I'd loved plenty of people but current… damn, the current that failed to arc. I guess what they say, you can't force love, is true because I'd tried and failed so many times to shuffle my feet and force an electrical shock – to make people love me - only to be met with disappointment when they failed to love me in return.

Why was it evading me when I was so filled with electricity I could practically set myself on fire? People were hard to understand and love, well, that was even harder. I gave up looking for my perfect match and went back to the science. It was easier – it had rules and laws that were clear and precise. I didn't give up on love, but I stopped trying to force it.

And with a hope that when the time was right love would

find me, I devoted my life to voltage and current.

CHAPTER ONE

Bianca

"No, NOT THAT one. The one next to it." My mother pointed to a large box on the top shelf of her closet. My brother, Donnie, awkwardly lifted the heavy cardboard and dropped it onto the bed.

"That it?" he asked and shifted anxiously toward the door.

She opened the flaps and as the pastel and floral prints peeked out, my mother grinned. "Yes. This is the one."

"Cool, I'm out of here. Leo and I are going to the park to shoot hoops."

Standing taller, my mother turned to face Donnie. "Did you make your bed and clean the hall bathroom?"

"Yes and yes," he muttered. "All my chores are done."

"Alright, say goodbye to your sister. And don't be out too late."

While Donnie wrapped one arm around my back and

leaned in – his version of a hug, my mom called for Leo. My brothers collided in the doorway.

Twins, but not identical, Leo and Donnie had the same build and height. Among their differences were hair styles and clothing. Donnie kept his hair cropped short and styled and preferred collared shirts and skinny jeans. Leo's hair and clothes were untidy, in a word, but he was attractive enough to pull it off in a carefree, too-cool-to-care-about-appearances way. Both sets of their light eyes, the same shade of laser blue as mine, turned to me.

"What's up?" Leo asked as he pulled a hoodie on over his head.

"I'm heading out in about an hour." I stepped forward and hugged Leo tightly. He hugged me back, using both arms – another noted difference between the twins. "Stay out of trouble." I pulled back and ruffled a hand through his long, unkept hair.

When we were alone, my mom started pulling out the clothes stashed away in the box.

"I finally went through my closet again and got rid of everything that doesn't fit or is too young for me." She rolled her eyes dramatically like the idea she was too old for anything was outrageous. At fifty-two, my mother was still beautiful. The last five years had brought more lines to her face and her body had softened, but the light in her eyes and the determined and confident way she held herself was timeless.

Her clothes, however, were not.

"These are just the spring and summer items," she said as she laid out a series of dresses that were circa the late nineties.

I smiled as I stepped toward the mountain of clothes. Lifting a long, pink sundress with large white and blue flowers, my mind skirted to our family photo album. A picture from my sixth-grade graduation where my mother wore this dress while sandwiched between me and my father flashed vividly in my mind.

Every piece of clothing told part of a story. Our story. And I inspected each article the same way, letting the memories of my mother standing beside me through important life events warm my insides.

Her scent clung to the fabrics and I lifted the dress to my face.

"Try this one on. It was my favorite." She tossed a shorter blue dress with another floral pattern my way.

While I pulled the dress on over my tank and leggings, my mother continued to pick through clothes and lay them on the bed for my inspection. Trying on my mother's worn and outdated clothes always transported me back to when I was younger. I'd sneak into her closet and rifle through each item, try on shoes or jewelry to make a complete outfit. I couldn't wait for the day I'd be able to fit into my mother's clothes and even though I'd been wearing her hand me downs for years now, it was still just as exciting every time she had new items for me.

"Hmm." She considered me and the dress. "It's a little big. You're more petite than I ever was, but I could take it in a bit in the waist and shoulders." Her hands pulled at the fabric to show me how it would look. "What do you think?"

I stared at my reflection in the floor length mirror of my parents' bedroom. She was right, it was a little big, but making do was practically my life's motto. "Not necessary. I'll wear a belt with it."

"It's really no big deal. The alterations are easy. I could pin it this afternoon and then mail it and any of the others you want."

With an exaggerated gasp, I gripped the skirt of the dress in both hands. "No way. I want to wear this one back to school today."

Her pleased smile was my reward.

I tossed a few other dresses over my shoulder and motioned toward the remaining clothes. "I'll put the rest in my closet for this summer. These will be perfect for work."

I leaned in and kissed her cheek before scooping everything into the box. I texted my roommate and best friend Tasha while I packed. A week in New York for Spring break had been amazing, but I missed my friend and our cozy apartment.

> **Me:** *My flight gets in at four. When do you get back?*
>
> **Tasha:** *Just got in! Can't wait to see you. I missed your face! Party at Todd's tonight so get your dancing shoes on! No excuses!*

Her excessive use of exclamations points was a good indicator of her state of mind. There would be no denying her tonight.

With a smile, I tucked my phone in my purse and glanced around my old room. The walls were a faded pink and Einstein and James Clerk Maxwell decorated the wall with their genius and inspiration. The girl that had pinned them to the wall had changed, but my love for math and science had not.

In just a few months I'd finally be able to move back to New York City and start applying everything I'd learned in school. I was ready, but I was beginning to feel the loss of my carefree college life. Not that it hadn't been hard work maintaining grades and keeping up with the twenty thousand other students all vying for top spots. Still, I was allowed a certain sheltering from the real world. I could forget that I was from a low-income family whose parents hadn't gone to college or held down fancy jobs. With Tasha as a roommate and friend, I felt normal for the first time in my life. She'd taken one look at me in our introduction to psychology class freshman year and told me she had my back. And she had. Still did.

"Well, I'm off," I announced as I entered the living room, pulling my suitcase behind me.

"Cookies for Tasha on the counter and bagels from Kossar's for you."

"Thank you."

"Got everything you need?" My father asked, standing from his favorite easy chair and pulling out his wallet. "You need cash for the taxi or for a soda at the airport?"

"Nah, I'm good." I stowed the food in the front compartment of my baggage and then practically threw myself into my mother's arms. "Thank you for everything. I'll see you in a few months."

Her eyes were misty as I pulled away, but she nodded and smiled proudly.

"It's always too quiet in this house after you leave," my father said as he squeezed me tightly and placed a kiss on top of my head. "We sure do miss you."

"Miss you too."

"And, uh, be sure to thank Tasha's father for arranging the ticket for you again. I hope it wasn't too much of an inconvenience."

I winced at the look that crossed my father's face. He was old school and proud. He didn't like the idea that someone else paid my way, but Tasha's dad was a big wig at one of the airlines so getting me on a flight home for Spring Break was no big deal – her words. I was grateful to not have to take the bus and my family was grateful to see more of me.

"I will. I promise."

After another round of hugs and loving glances, I stepped out into the city and inhaled deeply. I wanted to soak up every drop before I headed back to Connecticut. I thought about how little time I had left before I'd return for good as a career woman.

Had I lived enough in the four years I'd been gone? Had I experienced enough late nights and partying so that I wouldn't look back on this stage of my life with regret? I knew the answer to both of those questions was a resounding no. Practical and worried about the ramifications of getting too carried away, I'd lived cautiously.

Tasha's text about the party tonight was fresh on my mind. Maybe with the last months of college, my grades secure enough to relax a tiny bit, I could start spending more time on the extracurricular activities I'd neglected. Namely, dating.

Tasha would be on board and maybe with her help and some research of my own, I could think about a real boyfriend. Someone to celebrate the end of one chapter and the start of another. And I had just the someone in mind.

CHAPTER TWO

Court

Flying coach was bullshit. The crying babies and the cramped seats weren't even the worst of it, although admittedly not a perk. The real problem with sitting in the back of the plane was the comradery among the other passengers. In first-class no one tried to chat about the weather or ask the dreaded "Are you visiting or returning home?". No, in first class we sat in our large, reclining seats with plenty of leg room, cold drink on the tray table, laptop open, and we minded our own damn business.

I didn't sit in first class because of some ego trip where I needed to flaunt my better than average salary around. I did it because I preferred the silence. Also, I traveled so much it was almost always a free upgrade. Not today.

At least I'd been lucky enough to snag an aisle seat. Unlike the girl sitting in 8B. She didn't look up as I shrugged off my suit jacket and placed it with my carry-on bag in the overhead bin. She stared down at the magazine in her hands, a pen gripped in her mouth.

Pink lips were wrapped around the blue pen and her eyebrows were drawn together in deep concentration. The only indication I had that she knew her seat neighbor had arrived was the way she shielded the magazine with an elbow as I slid into my seat. Her stance reminded me of those smart kids who strategically placed their arm around the edge of the desk so that no one could cheat off their test answers.

Intrigued, I settled in and peeked over her arm and down at the glossy pages only catching the headline: *How to Get Out of the Friend Zone and Land the Guy of Your Dreams.* My eyes trailed up to the young woman so enthralled with such a ludicrous title and I studied her closer.

She was beautiful, but not in an in your face way. I definitely couldn't see her being banned to the friend zone. Her blonde hair was piled up in a bun on the top of her head, face clear and tanned even in the dreary March weather we'd been having. A faded, oversized floral dress was worn over leggings and sparkly shoes completed a look that was a cross between a preppy sorority girl and an artsy free spirit. She dressed in a way that told me she didn't know she was beautiful or if she knew, she just didn't care enough to conform to a style.

Judging by her reading material I was sold on the first option.

As the other passengers filed into their seats, I found myself intrigued and unable to focus on anything but 8B. I glanced over politely, hoping she'd look up and make eye contact so I could get a better look at her. No luck. She kept her focus on the garbage reading material in front of her as the cabin doors were closed and the flight attendants prepared for departure. When we'd reached twenty thousand feet and she still hadn't so much as side-eyed me, I gave up and pulled out my laptop to do some work.

I stared at the reports in front of me for five minutes, not reading a word, before I gave up and closed the laptop with a snap. She jumped, startled, and I turned to give her my attention. When her eyes finally found mine, I inhaled sharply.

Bright blue eyes were outlined with a heavy hand on the eyeliner or eyeshadow, whatever it was called, in a striking blue. I couldn't decide if was a fashion statement or a fashion disaster, but her eyes held mine captive and my lips parted to speak, only no words came out. We stared for a moment too long, neither saying a word, until she glanced down at her exposed reading and flipped it shut.

"There's no such thing as the friend zone with guys," I said, finally finding my voice.

"Excuse me?"

Clearing my throat, I watched her cheeks pink with embarrassment. "With women, they tend to put men into categories like that: friends, guys they're sort of interested in, guys they want to sleep with, guys they want a relationship with, etc. Men, we don't do that. We don't fit women into tidy little categories. We're either interested or we're not. And it changes constantly. What that article should have said was "How to Be More Than a One Night Fling" because that's what you really want, right? To be more than a random hookup or friends with benefits." I used my fingers to make quotations around the last phrase. "I never cared for that expression."

A tiny noise escaped her mouth as she stared at me with a shocked look on her face.

"Want my advice?"

"No," she blurted and shook her head, closing her eyes and turning her head to face forward. The captain's voice filtered through the speakers giving the usual spiel and I drummed my fingers on the top of my computer waiting for him to finish so I could apologize.

"I'm sorry. I didn't mean to embarrass you. You don't want to waste your time on a guy that makes you read trash articles like that. He's an idiot, for what it's worth."

"I wasn't reading for me," she said with a defensive tone. "I read all the articles."

"Nah, not like that you don't. You were glued to that thing. I've been trying to get your attention for the last half hour."

"You have?" she asked, scrunching up her face in a way that created a cute little wrinkle between her eyebrows.

"Tell me about the article. What was their advice?"

Clutching the magazine to her chest, she looked up at me like she was gauging the seriousness of my question. I leaned back, giving her my full attention.

"It said not to hang out with a man you're interested in alone unless it's a scheduled date. No texting or phone calls except to make plans until after the third official date. No sexting, obviously."

"Obviously?"

"Well yeah, the article suggests it makes it easy for a guy to get what he wants without having to work for it."

"True, but he's probably not putting you in the friend zone if he's staring at your boobs on his phone."

"He's probably not thinking of me as more than a hook up either."

"Depends on the rack." I grinned. "But fair enough. No

sexting. Any others?"

She hesitated before answering, looking away. "Date men in his circle of friends."

"Who wrote this trash?" I asked, grabbing the magazine and flipping to the article finding the rules she'd just mentioned. *Dirty little trick: date his friends. When he sees that other men want you, he'll stop seeing you as a friend.*

"You want to know how to get out of the friend zone or not be a random hook up? Stop reading articles like this. This woman probably lives alone with fifty hamsters."

"Hamsters?"

"Yeah, I know people always say cats, but I like cats."

Smiling, she seemed to relax a bit. "You seem pretty sure. What are your credentials and why should I listen to you?"

"How old are you?"

"Twenty-two."

"College?"

She nodded.

"I'm thirty-four and I'm not sure that advice would even work on me. Look, guys your age are preoccupied with parties and fun. You're asking him to work for it when there's practically a buffet line of other, delectable options."

She scoffed.

"Look, I'm certainly no expert on relationships, but I know that," I handed the magazine back to her, "is crap."

"Okay, I give. What do you think a girl that finds herself in this situation should do?"

"Well without knowing the situation exactly, I'd say for starters this girl should find excuses to hang around the guy as much as possible. If you aren't around, he'll find someone else. And I don't mean hang out together playing Xbox in sweat pants, although, something tells me you could pull that off," I said, letting my eyes graze over her again. "You want to dress to get his attention – dresses or skirts, high heels, hair down, just a touch of makeup. And, absolutely do not sleep with his friends. It might make him jealous, but it also makes you just another easy lay."

"That's it?"

The unbelieving look on her face caused a laugh to rumble in my chest. "It's not a perfect list, there are always other considerations like personal preferences and chemistry, but we're simple creatures."

"A woman being in the same room as you, dressed nice, who hasn't slept with your friends. That's all it takes to get your attention?"

"My attention? Nah, but I'm not your target audience. Contrary to popular belief, we men do mature as we age."

"What does it take for a woman to get your attention?"

Surprised by the question, I thought for a moment not coming up with any good answers. "I'll keep you posted when I figure it out. So, tell me about the guy."

She hesitated for just a moment. "His name is Todd. We run in the same circles, have mutual friends, usually end up at the same parties. We've become friends, I guess, over the years."

"You guess?"

"I mean not friends exactly. We don't braid each other's hair and watch Gossip Girl, but we have some classes together and we've gotten to know each other over the years. We flirt, we always hang out at parties – it's like we've been dancing around each other for years."

"Interesting," I said wondering why this guy hadn't made a move. "He's never tried to get you in bed?"

"What?" She looked around like she was worried about

the sweet old ladies in front of us hearing our conversation. "No, of course not."

"Sorry, I forgot people aren't that up front in our twenties. Let me re-phrase, does he hit you up with texts at the end of the night or put himself near you when it's time for everyone to leave?"

Squirming in her seat, her unease was apparent. So was my answer. I had no doubt the guy in question was into her and was making a play, however subtle and indirect, to sleep with her. A heaviness settled on my chest at the thought of this beautiful and inexperienced young woman fumbling into bed with some jackass.

"You sure you want to be with Ted? He sounds like an idiot."

"*Todd*. And yes, he's great. He comes from a well-respected family, he's captain of the squash team, pre-med…" Her voice trailed off.

Nodding, it was my turn to squirm. I disliked the guy more with every new tidbit she threw my way. I knew Todd's type. Arrogant, rich, entitled. I'd dealt with them my entire life.

"Well," I cleared my throat. "A guy like Tim is going to have expectations and pressure to be with a certain kind of woman, at least one he plans to keep around long-term. Keep the clothing tasteful – no tube tops or miniskirts and nothing like whatever it is you have on now. No offense, but where did you get that dress?" I didn't wait for an answer, but the flush that had gathered in her cheeks spread down her neck.

I continued, "He's probably used to women fawning over him, so don't throw yourself at him, but stay in his line of vision and have something ready to say when he does approach you. Mention his last match or ask about his future plans. Be interested in him and let him see that there's more to you than a pretty face. You want to be good enough to introduce to his parents, but sexy enough to make him the envy of all his buddies. Give him a little physical contact – nothing too aggressive, just light touching to show you're interested."

"What if that doesn't work?"

"It'll work."

"How can you be so sure?"

I shrugged and bit back the obvious. He'd be a fool to let this girl get away from him.

"What's your name, Tad's girl?"

"Bianca. And his name is Todd."

"Nice to meet you, Bianca. Court." I offered her my hand which she took and lightly squeezed.

"What do you do, Court?" She withdrew her hand and pointed at the laptop still closed on my tray table.

"Risk assessment. I help companies identify potential risks that could lower cash flow or create higher insurance rates and then implement plans and strategies so neither of those things happen. Not as exciting as pre-med." I cut myself off, feeling ridiculous for feeling less than some egg head who, statistically speaking, was not very likely to actually become a doctor.

"You're travelling for work, or…?"

"Yeah." I nodded. "I live in New York, but I fly out every month or so to see a client. What were you doing in the city?"

"I went home for Spring break to visit my family."

"From New York City and you didn't go to NYU? Shocking."

"I wanted a more rigorous engineering program. Plus, my parents wanted me to get out on my own."

"Impressive. And an engineer, huh? Beauty *and* brains."

The speakers crackled, and the captain welcomed us to Connecticut while I watched Bianca bite her lip and wring her hands.

"You seeing Tom tonight?"

She raised her eyebrows at my failure to say the right name but didn't correct me this time. "Yeah, there's a party to celebrate everyone coming back from Spring break."

"Don't wear that," I said dryly, motioning at her outfit and wishing I could see her done up to impress.

She pulled out her cell and held it with two hands tapping furiously with both thumbs. "No tube tops, no miniskirts, have something to say, light touches..."

"You're taking notes?"

"I'm a good student."

Pulling out my card, I handed it to her, our fingertips touched as I held on longer than necessary. "How about you just call me if you need a refresher course."

CHAPTER THREE

Bianca

WINGING MY KEYS in the general direction of the kitchen counter, I kicked off my heels and growled in exasperation. And then winced as my childish voice echoed back to me in the empty apartment.

I pulled the conservative black dress up over my head and tossed it in the laundry basket still sitting in the living room filled with unfolded clean clothes. An annoying flicker of hope built inside me at the sound of multiple incoming texts. As quickly as it had built, it was gone when Tasha's name appeared on the screen.

> **Tasha:** *Where did you go?*
>
> **Tasha:** *Todd's an ass. You're hot. Don't let him ruin your night. Come back out!*

Another text appeared as I scoffed at the idea of leaving the apartment again.

> **Tasha**: I'm staying at Lance's tonight. Netflix and pizza when I get home tomorrow?
>
> **Me**: Sounds great.

Sighing, I slumped into the couch feeling sorry for myself and irrationally angry at the world. An image of the beautiful girl in a mini-skirt and heels so high I was afraid she'd break an ankle that had sashayed around the party on Todd's arm made me clench my jaw and I stood quickly, knowing exactly who to lash out on.

Walking back to the counter where my purse lay, I rummaged through it pulling out the business card I'd stashed this afternoon. I held it in a shaky hand and without allowing myself to think beyond dialing, I punched in the numbers on my phone.

On the third ring, my anger at Todd started to feel irrational and I breathed a sigh of relief that the man I'd late night dialed hadn't answered. I pulled the phone away from my ear and reached to hit End as a gravelly voice answered.

"Hello?"

Fumbling, I hit the video button instead of End and with a screech I came face to face with the handsome stranger I'd left at baggage claim.

It was dark, but I could make out his face in the light from his cell and the hint of a smirk appeared as he stared back at me.

"Sexy bra, 8B. Please tell me you aren't calling me from Tim's place to tell me my advice worked. You could have waited until morning."

I screeched again and sat the phone down with a clunk on the counter and stepped back covering my mostly exposed chest with both arms.

His laugh rang through the silence of my apartment and I picked up the phone and held it close to my face to keep him from seeing anything else.

"No, I am *not* calling from Todd's apartment because *Todd* is at the party with another woman. The kind of woman *you* told me not to be – ridiculously short skirt, loads of makeup, throwing herself all over him. She broke all the rules and he picked her."

Letting out a deep breath, I finally forced myself to take a moment and chill. Court stared back at me through the screen. His mocking smile was gone, and his eyebrows pulled together with what looked like anger or concern.

"I'm sorry, were you sleeping? I should go. I am so sorry I called."

I was ready to crawl into bed and pull the covers over my head.

"Shit, *I'm* sorry 8B."

"8B?"

"The seat you were sitting in – on the plane."

"Oh." I furrowed my brow and thought back to the plane. I'd purged the minor details of the flight, like seat assignment, to memorize every word of the advice and wisdom he'd given me about Todd. Some good that had done.

He ran a hand through his dark hair, bringing my attention back to him and to the muscular bicep crooked up behind his head. He moved, the background behind him changing until light flooded around him and I could clearly see his five o'clock shadow and disheveled hair.

"Tom is an idiot," he mumbled and sat down in a red arm chair. "Give it to me from the top."

The alcohol and humiliation had made me vulnerable and so I did. I told him everything. I left nothing out. From the conservative, yet tight, black dress I'd worn to the way I'd sought him out and complimented Todd on a great season while standing so close my arm brushed up against his. I'd thought everything was going great. That my attention to detail was paying off and Todd was finally going to make a move.

"We were having a good time, flirting and laughing, until she brazenly came up, snaked a hand around his arm, and asked him to play flip cup," I muttered with annoyance dripping from my voice. I wasn't really mad at the girl. I couldn't blame her for having good taste in men, but it still stung that he'd walked off with her and left me standing alone.

"Mmm," he responded like he was carefully picturing the scene.

"What?"

He was quiet for a moment and my confidence in the way I'd played things with Todd dwindled with each second of dead air. "You did exactly what I told you. You're a good student."

"But?"

"But you forgot to have fun."

"Excuse me?"

He looked at me through the phone like I was a fragile child which is exactly what I felt like.

"Let me ask you something, why didn't you ask him to play flip cup?"

My brows pulled together. "Because I was trying to have

a conversation with him."

"Couldn't you do both?"

I sat there for a moment, considering his question. Why was this so hard?

A low chuckle brought my attention back to the screen. When Court laughed, it lit up his whole face and made him look young enough that I could almost picture him drinking cheap beer out of plastic cups on a Sunday night instead of holed up in a hotel room getting ready for work the next day.

"Just tell me this, 8B, if Taz hadn't been at the party tonight, would you have been over playing flip cup?"

"I went to the party to see him, not to get wasted."

"And there is the problem. However unperceptive we may be, men are drawn to women who are having fun and even more so if they want to have that fun with us. We're like little kids hopped up on sugar looking for the next rush of excitement."

Walking into my room, suddenly feeling older than I ever had, I threw myself onto my bed.

"I'm terrible at this. I'm going to die alone in a house full of hamsters." I grinned despite my despondent state when I realized I had swapped cats for hamsters like Court had done earlier. I liked that he liked cats. It said something about a man to admit they liked cats.

"Nah." He shook his head. "You just need to forget about what's his face and have some fun."

"Fun," I repeated the word back as I already began to dismiss the idea that it was that simple.

"Yeah, that thing most college kids live for."

My stomach dropped. Fun wasn't exactly my default setting. "I'm not some bimbo, party hopping, college girl."

"Those things aren't mutually exclusive."

"I'm here on scholarship. I can't afford to screw around."

"I get it. I know all about hustling to get by, but you can have a little fun and still be responsible. At least I think you can. Admittedly my college days are a bit of a drunken haze."

"Why am I not surprised to hear that?"

He grinned, a boyish charm overtaking his face again. "What do you want with this guy anyway? You're young. You're supposed to date around, kiss a lot of frogs or whatever that cheesy saying is."

"I don't want frogs."

He nodded, and his features transformed into a serious regard. "Alright if we're gonna do this, I'm going to need more intel. Tell me everything you know about Tonto."

"We?" I asked, ignoring that he'd gotten Todd's name wrong. Again.

"Clearly you need my wisdom and male perspective."

"And what's in it for you?"

"Let's just call it a service project. It's been awhile since I've helped anyone but myself."

Too tired to question the sanity of letting a near stranger help me, I did exactly what he'd asked. I told him nearly everything I knew about Todd. At two in the morning when my eyes were so heavy I couldn't keep them open any longer, we finally said goodnight and I went to bed exhausted, but hopeful.

The next afternoon, I was making a list of all the things I'd already learned from Court when Tasha got home. We decided on tacos instead of pizza and then settled in front of the TV to watch a cheesy horror film. Tasha had a thing for them and I cared more about her company than what we watched to protest.

"Have you heard from Todd?" she asked around a

mouthful of taco.

I shook my head and finished chewing before I spoke. "No, nothing."

"He's such an idiot." She rolled her eyes. "I don't know what his problem is."

"He's not an idiot."

Tasha gave me an "Are you kidding me?" look. "I know you two are friends, or whatever, but he's *acting* like an idiot. Either that or he's purposely stringing you along. Even I can see that he's totally into you. I don't understand why he doesn't make a move. Maybe you should take matters into your own hands."

"What, like ask him out?"

"Why not?"

"No way. I'm not going to be one of those girls that throws myself at him. And not because I'm universally opposed to women asking men out, but that's exactly the kind of women he's used to, and I see how easily he discards them. I don't want to be a one-night stand."

"So, what's the plan?" she asked.

Tasha knew me too well. Of course, I had a plan.

"Well, I found a sort of mentor?"

Her eyebrows lifted.

"So," I started, shifting so my feet were under me on the couch, "on the flight back yesterday I was sitting next to a guy and somehow we got on the topic of dating and I briefly mentioned my current frustration with Todd and he gave me some advice." I avoided her eyes, certain she could see right through the sugar-coated version of the story.

"That is totally random but continue. What was his advice?"

"He told me to make a point to talk to him at the party

and to dress sexy but not slutty."

"And? That's it?" she asked as unbelievingly as I had.

"That was pretty much it, but I sort of drunk dialed him last night after it didn't work."

"Oh my God, you called some strange man you met on a plane? How did you get his number? This is sounding more screwed up than this movie." She motioned toward the TV and then shoved the last bite of taco into her mouth.

I stood and crossed the room to my planner. I pulled out his business card and handed it to her. "He gave me this on the flight and told me to contact him if I needed more advice."

"This is insane," she said, but smiled as she read his name. "Court Adams, Senior Risk Analyst at Harrison and Mac. Fancy."

"He seemed nice. Anyway, I made a total ass of myself, but we ended up talking most the night – or morning, rather."

"This guy has got to be into you."

"No, it's not like that. I think he just feels sorry for me or something. I told him about Todd and he gave me some rules."

Tasha snorted. "Rules?"

"More like principles, I guess." I shook my head. "Mock all you want, but I am going to win Todd over by following these," I said holding up my planner.

"Let me see that."

Tasha flipped it open to the bookmarked page. "Number one, there is no such thing as the friend zone." She peeked up at me with a smirk, but continued, "Number two, men just want to have fun."

I pointed at my planner. "See that's where I went wrong

last night, I was so focused on him I forgot to have fun."

"What's been your excuse the last four years?"

"Hardy har," I said. "It's an area I need improvement on, I know, but you know how hard I've had to work to be here. Plus, I get sort of goal focused, even with men." I gave her a small smile that she returned with a laugh.

"I get it. All I'm saying is I agree with mister mentor on number two." She settled back into the couch, planner and business card still laid out in her lap. "Tell me more about *this* guy," she said motioning her head to Court's business card.

"I don't know much. He said he was thirty-four. He lives in New York and is here for business. He talked a little about his job, but we mostly talked about Todd and me."

"Is he good looking?"

I bit my lip. Was he good looking? It was like asking if New York was the greatest city in the world. He had been devastatingly handsome in his business suit and even better looking last night when I'd woken him shirtless and disheveled.

"He's nice looking for an older guy." I don't know why I threw the last part in. Court wasn't just good looking for an older guy, he was good looking *because* of his age. He had that mature look men got when they settled into their height and build and started taking care of themselves instead of downing beers and fast food. Court put every man on campus to shame in the looks department, and the men here were not your typical pimply faced, freshmen fifteen, college kids.

Tasha shot me a look of impatience to continue. "He's tall – I'd guess over six feet, dark, thick hair – the kind that sticks up but looks like it was styled to do so, and hazel eyes."

The smile on Tasha's face was wide and knowing.

"What, I'm trying to paint a picture." I tossed a throw pillow at her, which she dodged easily.

"Oh, I'm getting the picture. It sounds like you met a total hottie."

I rolled my eyes. I wasn't going down this rabbit hole. If Tasha thought I was harboring some secret crush on Court she would be unrelenting in her peer pressure to call him.

"I guess so, but I'm telling you it wasn't like that," I said in the most convincing voice I could muster.

Tasha gave a half shrug and shut the planner with Court's card tucked inside. She handed it back, but watched me carefully as she said, "If you say so."

Hugging it to my chest, I let myself imagine a world where someone like Court was interested in someone like me. But the idea was so ludicrous I couldn't even fathom it. No, Court wasn't into me, but just maybe, he could help me secure a future with Todd.

CHAPTER FOUR

Court

I RESISTED THE urge to press snooze. Three hours of sleep was all I'd gotten thanks to Bianca's late-night call. I wasn't exactly sorry, even though it was gonna be a long ass day. Talking to her made me feel like a hell of a lot better man than I actually was. I wanted to soak up all her sweet innocence.

Listening to her talk about how great Todd was – yeah, I knew his name – made me hate him even more. Todd was the kind of guy that breezed through life getting everything handed to him. He walked the yellow, brick fucking road to Oz while the rest of us clawed our way for every scrap of success. I sensed that Bianca and I had that in common. What she wanted with a tool like Todd was beyond me.

After I'd dressed in gym shorts and a long-sleeved t-shirt and pulled on my socks and sneakers, I decided to hit the pavement instead of the hotel gym. Cold air burned my lungs as I breathed in the crisp, early morning Connecticut air, shocking my tired limbs awake.

As it always did, my brain turned off and my body took over. Exercising, running in particular, was an outlet. While my muscles did the work, my brain relaxed. I was at peace here.

It's not to say I didn't think at all, but instead of the usual clutter – the memories, the to-do list that stayed front and center reminding me what had to be done, and the sense of urgency to stay one step ahead of whatever ghosts lurked – it all became white noise.

When I ran, my brain functioned in snapshots – fleeting images that even when not pleasant, were gone before they could cause any real damage.

Fleeting images.

The report I'd finished for Mr. Sterling.

A picture-perfect family smiling from the front of their beach house.

The steak and vegetables I'd had for dinner last night.

Bianca in her ugly flower dress hunched over a magazine.

Bianca's fiery expression as she'd stood in that lacy, black bra.

Bianca pulling her bottom lip behind her teeth as I told her my thoughts on Todd.

I'd turned on to College Street and was passing the university buildings before I'd realized I'd run directly where my brain was wandering. Toward Bianca.

She hadn't called me from a sorority or dorm room, so I waved off the notion that she lived in campus housing, but knowing she'd walked these same streets made me really stop and think about Bianca and what her life was like here.

I slowed as I passed the courtyard. It was too early and too cold to be filled with students, but I could picture it.

Bianca and I might have some things in common, but the simple fact that she fit in here, at a friggin' ivy league school, divided us in a way that had me resenting my life all over again.

Turning around, I picked up the pace, running back to the hotel until my legs and chest ached.

Stifling a yawn, the nagging reminder of Bianca stayed with me while I listened to Allen Sterling lavish his fifth wife over lunch. Still tanned from a recent trip to Barcelona, they were very much in the honeymoon stage. The only stage Allen seemed capable of.

In his mid-fifties, Allen had been born into money and a company that he tirelessly needed backing out of trouble. I guess I shouldn't complain since he kept me in a job, but from someone who had pushed their own luck pretty damn far, Allen was borderline insane with how he risked his company and money by marrying women half his age without a prenup. Even without a law degree, I knew that was a risky move. Even more volatile, he paraded each one into his company directly by making them his assistant. What made a man so insecure that he needed to stay tied down and keep his wives with him twenty-four-seven?

"What about you Court, do you have a girlfriend back in the city?"

I shook my head in answer to his question and to the idea that I'd tell him shit about my life even if I did. "No, no girlfriend."

"Smart man," Allen said and received a playful swat from his newest wife. Margaret was a curvy, bottle blonde. I didn't know what kind of life she'd been living before she'd sold her soul to become Mrs. Sterling, but I wondered if she'd still think it was worth it in six months or a year when he kicked her out for a younger model.

"But seriously, a successful young man living in New York should have women lined up. You're not batting for the other team, are you?"

Brushing off his less than tactful insult to an entire population of gay men, I answered as vaguely as possible. "I guess I just haven't slowed down enough to meet the right woman."

I wasn't about to get into my preference of casual relationships with a serial monogamist and a client, least of all Allen Sterling.

Margaret perked up. "Ooooh, you know Isla is single and –"

Lifting a hand, I cut her off before she could go any further. "I appreciate it, but I'm not interested in dating right now."

Sometime over the past decade, I'd become a man that couldn't just be single without a barrage of questions or setup attempts. Being a single thirty-four-year-old man was no longer socially acceptable. With only a slight pout of her lips, Margaret nodded and sat back into her seat as Allen dove back into business.

Margaret looked as dissatisfied with the change in conversation as I felt relieved.

"You're coming back next month," he stated rather than asked but I nodded in confirmation anyway.

"Yeah, I'll be back to do a comparison and make sure everything is moving in the right direction."

"The end of the month?" Margaret sat forward. "You simply must attend our reception at the Omni." She placed her elbows on the table and without pausing or giving me a second to respond added, "We won't hear of you not attending."

With a chuckle Allen pulled his bride closer. "Might as well agree. She usually gets what she wants one way or another."

"I thought you two already had a reception," I said by way of bypassing the invitation entirely.

"We did, but Margaret's family in West Virginia wasn't able to make it so we're having another one now that her sister is out of rehab."

Margaret's face paled in shock as if she was horrified that Allen had given away so much. I wanted to tell her not to bother being appalled, the way she covered herself in designer labels and expensive jewelry like armor made it clear she'd come from a less than prim and proper upbringing.

"So, you'll come?" she pleaded in a tone I'd wager she used to get her way with Allen.

I got her. We were more alike than she knew.

"I'd love to."

As soon as the bill was paid, Allen and Margaret made their excuses and I caught a cab back to the airport.

Bianca's first text came just as I'd started to doze off in the back of the taxi.

Bianca: Emergency! 911!

Without thinking I called her, more eager to hear her voice than I was worried. Bianca didn't strike me as the dramatic type, but something told me I wasn't the person she'd be calling for help if she was in real danger.

"Hi," her breathy voice came through after the second ring.

"Are you all right?" We were pulling up to the airport

and I cupped my free hand over the mic on my phone and instructed the taxi to the right airline stop.

"I'm sorry to bother you again."

"Are you all right?" I asked again. I wanted to see her face, her surroundings, to get an idea of what the problem was.

"Yes. It's just he asked me to hang out tonight. I mean it's a bunch of people – a small party, but he asked *me* to come," she said in a rushed whisper.

Words stuck in my throat. I wasn't nearly as shocked by her news as I was disappointed that this douchebag had her so excited with an invite to a party. He really didn't deserve her.

"Court? Are you there?"

I cleared my throat. "Yeah, sorry, I'm just getting to the airport. That's fantastic. Congratulations 8B, you got exactly wat you wanted. Looks like you didn't need my advice after all."

"You're leaving already?" the panic in her voice was more pronounced.

"Yeah, it was just a one-day trip."

"But I need you."

The thought of her needing me loosened a smile. "Finally decided Tom was a schmuck and decided to go for someone a little older and way better looking?"

"Be serious," she screeched. "What am I gonna do?"

"I don't understand the problem. I thought this is what you wanted?"

"It is, but –"

"But?" I prompted.

"What if I screw it up?"

"You'll be fine. He wouldn't have asked you out if he

wasn't interested. Men are straightforward that way."

"It's just… I don't know how to just go hang. What do I wear? Do I show up on time or be fashionably late? Should I bring a friend with me?"

The exasperation and candor in her voice was authentic and charming. Todd had better not be fucking with her. I'd track his pretentious ass down if he hurt her. I didn't make a habit of getting myself emotionally involved with people like this, so to say I had no clue where these protective thoughts were coming from was an understatement.

"Don't overthink it."

"Too late," she muttered.

Adjusting my tie, I checked my watch before I asked, "What time did he tell you to show up?"

"Nine."

"Seven hours is plenty of time," I reassured her and shook my head. Anything was possible in seven hours. "Show me the options."

"I was planning on wearing jeans. I think it'll be pretty casual."

"Show me," I instructed.

"Like you want me to snap a picture of my jeans?"

"I want you to send me a picture of you *in* the jeans."

"Oh, okay. Hold on," she said.

The faint rustling of clothing being taken off and discarded was followed by silence. My free hand laid restlessly on my knee and I tapped my thumb. How long did it take to put on a pair of jeans and take a picture?

"Okay, I sent it," she said breathlessly as a text alert pinged in my ear.

Pulling my phone away from my ear, I opened the message and inhaled. Letting the breath out slowly, I drank in her long, denim-clad legs. The picture cut off at her bare navel and dark jeans slung low on her hips and hugged them so tightly all I could think was how much I wanted to turn them inside out. The young girl I'd met in a frumpy, faded dress that hid her body and made her blend into the background was gone.

The taxi stopped in front of the American Airlines departure doors and I exited the car before I held the phone back to my ear.

"Are there other options?"

"Oh," she said, sounding surprised and then determined. "I knew those were no good. They're so tight I can barely bend over."

Fuck me, now I was picturing her bending over in those painted on denim jeans.

"You look great. I just want to see all the options. Shirts too. Something that shows just a bit of skin."

"Alright, give me –"

"Actually, I just arrived at the airport, so I need to hang up. Text me the options." I had nearly two hours until the plane boarded, but I needed to get off the phone before I said something stupid.

"Are you sure? My roommate is going to be home soon, I can ask her."

"I'm sure. Send me the options."

"Okay," she said and let out a small huff like the feat of getting dressed was more than she could manage.

"You're hot 8B. Stop stressing. Now get to work finding an outfit. There's still hair and shoes to iron out."

CHAPTER
FIVE

Bianca

Court said I was hot.

I used his words as the boost I needed while I picked through every article of clothing in my closet. Despite the fact that I lived in mostly hand me-down clothes, my closet was filled with lots of newer, stylish, and more expensive clothes, tags still intact.

Tasha liked to shop. More specifically she liked to use her dad's Visa card to somehow try to get back at him for not taking a more active interest in her life. I wasn't sure her approach was working since they hadn't seen each other all semester, but she shopped, and I often ended up on the receiving end of expensive, spur of the moment purchases.

I wasn't sure if she bought the items for herself and then felt too guilty to actually wear them or if gifting them to me was her subtly trying to get me out of my mother's old dresses. I appreciated the gesture either way. Plus, she had really good taste. Fashion, art – she had an eye for all of it.

I tried on three more pairs of jeans hoping one of these would get the Court seal of approval. The first pair was a light denim with holes at the knees that I paired with an off the shoulder black shirt. It was the most me of the outfits, but since the whole point of this was going out of my comfort zone, I figured this one wasn't it.

I went sexier with the second outfit. The black jeggings were tighter than the first pair of jeans Court had vetoed, but I pulled on a low cut red top that I hoped made me look sexy and didn't put me into the *trying too hard* class.

Last, I tried on a pair of pink skinny jeans that Tasha had bought just last week and pulled on a crème boat necked shirt. It was the most expensive looking outfit of the three and a quick glance at the tag told me why.

"$200 for a shirt?!" I said aloud to my reflection.

Pulling at the hem, I fidgeted but wasn't all together unhappy with how I looked. It felt like a compromise of who I was and how Court said I should look.

Stripping down and placing the outfits neatly on my bed, I sent Court the photos I'd snapped of me in all three options. I squeezed my eyes shut and let out a little squeal after pressing send. I was nervous.

His approval meant more than it probably should. I wasn't totally convinced that even with his help I could capture Todd's attention for more than one night, but I was pretty confident that if Court couldn't help me – no one could. He oozed self-confidence and there was no way a guy as good looking as him didn't have his pick of women.

While I waited for his response, I pulled out my laptop and entered his name in the search engine. Google returned almost no more information than I already knew about Court.

A link to his bio on his company's website affirmed that he was a NYU graduate who worked in risk management. The picture was a standard headshot with a grey background that should have made him look like all the other middle-aged men in suits. It didn't.

I pulled up his Facebook account next. His profile picture hadn't been changed in over two years, but it was a candid. He wasn't looking at whoever had taken the photo, but he smiled with a beer in hand wearing a white button-down shirt that was open at the neck. Everything else was locked down, but I had a suspicion that even if I had full access, his profile wouldn't provide me with the nitty gritty details I was after. Who was Court Adams?

My phone pinged from where it lay on the comforter beside me and I picked it up with greedy hands, both anxious and dreading his feedback.

Court: Option 3. Wear your hair up.

I let out a small sigh of relief that he hadn't chosen the most revealing outfit because I was pretty certain I'd never be able to convince myself to leave the house wearing it. I let my fingers hover over the message trying to decide how to respond. I wanted to know more about Court, but I treaded carefully, keeping the attention on our task at hand in hopes to gain some details about him.

Me: How often do you travel to CT?

I clutched the phone in my hands, eager for his response. The three dots indicating he was typing appeared.

> *Court*: *About once a month. What shoes are you wearing?*

I snapped a quick photo of the three shoe options I'd laid out. My sparkly flats, a brown sandal, and a pair of death trap five-inch platform heels that Tasha convinced me to buy last year telling me and I quote "those shoes are every man's wet dream".

> *Court*: *Wear the sparkly flats.*
>
> *Me*: *Seriously?*
>
> *Court*: *Seriously. The brown shoes are boring and the only place those other shoes belong are around a guy's shoulders.*

I blushed. Hard.

> *Court*: *Besides, you want to be comfortable and I have a feeling those shoes are your happy place.*
>
> *Me*: *They're my favorite.*
>
> *Court*: *They suit you.*

I liked that he thought so. It gave me a false confidence that maybe he somehow got who I really was and was going to help me without trying to make me into someone I wasn't. I was perfectly happy with who I was inside, I just wanted Todd to give me a chance to show him that person in some flashy new clothing.

CHAPTER
SIX

Court

I WAS RESTLESS throughout the flight. An hour with no communication to Bianca, and I was antsy. Irritated. Nervous. I'd helped her get all done up to impress and instead of feeling good about what I'd done, I was a half-hoping Todd was too much of a prick to see what was right in front of him.

He'd invited her there for a reason though. A reason I was sure had everything to do with getting her naked.

My irritation sent an unsettling cloud over me so when I made it back to New York I kept my phone off and grabbed dinner before heading to my apartment.

When I finally dropped my overnight bag in the entryway of my apartment, I allowed myself to turn on my cell. It was quarter past nine and for as little as I'd learned about Bianca, I knew she was already at Todd's. She was a girl that arrived on time. Probably five minutes early with a gift for the host.

Fucking Todd didn't deserve her.

Or maybe I was projecting. I didn't deserve someone like her and that made my chest constrict with emotions I hadn't tapped into for years.

I opened our text message conversation and flipped back to the pictures she'd sent. I'd chosen her outfit based on what I knew about Todd, but it wasn't the one that I went back to.

No, I wanted Bianca just as she'd been the day I met her. Fun. Carefree. A beautiful mess. I stared at her unsmiling face. She'd taken the photo with her phone using a full-length mirror in what appeared to be her bedroom. She looked down at the camera in her hand, but the image that reflected back in the mirror was a casual Bianca in worn jeans and an off the shoulder shirt.

Her easy beauty was hard to turn away from. I liked that she was more comfortable this way as much as I hated that she was trying to win over someone that needed to see her another way in order to get his attention. And I was helping.

My jealousy gave way to a genius idea and I typed out a quick text to Bianca with a smug grin. She was gonna be pissed as hell. I'd gotten a glimpse of her fiery side the night Todd had dropped her for another girl and I figured my instructions were going to go over about as well.

When she didn't immediately reply, I typed out another text to Leika to see if she could meet up for a drink. She responded immediately, and I hurried out of my apartment to meet her.

Leika and I had spent four years in the same foster home and she was as close to family as I had. She understood me. Understood who I was then and who I am now. She'd been one of the few from our circle, besides me, to go on to college and hold on to a full-time job. We were the lucky ones. The kids who had been blessed with enough grit and determination to not let our shitty past determine the rest of our lives. At least not in a way that was obvious.

My phone pinged, and I smiled before I even read the message.

> **Bianca**: LEAVE? Why? I just got here.
>
> **Me**: Be polite, but vague. Tell him you're sorry but you have somewhere else you need to be. And this is important... say something like 'we should do this again sometime' and then get out of there.

When my phone rang two minutes later I was expecting it. It didn't stop a victory grin from spreading across my face though.

"Hello?" I answered like I wasn't expecting her.

"What the hell?" Bianca's voice came in a raspy whisper.

"Did he look disappointed?"

"I think confused is a better word. I am too. What was that all about?"

"You don't want to be too available."

"I thought you said I needed to be around or he'd find someone else."

"That's true, but it needs to be a little bit of a challenge. He should be texting you any minute."

"I don't think so. Todd doesn't do that."

I rolled my eyes at the shit this dude had been filling her head with. "He doesn't text? Bullshit. Maybe he says that as an out for blowing people off, but everyone texts when it suits them."

"I feel like I just completely screwed up any shot I had with him. What if that was my one chance?"

"Trust me, 8B."

The line crackled with what sounded like Bianca letting out a breath.

"I –"

Silence and then I heard Bianca gasp, and I knew. I *knew* she'd just received a text from Todd. Feeling like I'd just hit a grand slam, I raised both hands in the air, mentally taking my bases before I put the phone back to my ear.

"Oh my God. It's him."

"What'd he say?"

"It says, 'Way to leave a guy hanging' with a wink smiley face."

God this guy grated on me with his every move.

"What do I text back?"

"Nothing. He texted you because he realized he isn't your top priority. He doesn't like that, but he respects it. If you text him back you're negating that. Listen I gotta go. Good job, Bianca. Remember, no texting him back until tomorrow."

I hung up the phone and nodded to Leika who was already sitting at our usual table in the back of the bar. Her boyfriend, Jeff, sat next to her and for a moment, seeing them together and happy, made me pause in appreciation. Too much time at work, rubbing elbows with people that had no clue there was a life outside of their penthouse and seemingly-never-ending cashflow, made me itchy and claustrophobic, but Leika and Jeff were good people and I could always relax around them.

"Look at you all fancy and shit." Leika stood and eyed me with a smirk.

Loosening the tie around my neck, I wrapped my free arm around her and she molded her petite body into my side.

"I just got back."

She pulled back and gave me a wary look as we took a seat across the table from each other.

"How've you been?" I asked as I poured a beer from the pitcher sitting between us.

Leika leaned back into the booth and crossed her arms over her chest. Dressed in jeans and a U2 t-shirt, she looked younger than thirty. She ate that shit up, taking full advantage of people underestimating her.

Pushing her red-framed glasses up with one hand, she narrowed her gaze on me. "I'm fine. Good. The same. Work is busy, blah blah. What's up with you? You look like shit. Are you really going to keep going to Connecticut to work for that man?"

Quirking an eyebrow up, I took a long pull from my glass before I responded to the mouthful she'd just shot at me.

"I didn't get a lot of sleep last night." I purposely avoided her other questions.

"How'd it go?" she pressed, and I didn't miss the concern hidden in the question.

"It was fine. No, it was good. He invited me to his wedding reception next month."

Leika's eyes went wide. "Please tell me you're not going."

I gave her a big smile, lips pulled up and teeth on display. Unease etched her features, but I ignored it.

Jeff wrapped an arm around her shoulder and I turned my attention to him. "So, you two are still together, huh? I figured you'd have gotten tired of her sassy mouth by now." I lifted one finger from the hand cupped around the glass to point toward the two of them snuggled up together.

Leika looked embarrassed for a split second but turned the tables quickly back to me. "Maybe you should try spending more than one night with a woman before you start doling out relationship advice."

I cringed a bit at her words. She was right, and I suddenly had a wave of guilt for the way I'd inserted myself into Bianca's life. What the hell did I know about love or relationships? Too bad for her she hadn't been sitting next to someone on that flight that had actually been in a real relationship.

"You alright man? She was just busting your balls. We know how hard you're working, traveling all the time, working shit hours when you are in town. You'll meet someone when the time is right."

Leika rolled her eyes at him.

"I dunno. I'm not sure I'm cut out to be tied down."

Leika reached across the table and grabbed my hand for only a second. A quick squeeze and then she pulled her hand back to her side. Physical contact like this between us was rare and I knew she was making an effort to make a point. "You are, or you will be when you meet the right woman."

Leika knew my past better than anyone. Knew the abuse – physical and emotional that came from being bounced around through the formative years. Jeff had grown up with a happy childhood, but he seemed to understand where we came from. Or at least respected it. I might give them shit but it was amazing that they'd found each other. He was good for her and my big brother instincts knew he'd take care of her.

I'd been wrong to come here, though. I needed to be alone to remember who I was and why I lived my life the way I did. Leika wanted more for me and Bianca's sweet innocence had triggered something that had me questioning if I was as happy with my life as I'd thought.

I waited for the first lull in conversation, which felt like an eternity even though the evening had been pleasant enough, to excuse myself. Downing the rest of my beer, I stood and tossed a twenty on the table. "Thanks for the drink and pep talk. I'm tired as shit. See you two later."

I walked the two blocks from the bar to my apartment slowly. I hadn't lied. I was exhausted, but I wasn't ready to go home.

Home. The word didn't mean much to me. It had never been a place for me and if it was, it wasn't the safe, comforting haven that others associated with the word and place.

Maybe it was why I'd chosen a career where I traveled so much and why I preferred isolation to committed relationships. What could I possibly offer another human being?

I didn't know the first thing about love or relationships, but I knew people and how to do what was necessary to get by. It was what made me good at analyzing risks for companies and it was what made me good at reading people like Todd.

I might not be able to find it for myself, but I needed to do everything I could to see that Bianca found hers. I had a feeling she deserved it and I wanted people like her, people like me, to come out on top for once.

CHAPTER
SEVEN

Bianca

I'D ALWAYS BEEN secretly jealous of my friends who sexted with their boyfriends or random hook ups. In part, my jealousy was admiration. Regardless of the potentially damaging and incriminating things they sent or said, it took real guts to participate and to trust someone with that side of yourself.

Tasha said that I was reading too much into it that it was usually drunken messages that only half made sense and that the sender usually regretted it the next morning. She also suggested I clear my text history every night before bed, so I couldn't punish myself with the damning evidence the next day. This was the part that gave me pause. What was the point of sexting if I wasn't going to be able to live out the fantasy? I didn't want to type up some racy message only to have it forgotten with the morning light.

It was for all of the above reasons that I hadn't texted Todd back. Some part of me knew that once we started texting it would lead somewhere I wasn't prepared. Also, Court had told me not to and I was beginning to trust his judgment.

> **Me**: I need help texting.
>
> **Court**: Looks like you've mastered it to me.
>
> **Me**: You know what I mean – flirty stuff.
>
> **Court**: You can't even type the word. Baby steps.
>
> **Me**: Sexting. I need help sexting.

Rubbing my palms down my legs, I waited for Court's response. It didn't come right away and as the seconds turned into a full five minutes, I panicked that I had taken this thing too far. Of course, this gorgeous man didn't want to teach an inexperienced college kid the art of sending sexy text messages.

As I tossed the phone aside it finally beeped. Lunging, I grabbed the phone and squinted while I opened the message in case it was a full out rejection and Court was cutting ties and ending whatever weird mentorship thing we had going.

> **Court**: Thinking of you...

The words were a blur as I scanned the attached photo. My mouth went dry and my entire body burned with a thousand fires. I was positive it was Court's body even with the head purposely cropped out. This wasn't the body of a twenty-two-year-old throwing back wings and beer every night. It was the body of a man who took care of himself and probably worked out more than my sporadic attempts once or twice a month.

It was only when my eyes drifted to the bed he was lying in did I remember it was after midnight. I seemed to have a knack for interrupting his sleep, but I couldn't bring myself to care as I continued to stare at the photo.

Leaned back on his bed, Court laid on top of crumpled white sheets that provided the perfect backdrop to his naked torso. Abs that shouldn't be real disappeared into grey sweat pants that were slung low on his hips. While the picture wasn't provocative in itself, combined with his words and the bed… the whole thing had my body tingling like his message was meant only for me.

I was certain it was a test and that I was meant to respond, but holy crap I couldn't even get my brain to function enough to make coherent thoughts let alone text.

"Deep breath in and let it out. Deep breath in and let it out," I chanted quietly as my fingers punched out a response.

> *Me*: Want some company?

I added a winking smiley and pressed send before I could talk myself out of it. His response was embarrassingly fast… and embarrassingly hurtful.

> *Court*: No, never respond with direct questions. Direct questions require answers which takes all the fun out of it. Keep it vague and detached. Try again.
>
> *Me*: Good thoughts, I hope.
>
> *Court*: Perfect. That was much better.
>
> *Me*: Hooray!
>
> *Court*: Don't get too excited that was tame.
>
> *Me*: I'll take my small win.

> *Court: Fair enough. Just remember, keep it vague, keep it classy (no vag shots), and only send what you're comfortable with.*

I wanted to ask him about his sexting experience. Did he sext women or did he just know all of this from his younger days? And had women actually texted him photos of their vagina? I decided to steal his advice and keep it vague.

> *Me: How did you learn all this?*
>
> *Court: What do you really want to know 8B?*

Of course, it was just like him to know I wasn't being direct.

> *Me: Are you some sort of player or something? How do you know all this?*
>
> *Court: Nah, I'm not a player. I just crush a lot.*
>
> *Court: That was a rap song reference for you, young pup.*
>
> *Me: I know who Big Pun is and you completely dodged that question and used the radio version. He doesn't say crush.*
>
> *Court: Nice catch. No, Bianca I'm not a player. I just prefer casual dating to relationships.*
>
> *Me: Why?*

His response took longer this time and I tried to guess what he'd say next but couldn't come up with a single reason why he wouldn't be attached. Court was an enigma.

Handsome, successful, smart – how had he not been swooped up by some beautiful woman in the city?

> *Court*: *Relationships take a lot of work and I've been focused on my job. I don't have time for another one.*

It felt like a bullshit response, but I didn't pry, and I didn't text back. I didn't text Todd either, but instead crawled into bed filled with thoughts of two men.

The next day after classes, I decided to attempt a deliberate run in. After changing into yoga pants and a fitted shirt, I threw on my sneakers and headed out the door. I wasn't much of a runner or even a jogger, but I could power walk for days and I knew that Todd would be finishing his daily work out about the same time it would take to walk to the courts.

Responding to Todd's text message today had felt wrong, like I'd waited too long but I didn't want to wait until our next class together to bump into him either.

I put my earbuds in under the guise of a relaxing walk on a Tuesday afternoon. Fate was on my side and Todd was walking out of the multipurpose building that housed the courts as I came around the corner, putting me in his direct line of vision.

"Bianca, hey." He lifted a hand and walked over, bypassing his car.

Removing an ear bud, I forced myself to keep my facial expression as unaffected as possible. "Hey, Todd. What a surprise. Just getting out of practice?"

"Yeah. What are you up to? Classes done for the day?"

I nodded. "Just taking a break from studying for a diffey-q test."

"Killer. It was really good to see you last night. I was bummed you had to leave so early."

"Sorry about that," I murmured, and guilt instantly nagged at me for the little white lie.

"Well, hey, some of the guys and I are going to the library tonight at six to study for an anatomy test if you want to come by. I'll save you a spot on the comfy couch."

"The one by the bathrooms or the vending machines."

"Definitely the vending machines."

I couldn't stop the smile from breaking out on my face. Not because the couch near the vending machine was prime library seating, which it was, but because he'd invited me to hang out for a second night in a row.

"Sounds good." I tried for nonchalant and moved to put my earbuds back in and walk away, but Todd reached out and grabbed my hand with his larger one. His touch threw me off balance. It was warm, damp – probably sweaty, but it felt... nice.

"You'll come, right?"

Vague. Keep it vague. Leave him wanting more. I could hear Court's advice just over the cheerleaders jumping up and down and screaming "be aggressive, b-e aggressive."

"Y-yeah," I said softly. "I'll try to be there."

CHAPTER EIGHT

Court

I LEFT THE office at seven, turning out the lights behind me. I was the last one to leave. Always was. I bypassed the subway and started in on my ten-block walk. I'd done it plenty of times before. I liked to be out on the street in New York. No matter the time of day, it buzzed with an excitement and hurried tempo that matched my own. It made me feel like I was part of something. Made me feel normal.

Slowing down as I got within eyesight of my building, I decided to stop and get groceries for dinner. Contrary to the bachelor stigma, I didn't eat takeout every night. Not even every other night. Growing up where the only chef on hand was Boyardee and ramen noodles were considered a weekly staple, I had been eager to start teaching myself to cook as soon as I got my own place. It was my favorite part of the day.

Beer on the counter, knife in hand, and an array of

ingredients scattered around me. Light music played from my phone and all of it was almost enough to make me forget that I was alone.

Once the fish was in the oven and the rice and vegetables were cooking on top of the stove, I grabbed my beer and the mail stack and sat down in front of the TV. A few bills from stone age companies that refused to go paperless, junk mail, and on the bottom a crème envelope with Mr. Court Adams written in fancy penmanship. Flipping the heavy cardstock over, the Connecticut address stared up at me.

I pulled out the invitation and read it over, noting the date and time for Mr. and Mrs. Allen Sterling's reception take two. There was no way I could get out of going even if I wanted to. Allen, for all his bullshit, had been a faithful client and snubbing him wouldn't look good on me or the company. I cared less about how it'd look for me, but Harrison and Mac had been good to me giving me a job right out of college and letting me work my way up. My boss Teddy Harrison hadn't even batted an eye when I'd asked to take on one of their biggest accounts, Allen Sterling.

Tossing the invitation aside, I grabbed my laptop from the coffee table in front of me and opened it. I put the reception on my calendar and sent an email to our company travel agent to make sure my next trip coincided and let her know that I'd be staying through the weekend.

With nothing left to do but wait for my food to finish cooking, I picked up my phone and scrolled back through the last texts from Bianca. Sending her a photo of myself had been fun. I wasn't one for sexting in general, maybe because my relationships went straight from drinks or dinner back to her place and they ended when I walked out the door. The buildup was fun, exciting even.

God, I'd loved to have seen Bianca's reaction. Did she like what she saw? I'd been with enough women to know they generally did, but Bianca was barely a woman.

I pulled up my Facebook account for maybe the third time in the past month and typed her name in the search bar. Surprisingly, I was greeted with a selfie of Bianca. I hadn't pegged her as the type to take selfies. She stared into the camera, unsmiling. She was done up and from what I could tell of the background of the photo, she was at a bar. People sitting at tables, beer bottles scattered around, but no one was looking in the direction of the camera.

Had she taken this photo in a happy moment or sad? Was she feeling alone even though she was out surrounded by people? Without thinking I sent her a text. It was the first time I'd initiated contact and I hoped I wasn't coming across as the creepy old guy.

> *Me*: How'd the sexting go?
>
> *Bianca*: I chickened out.

The relief that coursed through me was unsettling. I didn't like the idea of sweet Bianca sending sexy messages to Todd or anyone else. Still I wanted her to feel confident enough to be able to when the time was right.

> *Me*: You'll have plenty of other opportunities. Guys are pretty much always up for a good sexy text message.
>
> *Bianca*: We're at the library studying so probably not the best moment.
>
> *Me*: You're with Tom?

I got a kick out of getting his name wrong and the reaction it stirred in Bianca.

> *Bianca*: Todd. His name is Todd. Do you have some sort of short term memory problem? We're hanging out at the library with a few other people.
>
> *Me*: My memory is just fine for things worth remembering. Did he ask you?
>
> *Bianca*: Yes.
>
> *Me*: And you're actually studying - that's not code for making out or something?
>
> *Bianca*: Yes, we're actually studying. I have a diffey-q test tomorrow.
>
> *Me*: What did you wear?
>
> *Bianca*: Leggings, t-shirt, flip flops. We're studying I didn't think dressing up was a requirement.
>
> *Me*: It's always a requirement if you're looking to get laid. What's he wearing?
>
> *Bianca*: Jeans and a polo shirt.

Of-fucking-course he was wearing a polo shirt.

> *Me*: Is he wearing sneakers?
>
> *Bianca*: This is the strangest conversation I've ever had over text. No, he's wearing loafers.
>
> *Me*: So, he's more dressed up than you?
>
> *Bianca*: Yeah, I guess so
>
> *Me*: Don't ever let the guy be more dressed up than

you. However masochistic and unfair it is, men want a
trophy to look good on their arm first and foremost.

Okay that wasn't strictly true. I tended to prefer my women mussed and undone – it felt more honest. More real. But men like Todd who grew up with money and worked in highly revered professions like doctors or CEOs lived in an archaic world where women were meant to look pretty and do as they were told. Maybe that was harsh and maybe it wasn't even true. But it looked true for all I'd seen and if we were airing on the side of caution here it was better to be dressed up than down.

> **Bianca**: Ugh, my brain hurts.
>
> **Me**: He invited you to do something two nights in a row. He seems to like you regardless of his moving slower than a tortoise. Now put your phone away and get to work on making physical contact. Footsie under the table? If you're sitting next to him make sure your legs are touching – something. Don't leave that library until you've touched him intimately.
>
> **Bianca**: Aye, aye.
>
> **Me**: I like it. You can call me captain anytime

As I sent the last text the timer on the oven went off. With a sigh I placed my phone on the coffee table and moved to plate my dinner. Back to reality. Alone.

CHAPTER NINE

Bianca

Todd drove me to my apartment, even though it was only a few blocks away. The campus was well lit and lots of people were out, but I appreciated his attempt at chivalry anyway. Plus, it meant some time alone with him. The end of the term was less than two months away and the craziness of final projects and the upcoming finals had everyone cramming a semester worth of good intentions into ending the year on a high note.

"Any interviews lined up for next week?" Todd asked, bringing my thoughts back to my own future. Career day was next week and companies all over the northeast would be coming to look for new hires and summer interns.

"Yeah, I have three scheduled. Have you finalized your plans for med school yet?"

"Yep," he grabbed my hand and held it on top of my thigh. "Looks like I'll be staying right here for a while longer."

"That's great. Congratulations."

I tucked a strand of hair behind my ear to keep the disappointment from showing. He was already making plans for next year and I was still trying to make the most of this one.

"Any chance the companies you're looking at are nearby?"

The sincerity in his tone made my body tingle and I peeked over at him with what felt like a goofy grin on my face. "I'm not sure. New York isn't too far."

We'd reached my apartment and I unfastened the seatbelt and moved to open the door.

Todd grabbed my elbow and pulled me back toward him. I turned in surprise as he leaned over the console with a smirk.

"Well here's hoping I'll be seeing more of you." He brushed a kiss on my unexpecting lips so quick and light it was over before I could even reciprocate. Before I could feel the spark.

He sat back in the driver's seat and moved his hand to the gear shift. "See ya later, B"

I walked from his car to inside the apartment in a haze. A scribbled note on the counter told me Tasha was at Lance's house. We'd barely seen each other over the past month and with reminders of the looming graduation I was sad that we'd spent our final semester barely able to spend time with each other.

I was desperate to tell someone about Todd and there was only one other person that I knew would share my excitement. I texted first just in case it wasn't a good time but no sooner had I pressed send did my phone ring, giving me my answer.

"Hey," I answered trying to keep myself from squealing

into his ear.

"8B, I'm surprised to hear from you again. I thought you'd be studying until late in the night. Differential equations are no joke."

"You took diffey-q?" I asked as I sat down on my bed and leaned back on to the mountain of pillows. I couldn't get too comfortable. Studying with Todd hadn't been very productive – at least on the upcoming test front.

"What, that surprises you?"

Feeling a bit sheepish, Court's deep laugh eased the tension. "I thought I might want to be a mechanical engineer for a while. That class nearly killed me, and I decided to go a different way."

"I didn't know that."

"Lots of things you don't know about me, 8B."

That was the understatement of the year. I felt like I'd barely scratched the surface of who Court was.

"So, you're good at diffey-q, huh?" he asked. "Why am I not surprised."

"I'm good at math. Not so good at people and relationships apparently."

"Uh-oh, did the study session not end so well?"

"Actually, it ended great. He kissed me."

"In the library?"

"No, he drove me home."

"And…"

"And what?"

"Well did it live up to everything you hoped it would be? Unicorns and rainbows and shit?"

"It was nice," I responded and shifted uncomfortably on my bed.

"Nice?" his voice was unbelieving.

"Yes, it was nice," I said with more resolve this time.

"Oh, I believe you. I'm just a little disappointed that you're so excited about a *nice* kiss."

"Disappointed? I'm ecstatic. I mean I really didn't think blowing him off last night was going to end well. Your advice worked."

"Yeah and I gotta live with that," he muttered.

"What are you doing over there?" I asked, finally zoning in on the background noise that sounded like a shower running. Court in the shower was a mental picture I'd have to revisit later.

"I'm doing the dishes."

"Interesting. Don't you have a dishwasher?"

"I do, but there's only a few things to wash so this is faster."

"Do you cook?"

"You know, the way you asked that is almost as if you don't think me capable."

"Just surprised is all. I can barely boil water. What did you have for dinner?"

I failed to picture Court in the kitchen, but I was intrigued.

"Salmon, rice, vegetables – nothing fancy."

"Wow, I'm impressed," I admitted. "I guess I should have known you wouldn't be a stereotypical bachelor living on TV dinners."

"Why's that 8B?" he asked, and the background noise stopped like he'd turned off the faucet.

I shrugged even though he couldn't see me. "You continually surprise me. I guess I've been living with really bad assumptions about men my entire life. I should have been gathering information and figuring it all out, but I figured eventually it'd just happen. Guess not."

The truth of that statement made me sink back into the bed. Why hadn't I spent more time analyzing and researching men and relationships? And had any of my assumptions about men been accurate? Where did I even get my views? From my father? From his relationship with my mom? I'd grown up firmly in the lower-class bracket. There'd been months and years of stress as we struggled to pay bills or keep landlords at bay, but it hadn't been a bad childhood by any stretch of the imagination. My father adored my mother. He treated her with respect and love – the same way he treated me and my brothers.

"Not the worst thing to find out."

"Are you kidding me? I've been completely wrong about so many things. So many wasted years – I could already have all this data."

"Don't be so hard on yourself. Besides, think of all the amazing things that open up to you now that you're aware. Things that are better to find out with a little age and wisdom."

"Like?"

"Well sex for example."

I scoffed but he kept going.

"No seriously, Bianca. You're still plenty young. Most people have a rap sheet of shit they wish they could take back by now. You may have been naïve and even missed out on some experiences, but now you're a responsible adult and you'll have a degree behind you and be ready to conquer men, business, the world – you name it. You're just getting started."

"I don't want to have a different experience from everyone else. I just want to fit in."

REBECCA JENSHAK

"You'll never fit in."

The way he said that, I was sure it wasn't meant as a dig, but it still stung.

"It's not a bad thing," he said, confirming my thoughts.

"But what if –"

He interrupted. "What if it's too late? You're twenty-two. Save the melodramatics for your thirties. That's when women typically start freaking out about getting old."

I laughed, a hollow sound.

"Are you a virgin 8B?"

His question caught me off guard and I inhaled sharply, cheeks flaming with heat.

"No!" I responded a little too loudly. "Of course not."

"Just checking. You don't need to get all defensive. So, you've had sex. Then what's kept you from putting yourself out there more?"

"I guess I thought the right guy would just land in my lap and everything after would be perfect."

"A romantic, huh?"

"Isn't it obvious?"

"So, the men you've been with – why weren't they the right ones for you? Why did it end?"

I hesitated. How much could I tell him without sounding utterly pathetic?

"It just wasn't…"

"No judgment here. It just wasn't what?"

"It wasn't good, okay?" I placed a palm over my eyes and cringed as I forced myself to continue. "I've never, you know, gotten off during sex."

"Never?" His voice was disbelieving.

"I mean I have by myself just not… oh my God this is humiliating," I groaned.

"The only person that should be humiliated are the guys that failed to get you off."

"Maybe it's me."

"Maybe it is."

"Hey," I chuckled. "I just meant maybe I'm holding back somehow. I need to get out of my head and just go for it, stop analyzing everything."

"I'm in. Let's do it."

"Do what?" My voice trembled. I had no idea what I'd just talked him into.

"Let's get you out of your head and ready for the real deal."

"I –"

"Think of it as practice for what's his face."

"What exactly are you suggesting?"

"The same thing we've been doing, but we'll spend more time talking like we're in a real relationship instead of me just telling you what to do."

"I dunno."

"It worked for the sexting bit – you picked that up quickly with a little real-life practice."

"That wasn't real life."

"Speak for yourself." He chuckled.

I bit my lip and tried to come up with any reason why I should say no. The only thing that truly came to mind was Todd. What would he think if he knew I'd stooped to this level to get his attention? I trusted Court and I thought he was sincere in wanting to help me for some reason. What that reason was, I couldn't fathom. There was no way he was hard pressed for women.

"See before I was telling you what to do, but the only feedback I got on how it went came from you. This way I'll get to experience it authentically. I can steer you in the right direction or just give you some confidence that you're doing it right."

"So, I'm supposed to treat you like a guy I'm interested in?" I shook my head trying to wrap my brain around what it was he was asking for us to be. Was this strictly a virtual arrangement? He lived in NYC, so it wasn't as if he was going to be close enough for real dates.

His deep laugh came through again and goosebumps spread over my skin. This older, handsome man wanted to do this… with me. I'd be a fool to say no even though *I* was probably going to look like the fool with my inexperience and lack of knowledge.

"We'll take it as it comes. No rules. I know that'll be hard for you Miss Rules," he said teasingly.

"Okay, I guess we could try it."

"Yeah?" he sounded excited and that put butterflies in my stomach.

"Sure, I mean it can't hurt to have the practice before I do it for real, right?"

"Exactly."

I let out a deep breath and sat up on the bed eyeing my backpack. "I hate to ruin the moment, but I need to study some more for my test tomorrow."

"What's the test over?"

Pulling my bag onto my lap, I grabbed my textbook and notes and flipped open to the last chapter. "Systems of first-order equations."

"Let's work some problems then."

"You want to help me study?"

"Isn't that what you'd want a boyfriend to do? Plus, I'm sorta curious to see that brain of yours in action."

CHAPTER TEN

Court

Her brain turned me on. It was incredible. She was way smarter than me – not that I'd admit it to her. I had the advantage of years of practical use, but she had a book smart like I'd never seen before.

"What are you going to do after college?" I asked when we'd finished working a handful of problems and it was clear she knew the stuff.

"The career fair is next week. I have some interviews and I'm going to try and get my resume in front of a few other companies while they're on campus."

"I don't think I ever asked you what kind of engineer you were studying to be," I said, wondering why I hadn't thought to ask her before. I didn't know much about her hopes and dreams outside of Todd. Shit, when did I start caring about other people's hopes and dreams?

"Electrical. I'm interested in signal processing, specifically machine learning."

"How very new age of you."

"You majored in finance, yeah?" she asked.

I paused because I'd never told her that. I was certain I hadn't. I didn't like talking about myself – specifically my degrees or awards because it felt fucking weird to be defined by something so unimportant as what I'd majored in. Had Bianca looked me up?

"Someone did her homework."

"Well, I had to make sure you weren't some crazy psycho-stalker."

"And my majoring in finance means I'm not a stalker?"

"No, but I didn't find anything alarming. In fact, I found very little."

This made me smile. "Good."

"Why did you go into finance?"

Scrubbing a hand over my face, I thought about my answer. "I guess I wanted to do something challenging, but practical. And I wanted a career path that had stability so there'd be less of a chance of being out of a job when times were tough."

"Wow." Her voice had a hint of amazement and I was afraid I'd said too much – given too much away about my past. What kid chose a career path based on the economy? Parents and adults would like to think we all did, but in reality, I thought we all chose our paths based on things that sounded cool or for lifestyles we desired. Engineers didn't want to dress up in suits every day any more than I wanted to roll into the office with cargo shorts and a t-shirt. I cringed at the thought.

"I guess that doesn't sound like a very cool way to pick a career."

"No, actually, I think that's amazing. I don't think very many people consider what life is going to be like after graduation. It's tough out there even for people with lots of work experience."

Her words soothed something inside of me. She got it. She got *me*.

We talked for an hour and every word out of her mouth captivated me more. My 8B was deep and thoughtful without being hokey or insincere. She saw the world through rose-tinted glasses but tackled decisions like the glass was half-empty.

I didn't know what to make of her, but I was intrigued. I wanted to know more. I wanted to know *everything*.

When she eventually yawned loudly into the phone, I looked at the clock noticing it was midnight. I felt like a dick for keeping her up so late the night before a test. It didn't occur to me until after we'd said our goodbyes and I'd stretched out into my bed that this was the first time I'd had a conversation with a woman like that. Without it even being planned, we'd had a phone call that had almost felt like a date – or at the very least the pre-cursor to a date. The getting to know you stage was a rush that I'd completely forgotten about.

The next morning when I arrived at the office, my boss was waiting for me. Still wearing the Bianca-induced smile, his presence didn't annoy me the way it might have on a different day. Teddy Harrison was a good man, a good boss, even, but his penchant for starting the day off by blind siding employees with impromptu meetings made us all scratch our heads in frustration.

"Good morning, Court. Sorry to catch you just as you're getting in, but I wanted to tell you Allen Sterling wrote a nice email on the good work you're doing for him.

I dropped my laptop bag onto my desk and took a seat. "That's great to hear. I sent travel directions to Mindy last night actually, he wants me back next month for another check in."

"Actually, that's partly why I'm here."

"Oh?" I raised my eyebrows as I searched his face for some indication of the news.

Teddy ran a hand over his grayed moustache. "I'd like you to go back to Connecticut next week."

"But Allen won't have anything for at least another three."

"Not for him, for us. Harrison and Mac wants to have a presence on campus this year. We got a last-minute invite to the career fair and we'd like you to go and do some head hunting for us."

"Why me?" I tried to keep the note of disappointment from my voice. This was not something a senior risk analyst should be doing. We had an entire HR division for this sort of thing.

"I know it's more of a human resources thing, but I'd like you to start leading your own team. You can pick them from the career fair, plus I'll have some local candidates brought in for you to interview. It's time for you to start mentoring a new crop of hungry kids."

I laughed.

"Plus, you're familiar with the area and the type of people there."

By people I was sure he meant snooty rich people or, more specifically, their offspring.

"Wow, thank you. I don't know what to say."

"Say you're getting on a flight to Connecticut next week."

"I'm not sure I'll be very good at conducting interviews."

"Nonsense, you're a top employee. Just talk to them about your career – how you got started, how you've risen in the company, things you like about working for Harrison and Mac. Far better for this to come from someone like you than one of us old people. It hasn't been so long for you. I can still remember you walking in fresh out of college."

"That feels like a million years ago," I told him truthfully.

Mr. Harrison chuckled and moved toward the door. "You're still young. Thank you for doing this, Court, and try and have some fun while you're there, eh? Some day you really will be old." A sad sort of look passed over his face before he left me alone in my office.

As if it'd been a sure thing, which of course it was, the travel details were already in my inbox. I guess that explained why he was waiting in my office first thing.

I ran a hand through my hair as I contemplated jumping on a plane so soon after getting back. There wasn't really anything holding me in NYC. My circle was small. I had an assorted variety of friends, or acquaintances, that I really only saw in one aspect of my life. Aside from Leika, they didn't cross over.

I had a guy at the gym who I worked out with. Not because we were friends exactly, but because our schedules and lifting styles were the same. We shared a small part of ourselves with each other. For an hour, three to five days a week, depending on my travel schedule, we shot the breeze, keeping our conversation to stock prices, the news, and weights.

I had a group of guys at the office that were good for an occasional lunch out or happy hour after a shitty day. Most of us had been with the company since college and years of familiarity, more than friendship, made our conversations deeper. Questions about how the wife or kids were, for those that had them, updates on new apartments or homes, vacations, and, of course, work. These people probably knew the details of what was happening in my day-to-day life better than anyone – even Leika, but it was a shallow understanding.

Then the college buddies who'd known the me I was fifteen years ago – wild and reckless and still coming to terms with an anger about my life that threatened to consume me. I think they were all surprised to see how well I was doing now. They probably chalked it up to luck that out of our crew, I had the most stable and lucrative career. They didn't see the hours they spent doting on wives or girlfriends the way I did – as an expensive distraction from work.

I didn't resent their lives. I even envied them a bit, but when I'd vowed not to let the past dictate my future I'd settled into a controlled life where my time was spent deliberately. This went hand in hand with my decision to date casually and keep people at arm's length.

I was second-guessing the way I'd siloed myself from meaningful relationships when I got a text from Bianca.

> *Bianca*: Good Morning, handsome. Hope you have a great day.

I smiled. It was a great text. It made me wish she'd meant it specifically for me.

> *Me*: You too sweetheart (Great text – probably only appropriate after you're officially dating so you don't come across as a stage five clinger, but the message itself is perfect)

I waited a full minute for a response, but when I didn't get one I put my phone away and got to work. The day moved at a hurried pace filled with meetings and client calls and lunch at my desk. When I checked my phone at five-thirty, I was excited to see another text from Bianca.

Bianca: Aced the test. Thanks for helping me study.

The small gesture, thanking me for something that I'd never even considered a favor – even as her fake boyfriend, filled my chest with a warmth I didn't understand. My mind wandered to Bianca and what part of me I'd shown her. And what part of her she had shown me.

I wanted to be a part of her life in a real way, even if I had to do it under the guise of helping her with Todd. And hopefully when she landed Todd, which I had no doubt she would, we could be... fuck, I didn't know. Friends?

I packed up for the night with thoughts of Bianca and the trip I'd be making back to Connecticut next week. I was torn about telling her we'd be in the same city again, so I decided to hold off. My little 8B might pull back if she thought she was going to have to face me. If things went well over the next week, I'd tell her once I got there.

I hoped she would be ready to see me again because for the first time since I'd learned of the last-minute trip to Connecticut, I was looking forward to it and the only reason I could come up with for my unexplainable feelings... Bianca.

CHAPTER ELEVEN

Bianca

"Bianca, get out here!" Tasha yelled from the living room.

I opened my door just a crack. "Give me five minutes. I just got out of the shower."

My already speeding heart rate quickened as I dropped the towel and stood in front of the mirror in my bedroom. It wasn't a lie, I *had* just gotten out of the shower ten minutes ago. But I'd already applied my makeup, going intentionally heavier on the eyeliner and mascara and gotten dressed – or half-dressed anyway. In just a bra – the black lacy one I'd accidentally given Court a glimpse of that first night – and a pair of jeans worn with holes and permanently stretched out from wearing them so much, I tried to remember everything Court had told me about sexting.

No vag shots. Gross, that definitely wasn't a problem.

Keep it vague.

What else had he told me?

I pulled my comforter taught, giving the appearance of a made bed and laid on top of it holding my camera above me. I angled it left, right, up, down – ugh, how the hell had Court made it look so effortless?

I snapped a few photos, trying to capture the same pose Court had. I didn't see the appeal of a little cleavage and bare stomach, but he had told me guys were always up for sexting, so I couldn't go wrong, could I?

I selected the best of the photos and sat up in my bed to come up with a message to go with it.

Me: *Whatcha doing, handsome?*

I jumped off the bed after I pressed send and pulled a tank top on over my head. Court and I had continued talking every day. My days started with sending him a good morning text and ended with him telling me good night and sweet dreams over video chat. It had been awkward initially, to treat him like someone I was dating, but he'd been right – it had made me feel more confident. Court was a fun fake boyfriend. And now I was ready to conquer sexting.

My phone rang with an incoming video call and I smiled as I answered. "Hey."

Court's face filled the screen. A smile pulled at the corner of his mouth and, as usual, my stomach flipped at the sight of him.

"Hey, sweet girl," he crooned above the background noise.

I couldn't make out his location, but it was loud.

"Hey," I repeated self-consciously.

His eyes wandered down to my now covered chest. "Looks like I missed the free show."

"Ha. Ha. So, how'd I do?" I bit my lip nervously.

"Perfect."

I grinned wide, mentally giving myself a gold star.

"*If* you were a dude and trying to send a chick a picture of your non-existent six pack abs."

Okay, so no gold star.

"Take your shirt off and stand in front of a mirror."

My face must have shown the panic I was feeling.

"Relax, 8B. You can keep the camera pointed at your face. I'll walk you through it."

Awkwardly, I pulled the tank over my head with one hand while I kept the camera pointed away. I brought the phone back up to my face as I stood before my mirror.

"Okay."

"Alright, 8B. Ever heard of T and A?"

"Umm, what?"

He chuckled. "Tits and ass. These are the two focal points you want to remember when sexting. Okay, now, position yourself so that you're standing not quite perpendicular to the mirror - let's call it forty-five degrees since I know you're going to want specifics. Now turn your upper body, without moving your feet so that your chest is square with the mirror. Got that?"

I did as he said feeling more like a contortionist than a sex object. "Yeah, I think so."

"Now pop that booty out by tilting your hips toward the ground." He nodded as I manipulated my body around.

"This is ridiculous. What am I hoping to accomplish by standing all awkward and twisted around?" I tried to focus on moving my hips and lifting my butt. My side hurt from

holding the position and I felt utterly ridiculous. And then…
"Oh my God."

I had a waist – a small one and my boobs were on display without outright flashing them and somehow my mostly non-existent butt looked perky and round.

"You're a genius," I said as I let the camera fall so he could see at least a portion of the result.

Court's expression grew serious. "You look gorgeous. You *are* gorgeous. Good job. A-plus. When you do it for real, try it with something that shows off more leg."

I ignored everything but the praise. Gold star.

"Alright, thank you, Yoda. I gotta go study. Talk later?"
He nodded. "Later, 8B."

I'd planned on sending the image to Todd after it got the Court seal of approval, but it was going to have to wait for when I had more time. I slipped back into my tank and headed out to the living room where Tasha waited for me.

"Finally. I thought you'd fallen asleep in there."

"Sorry, sorry. I'm here." If only Tasha knew what I'd been doing, she'd have high-fived me instead of giving me a pouty look. But she'd also demand to know every detail, like she did every time she caught me and Court texting or talking, and I wanted to keep some of it just for me.

"Ready to study for your interviews?"

"Ready."

Twenty-five minutes later, my mood sufficiently deflated, Tasha was still drilling me with questions.

"Where do you see yourself in five years?"

I stared blankly at Tasha as she read the interview question from her laptop. We were sitting on the couch in our living room, legs tucked up underneath, so we could face one another as she attempted to prepare me for my interviews tomorrow. Tasha had already accepted a job offer in New York with an art gallery she'd interned with last summer. A friend of a friend of a family. It helped to know people – especially in a city like New York.

"These questions are dumb," I groaned. "I have no idea where I'll be in five years until I figure out where I'm going to work."

Undeterred by my pessimism, Tasha read the advice listed on the screen in front of her. "Talk about what type of responsibility you want – leading projects or teams, mention any certifications or additional degrees you're interested in obtaining."

"All of that. I want all the responsibility they'll give me, but I mean come on, it's an entry level job."

The truth was, I did have an idea of what I wanted, but I was skeptical that any of it really mattered for the purposes of the interview. I could tell them I planned to be the first female president and they'd probably just nod and ask about my previous experiences."

I stood and headed for our small kitchen, grabbing two waters from the fridge. "Actually, I've been thinking about applying to the master's program here for next semester. Just in case a job doesn't work out."

"Isn't it a little late for that?"

"Technically, yes, but Dr. Hassup loves me so I think he might be able to pull some strings."

"I don't understand." Tasha closed the laptop halfway and peered over at me. "I thought you were excited about graduating and moving back to the city to be closer to your mom – to your whole family."

"I am. I just want to explore all my options."

Tasha crossed her arms over her chest and glared, not

moving even to take the water I offered.

"It could be good to get a master's – more opportunities, higher pay. My mom is doing well, and I could still visit and eventually return there," I finished and set the water on the coffee table in front of her.

"This doesn't have anything to do with Todd staying here for med school, does it?"

"What? No, of course not." It was a perk, I admitted, but not the reason.

"Just… please make sure you're keeping Todd completely out of this decision," she said as she uncrossed her arms. The look of annoyance had left her face and was replaced with something that looked like sadness or pity. "Do what's best for *you*. And perhaps consider what's best for me – having you with me in New York." She looked up at me with a hopeful smile.

My phone beeped with an incoming text, saving me from hashing out future plans. I needed time on my own to think, weigh the pros and cons, analyze.

"It's Todd. They're going out. He wants me to come meet up with them," I said happily.

Tasha waved at the computer in her lap. "I thought we were prepping for your interviews."

"We did. I'll be fine. Seriously. I do some of my best work under pressure."

It was a lie and she knew it – or at least an unproven theory. I was never unprepared, but I was less concerned with my interviews than I was with the idea of trying out my potential girlfriend moves on Todd.

"Come on. Come with us. I miss hanging out. We have less than a month until graduation and I feel like I've barely seen you this semester."

I'd played to her guilt and I could tell it was working by the way she bit back a smile.

"You're not wearing that, are you?"

I rolled my eyes and went in for the kill. "Come on, I'll even let you dress me."

As I'd expected, her eyes lit up. "Where are they going?"

Thirty minutes later Tasha and I were on York Street just after ten o'clock. It was early by college standards, but the bar was already packed. I pulled at the hem of the too short dress while trying to keep myself upright on heels that were five inches higher than anything I usually wore. Maybe letting Tasha dress me had been going too far. She could pull this off with a confidence and general bad-assery that I didn't possess.

"How are we supposed to find him in here?" I shouted above the noise. We pushed through the crowd and stood sandwiched in at the edge of the bar.

"Hey," Tasha grabbed my elbow and gave it a little squeeze. "Chill out. We'll find him. Let's grab a drink and try and find a table."

I nodded as the bartender hustled in front of us asking our order while walking away. I was only half-listening as Tasha gave her our order. I scanned the crowd looking for Todd or his friends. They were a large – as in muscular – and loud group so I didn't think they'd be too hard to find. A peek at my cell revealed no new text messages and I refrained from sending one that made me look overly eager. I was, but I could almost hear Court's voice telling me to put away my phone and have fun.

Tasha handed me a glass and I took a sip of the rum and diet concoction as we squeezed away from the bar looking for a table. I continued my perusal of the place, spotting a few alumni in the crowd, in town for the career fair, no doubt.

We found a table near the front of the bar next to the karaoke table with an ear-piercing closeness to the speakers. Currently there was a trio of girls belting out Taylor Swift's *We Are Never Ever Getting Back Together*. I had twenty bucks that at least one of them ended the night tangled up with the very man she was singing about. No one sang that song with that much passion unless they were still hung up on someone.

"Stop it," Tasha said, snapping my attention back to her. "He'll show. Until then…" She raised her glass and a smile pulled at her lips.

"Cheers," I said, clinking my glass against hers.

I gave up the look out and focused on Tasha. We drank. We caught up. We laughed. God, how we laughed.

"I miss this," I said after our second drink.

"Well if you take a job in New York, we could keep rooming together and we'd be able to spend a lot more time together once our evenings aren't filled with homework and cramming for tests."

"What about Lance? I thought you two would be shacking up together?"

"He hasn't asked yet, but even if he does, New York is expensive. The three of us could get a place."

Almost before I could give her my best no way in hell face, she continued. "I promise it wouldn't be weird."

"Says the girl who wouldn't have to listen to her best friend getting it on."

"Just think about it, okay?"

"Okay," I agreed.

Tasha's gaze went past me, and I used the opportunity to

check my cell again. Still nothing.

"There is an insanely hot guy at the table behind you. You should go introduce yourself."

"Okay first off, I can't just walk up to some random guy and make casual conversation and second, I'm meeting up with Todd." I resisted looking behind me knowing it would only encourage her more.

"Oh please, there's no harm in some flirting and this guy, trust me, he's worth getting out of your comfort zone. Besides, Todd has made no claim over you. Don't put all your eggs in one basket," Tasha said as her eyes went wide. "That's good, put that on your list!"

Before I could protest, Tasha was up and pulling me behind her. My whole body warmed as I kept my eyes focused down on my drink. I was grateful at least that I had a fresh one. I fidgeted with the straw as the chatter at the table died down at our approach.

"Hello, boys," Tasha said by way of greeting. "I'm Tasha." She bumped her shoulder against mine, making my drink nearly tumble out of my hands. "And this is –"

"8B."

CHAPTER TWELVE

Bianca

His deep voice sliced through the noise of the bar and I snapped my head up to meet his eyes. I'd forgotten the depths of those eyes in person. Over video chat they were beautiful, but in person they drew me in and I couldn't look away.

The corners of his hazel eyes crinkled in surprise and happiness. My mouth went dry at the sight of him. He was better looking than I remembered. Taller. I guess since most of our interaction had been while sitting, or over the phone, I hadn't fully realized how he towered over me, even in heels.

He was dressed more casually than our last in person interaction. Instead of the suit he'd worn on the plane, his muscular frame filled out a pair of dark jeans and light blue V-neck sweater that showed the most amazing hint of chest. A promise that what was underneath was even better than what covered it. What covered it was pretty damn good, but then again, I'd seen what was underneath too. I had a feeling seeing it in person would be sinful by comparison to the photo.

"You two know each other?" Tasha looked to me with a glare that demanded to know how on earth I knew this gorgeous man.

"Court." His name came out in a whisper.

"Oh my God, you're the guy from the plane!"

Court's eyes left mine as he gave his attention to Tasha.

"Court Adams." He held out a hand which Tasha took all too eagerly.

"I'm Tasha. Bianca's roommate. Oh my God, the rule book you two are creating is amazing. Seriously, you could write a dissertation on human behavior with that thing."

"What are you doing here?" I squeaked out, finally finding my voice.

A small shrug of his shoulders had my eyes falling to the muscles that were on display through the light material of his sweater. I was going to have to create my own Court-specific rules, like don't ogle and use your damn words.

"I'm here for the career fair," he said simply and then. "What's this about a rule book?"

My face burned, and I glared at Tasha. "I, uh, have been writing down all your advice as a sort of how-to." Tasha winked at me and then waved to someone at the end of the table. I didn't follow her gaze, I was transfixed on Court.

"Such a good student," he said, but his voice didn't sound mocking. It was almost proud.

He'd been standing on the other side of Tasha – a safe distance away from me and my bumbling hormones, but as she moved away in the direction she'd waved, Court stepped forward. His woodsy, masculine scent floated around me making me forget the musty, alcohol and sweat odor that overpowered the bar.

His eyes scanned my body slowly sending goosebumps over my skin. "It's good to see you 8B. You look great."

"Thanks. I'm a little shocked you're here. Oh my God were you here when I was talking to you earlier?" I covered my chest as if I were still half-naked.

A sheepish smile crossed his face. "Yeah, I'd just landed."

"Why didn't you tell me you were coming back – that you were here?"

He didn't answer, and I drained my glass while I waited for him to explain, only realizing it was empty when the straw slurped in protest.

"I think that one's cashed. Come on, I need to get a refill too."

He moved toward the bar, but I stayed firmly frozen in place. I looked to Tasha who had completely abandoned me. Not even a glance back to see the look of desperation on my face.

"Come on, she's fine."

She wasn't my concern. *I* wasn't fine. How was I going to keep from making an utter fool of myself?

His hand moved to my side and I warmed under his touch. "I promise I'll bring you right back."

He led me to the bar, pushing through the crowd easily as if they'd parted just for him.

"What can I get ya?" the bartender looked Court over like she wanted to devour him.

"Can I get another one of these." He placed his empty beer bottle on the bar top and looked to me, pulling me closer with the hand that still rested at my hip. "And whatever she wants," he said looking back to the bartender but not loosening his hold.

I struggled to speak. With his hard body pressed at my side, I was beyond the ability to form complete sentences. Or think them.

"Is that a Rum and Coke?"

I nodded. "Diet."

The bartender flited away, but not before another long, hungry gaze pointed at the man next to me.

"How've you been?" Court asked, letting go of me and leaning his tall frame against the bar. He settled in like we were old friends and he wanted to hear every detail that had happened in my life since the last time he'd seen me. It was the same sort of posture I recognized all over this bar from alumni catching up with old friends. But Court and I were hardly old friends. We'd spent all morning sending flirty texts back and forth and now here he was.

My body chilled without his and I inched forward seeking out the warmth that radiated off him. "Good. I – I'm sorry. I'm a little thrown that you're actually here. I never thought I'd see you again. You know what I mean – like this, standing in front of me."

It was true, I realized. Would I have told him the intimate things I had if I thought there would ever come a time he was standing in front of me again? I knew the answer before I'd even finished thinking it. There was no way I'd have admitted to this gorgeous, experienced man that I was a hopeless case or hadn't sexted before. Oh, God. I'd actually told him I'd never had an orgasm during sex. And he'd seen me twice now more naked than anyone had seen me in…

"Whoa. I got you." Court steadied me as I tumbled into him. He looked to my shoes and smiled. Leaning so that his cheek rested against mine, he whispered, "What did I tell you about those shoes? Those shoes are against the rules."

My face flushed hotter as I remembered his words. *The only place those shoes belong is around a guy's shoulders.*

He stood upright, and I missed the feel of his stubble against my skin.

"You remember the shoes?" I was impressed that something as insignificant as my wardrobe had been retained in his memories.

Our drinks arrived, and he took his and then handed me mine, keeping his fingers tight around the glass after I'd taken hold of it. He leaned in and the moment hung in the air thick and alive. Our fingers were live wires and the longer they touched the more sparks fizzled around us.

"I'll remember those shoes," he let his eyes fall back to my feet and then brought them up my body slowly. His voice gruffer when he spoke again. "until the day I die."

"There you are." Tasha appeared at my side and Court pulled back.

"What can I get you to drink?" he asked her, stepping back to the bar.

"Let's do a round of shots. Rule book guy being here is cause for celebration."

"Shots?" Court gave me a surprised look. "What's your poison?"

"Lemon drops," Tasha answered.

"Three lemon drops," he told the bartender. "And another rum and diet."

Court looked between Tash and me as she looped her arm through mine.

"So, Court," she paused. "What's that short for? Courtney?"

He grimaced and then nodded as he took a swig from

his beer.

"I didn't know that," I said as I filed away the information. I was certain that every scrap of information I'd found on him had called him only Court.

"Nobody calls me that. I've gone by Court since as long as I can remember."

"Not even your parents?" I asked, feeling more comfortable with him in the hot seat. Also, there was something comforting about the way Court interacted with me. Despite how insanely hot he was, he didn't look at me as a pathetic girl he was taking pity on – he looked at me like he was interested in who I was and what I had to say.

The smile on his face disappeared and in its place was a look I didn't recognize. Before I could analyze it, the bartender arrived with our drinks and Court turned his back to us. When he faced me again, the smile had returned.

"I can't tell you the last time I had a lemon drop shot," he said as we raised our shot glasses together.

"What should we toast to?" Tasha asked.

He glanced down, a seemingly harmless gesture until I felt his eyes land on my legs and down to my feet. Lifting his gaze back to us, Court's mouth quirked up on one side before he said, "To rules and knowing when to break them."

He winked as he lifted the drink to his lips.

We'd barely set our empty shot glasses on the bar when Tasha was hugging me and giving her apologies to Court.

"I'm gonna go next door and see if I can convince Lance to come here. Text or call me when you're headed home and let me know you made it."

"You're not coming home tonight?" I hated the way my voice sounded whiny and disappointed. Of course, she was staying at Lance's place. She almost always did when we'd been out.

"I have a feeling Lance is going to want to peel this dress off with his teeth when he seems me." She shimmied her hips and shot a friendly smile at Court.

"It was nice to meet you," Court said.

Tasha looked from him to me and then narrowed her gaze back to Court. "You too. And good work with this one. Rules or not, she's come a long way since she met you. I mean look at her, she's smoking hot."

With that, Tasha disappeared and I let out a shaky breath at being left alone with Court.

"If you want to get back to your co-workers," I pointed over my shoulder to the table we'd left. "I should probably call it a night anyway."

"Are you kidding me, 8B? I want to see you in action."

"In action?"

My heart hammered in my chest and my mind raced to understand his meaning. Did he want me to pretend to be his girlfriend here? Now?

Grabbing my free hand and tugging me behind him, Court's intentions were only clear once we reached the karaoke signup table.

"Oh no," I shook my head fervently. "I don't do karaoke."

He raised both eyebrows at me as he took a pen and scribbled on a small piece of paper. Curiosity got the better of me and I craned my neck to try and make out what he'd written. No luck.

Like he hadn't just signed me up for public humiliation, he grabbed my hand again and pulled me away before I could ask questions… or grab the paper and tear it to shreds.

"Come on, let's go grab a seat."

Court was filled with a sort of contagious energy that

had me smiling despite the way he took charge and left me trying to catch up. I liked to be one step ahead, but with him I didn't even know which way we were going.

"How are things, Bianca?" he asked once we were seated at a table in the corner. Hearing him say my name made my pulse pick up.

I fidgeted with my drink, stirring the straw in circles and watching the brown liquid swirl and catch the light.

"Things are good. Great," I added in a voice that sounded more like I was trying to convince myself than him.

Court laughed softly and pulled his chair closer to mine. "You don't make it easy, do you?"

"Make what easy?"

"Getting to know you. You've got your canned answers down pat. You're less guarded over text."

I leaned back in my chair and I felt the weirdness of the night lift away. I liked that he called me out – challenged me. It was the reason I'd trusted him from the beginning. He didn't put on airs.

"Okay, fine. Things are too uncertain right now and it's making me feel unsure of everything. I have interviews lined up for jobs that I'm not even sure I want. All of this is coming to an end and I can't seem to figure out what's next."

He nodded. "You don't have a plan and you're freaked out."

"More like I'm afraid to make a plan. It feels like whatever decision I make sets off a string of events that is going to impact everything and how in the hell am I supposed to know what's the right decision?"

"Wanna know a secret?" He leaned in and the soft material of his shirt rubbed against my arm.

"Yes," I whispered, voice wavering.

He moved away, and his eyes fell to his beer. "None of it matters. What degree you get, what job you take – none of that is going to make or break your future. It just changes your location."

"And the people," I added.

He studied me for a moment and then his mouth pulled up in a knowing smile. "This is about Tonto."

"His name is Todd."

"And if you were basing the decision solely on him what would you do?"

"That's not what I'm doing," I insisted.

"Alright, but let's pretend you were. What's the best scenario for you and what's his face?"

I blew out a deep breath. "He's staying here for medical school so staying another couple years to get a master's means we'd be in the same city. It would buy me some more time to give him, give us, a chance to get to know each other and see if we have a future."

"You need to buy time to figure out if you want to be with the guy?"

"You're putting words in my mouth." I shook my head. "I already told you that's not what I'm doing. I'm basing my future plans solely on me and what's best for me."

And yes, for what was best for my family, but I wasn't about to drop my sad story on Court.

"If I did stay, though, it would make it more likely that Todd and I could be together. Is that so wrong?"

"No. No, 8B, that's not wrong at all. He's a lucky guy."

CHAPTER THIRTEEN

Court

Hᴀᴛɪɴɢ Tᴏᴅᴅ ʜᴀᴅ become the only emotion I was certain of anymore. When I was eleven, one particularly empathetic family (at least until I'd caused so much trouble they couldn't handle me) had demanded I go to counseling. It had only taken three sessions for everyone, therapist included, to deduct that therapy wasn't going to work until I was willing to cooperate. Still, I had been listening to most of her garbage and right now I could practically hear her saying, "Identify your feelings. How does it make you feel that your parents abandoned you?"

"It fucking sucks," had been my response, as if there were any other way to feel about something like that.

But I was as crystal clear on my feelings for Todd as I had been about being abandoned. True, I hadn't met the guy and to hear it from Bianca, he was a good guy with a bright future ahead of him, still I hated that it had taken my interference for him to finally see how amazing she was. He should have seen it earlier and he absolutely shouldn't be letting her even consider sticking around for another year or two to get a master's degree. It was a bullshit excuse, no matter how she was trying to play it off to herself. She lit up when she talked about New York.

"Tell me about the companies you're interviewing with," I said before she could tell me more about her possible future with Todd.

"Qualcomm, Analog Devices, and a new company in New York that just won a big government contract."

"And that's the one you want? The one in New York?"

She nodded, narrowing her eyes a bit as if to decipher how I'd guessed her thoughts.

"It's the only one you said anything about other than the name."

"You wouldn't have known the company by name like the others."

"Maybe, but I don't know much about the other two either."

She shrugged, and I decided to give her a pass on telling me more about the New York job – for now.

"When are your interviews?"

With a sheepish grin she looked up at me through dark lashes. "Tomorrow."

"You're out drinking the night before your interviews?" I couldn't believe it. Everything I thought I knew about this woman had just been decimated by the thought of her irresponsibility at something so big. It also made me more pissed at Todd who no doubt was the sudden cause of her wavering personality. Her outfit gave her away.

"What happened to the 'You need to have a little fun'

crap you were spouting at me a few weeks ago?" she asked as she crossed her arms over her chest.

"I stand by that statement, but there's a time and a place. The night before interviews for your first real job isn't the time."

"And the place?" she'd uncrossed her arms and looked around at the busy bar. The place didn't look half bad. It wasn't my cup of tea per se, but I saw the appeal to college kids – cheap beer and free entertainment a hop skip and a jump from campus.

"The place is just fine. You come here a lot?"

"No, not really."

"So why tonight?"

She looked down and my interest piqued.

"Todd."

"You were hoping to see him, or…"

"He asked me to come. Said he and his friends were gonna be here, but I don't think they're here yet."

"Maybe he called or sent a text – wanna check your phone?"

"I, uh, have been." She slid her small purse across the table revealing her cell phone laying on the top, screen up. It shouldn't have been a big deal. It wasn't like she was my girlfriend. So, what if she'd been keeping an eye on her cell during our conversation? I knew it shouldn't rankle me, but it did. It cheapened our time together somehow. And then again, every conversation we'd ever had revolved around Todd in some way.

"I'm sorry," I said, my emotions pinballing all over the fucking place. "Can I ask you a question?"

"Sure," she responded immediately.

"What is it about this guy that you're willing to do all

this to get his attention. There are lots of guys out there. Why this one?"

She blushed, and I wondered how much of the truth she'd tell me. I had my guesses, based off everything I knew about the guy, but I couldn't help but wonder what it was about this guy that had her so hell bent on getting his attention. Shit, the lengths she'd gone to would make a normal guy feel like king of the world, and from where I was sitting, fucking Todd seemed like he was taking it, taking *her*, for granted.

"Have you ever had a conversation with someone and it just changed everything?"

A strangled sort of sound left my lips in acknowledgment. Her sitting across from me was proof of that.

"My conversations with him were like that early on. We talked about real things. Things that matter. It's easy to get caught up in the bubble that is this place." She waved her arms around. "The only thing people here are concerned about are parties and sleeping around. But with him, it was never like that. He asked the questions others never bothered to and so I've shown him a part of me that feels like so much more. Does any of that make any sense?"

"Yeah." I nodded and felt like a total ass. "Yeah, that makes sense."

I knew she hadn't meant to call me out as someone who couldn't be troubled to go beyond the surface, but it's exactly what I'd done. It had never bothered me to be that kind of person until now.

The karaoke DJ caught my attention as he announced the next singer and I was thankful for the distraction. "Ah, here we go. It's show time."

"What?" she asked, a look of panic before she whipped her head to the man walking toward the karaoke mic.

I shot Perry a wicked smile and tipped my beer to him. He shook his head like he was upset with me, but he didn't hesitate to grab the mic and start belting out Weezer's *Say it Aint So*.

"I don't understand. I thought you were writing our names down."

"Are you kidding me? I can't carry a tune. My buddy Perry though, this song was his specialty back in New York at a little dive bar we frequented throughout college."

"And you're both in town for the career fair?"

"Yeah, I have quite a few buddies from college here actually. We all graduated and took jobs in New York, but it appears our companies like to try and get a bit of fresh blood each year, so here we are."

"You should go hang out with them. I'm so sorry. I had no idea you had friends here. I just assumed they were people from your company."

"Nah, I'm the only one from my company. My boss thought I was the best fit since I have a client in the community. And Perry is just someone I partied with in college, we see each other often enough. Happy hours and parties on weekends occasionally."

She moved to stand, and I followed, putting myself between her and the exit.

"No, don't go. This is nice," I motioned between us with a hand. "Talking to you in person."

Her face flushed like it did every time I gave her even the smallest of compliments, but she nodded slightly. "Okay, but let's at least go over there so it's not like I stole you away."

"I think they'd understand," I muttered and chuckled to myself.

We grabbed our drinks and I led her across the bar and

introduced her to my buddies. Bianca shook hands, repeated names back and smiled up to the guys in such a sweet, charming way they were all eating out of her hand.

"How do you know this guy?" Aaron, a co-worker of Perry's that I'd only met twice, asked as he patted me on the shoulder like we were best buds.

I cocked an eyebrow at him but didn't push his hand off me like I wanted to.

"We met on a flight from New York awhile back," Bianca answered.

Aaron's eyes lit up as if that was all the information he needed to know she was available.

Wrapping an arm around her waist, I pulled Bianca to me in a possessive stance. She shot me a confused look but didn't pull away as I held her there making sure Aaron understood she was mine. It was petty and not even true, but I wanted to protect her. Needed to in some caveman, messed up primal desire.

"We've kept in touch," I added for no other reason than to make it clear I had put in the time with her.

Aaron nodded, glancing between us. "I see. Well, Court here's a great guy. You don't go through the shit he has without knowing how to appreciate a good thing."

I smiled a big, fake, toothy grin at Aaron and silently fumed at Perry for sharing shit he had no business sharing. Bianca's body molded into mine as if she understood my need for her sweet goodness. The anger rolled off me as I looked down at her. Even in those ridiculously high heels her head sat just above my shoulder. "What do you say we grab another drink?"

I pulled her behind me without waiting for her response, knowing full well she already had a nearly full drink in her hand.

When we got to the bar, she finally spoke. "Actually, I shouldn't have another if I'm going to be in any kind of shape for tomorrow."

I nodded.

"Tab?" I motioned to the bartender.

"You don't have to stop on my account. I'm just gonna catch a cab back to my apartment."

"You live far?" I asked as I signed the check.

"No, Orange and Grove."

"I'm staying at the Courtyard, we can share a cab."

"Those are in two completely different directions," she said with a smile.

I just grinned back at her.

She bit her bottom lip and her nervousness reminded me of why I'd found her so intriguing in the first place. She was innocence wrapped up in a tempting little package that she hid in plain sight. She'd been born in a generation that flaunted everything and balked at nothing and she'd gone unnoticed because she didn't try to be noticed. She didn't dress trendy or have pink hair. I hadn't spotted any piercing or tattoos – she was just your average college girl. But God, she was so much more.

I held the door to the bar open. The cool air greeted us, a welcome feeling after being in the hot bar. I inhaled deeply and let the door fall close behind us. Bianca smiled at me, stepping onto the sidewalk and freezing in place. I followed her line of vision to a group of guys piling out of a cab. It was clear they were already drunk from their loud and exaggerated movements, but they were put together well – rich, frat guys in polo shirts that cost as much as my entire wardrobe had in college.

"Ready?" I reached a hand out for her and she opened her mouth, her eyes darted from me to the group of guys.

"Bianca!" one of the guys called out and a look of uneasiness and panic took over her face. I stepped toward her just as the guy, wearing a striped Lacoste shirt and jeans that looked like they'd been freshly ironed – or probably dry cleaned I thought, reached us.

"Hey, sorry it took so long. Been quite a night. Wow, you look great," he prattled on, openly appreciating Bianca's bare legs without giving me so much as a glance.

"Hi, Todd," she said looking down to the sidewalk.

So, this was Todd. He looked like every other preppy asshole I'd seen in the bar tonight. I had him on height by a good few inches, but he was bulkier – maybe not more muscular, but broader – built something like a lineman instead of the squash player I knew him to be. He finally looked at me as if he'd just noticed Bianca wasn't alone. Strategic incompetence. He wanted me to know that I didn't matter.

"Todd," he stuck out his hand to me, giving me no other option than to shake.

"Court," I said, giving him one firm squeeze and pulling back. "So, I'll talk to you later?" I said, looking to Bianca. I was giving her the easy out. I knew she wanted to go with him. If she'd asked me what to do in this exact situation I would have told her going back in the bar for a drink was the right move. Hell, my being here probably made her all that more appealing. In Todd's eyes she'd be choosing him over me. The perfect setup. I couldn't have planned it better if I'd tried.

"I –" she stammered as Todd moved to her side and waited with an outstretched hand.

I leaned down, brushing my lips against her cheek before whispering in her ear, "Sweet dreams, 8B."

CHAPTER FOURTEEN

Bianca

Todd dropped my hand once we were inside the bar. I wondered if the way he'd so possessively taken my hand outside had more to do with Court than how happy he was to see me. Still I was excited.

I understood that appearances were part of the package with Todd. He wasn't malicious or ostentatious on purpose, sometimes it was just a side effect of the way he'd been raised. He'd grown up with a family who prided themselves on being perfectly put together. He'd admitted once that his father had actually inspected his outfit each night before dinner.

When I thought of the ratty play clothes my mother had insisted I wear at home – to preserve my school clothes – I'd felt a mixture of sadness and jealousy. Sadness because my best memories had been made when I was wearing those dirty clothes that were a size too small and filled with holes.

I was jealous for obvious reasons – what kid hadn't wanted to own a closet full of nice clothes? To stand out for looking nice. That's a desire that starts early on and I'm not sure it ever leaves us. If it does, I wasn't there yet. I tried to stay in the not pathetic enough to draw attention to myself zone. So, I hadn't looked ratty enough to draw attention and I was smart enough that I'd floated through school being mostly invisible.

"What are you drinking?" Todd asked as he tapped his credit card on the bar to get the bartender's attention.

He didn't look at me as he spoke, instead he bobbed his head around in that impatient way people do to draw attention to themselves without shouting 'Hey you' or waving their hands around. When it was clear that the bartender wasn't running over to take his order, he looked over my head – eyes scanning the place to see who was here and who wasn't.

It was petty to compare him to Court, but it occurred to me then, that in the entire time I'd spent with Court tonight he'd never once looked past me. He'd only been interested in me.

"I can't stay, Todd." That got his eyes back on me and suddenly I had his undivided attention. I continued, "I have interviews tomorrow morning and I've already stayed out longer and drank more than I should have."

The disappointment on his face only lasted a second until his buddies surrounded us, all vying to get the attention of the bartender who I was starting to think was avoiding them on purpose.

"What time are you done tomorrow? Do you want to grab lunch?"

"My interviews go until late afternoon. What about

dinner?"

"We have a team dinner tomorrow. How about Friday?"

"Sounds great," I said just as the bartender finally made her way to Todd. He waved to me as he spouted out their order and I slipped away. I moved toward the door in a haze of confusion. Why was I leaving? I'd been perfectly content to blow off the interviews at the beginning of the night, but now it just felt irresponsible and wrong. I wasn't even all that sad about leaving Todd.

Back at my apartment I slipped off my heels and groaned at the ache in my feet. Court had been right yet again – those shoes were only meant for one thing and it wasn't walking.

The alcohol was still buzzing through my body and although I knew I needed to crawl into bed and try and get as much sleep as possible, it's not what I did. I wanted to talk to Court.

I'd felt guilty about the way things had ended tonight. His manners had been impeccable as he'd graciously left without making a big deal of it. Still, I'd seen the way he'd looked at me tonight. I was almost sure there was something more to his interest in me than helping me with Todd.

Phone in hand, I plopped onto my bed and pulled up our text exchange. While I stared at the screen trying to figure out what to type, it buzzed in my hand.

> *Court*: Good luck on your interviews tomorrow, 8B.
> Let me know how they go.
>
> *Me*: Thank you.

I was still torn on what to say next when his reply came.

> *Court*: That was quick. You home already?

Me: Yes, just walked in.

How did we move forward from tonight? I didn't want to ask him about relationships or talk about Todd, I wanted to ask about him. Who was Court Adams?

Me: What's your schedule tomorrow? Are you at the career fair all day?

Court: Yep, 8-5. It's gonna be a long ass day. You gonna stop by and say hi between your interviews?

Me: While I would love to see you all professional, I don't think they'll let me in to see you without an interview.

Court: You could just say you want to see me in a suit again.

My cheeks hurt from smiling as I texted back.

Me: Such ego.

Court: Come by, I've got an open slot around eleven. I'll give you the whole spiel on why you should work for my company and I can test your interview skills.

Me: I don't think you'd want me for whatever it is that you do there.

Court: It's not so much about degree. It's a lot of on the job training since each client has different needs. Being comfortable analyzing numbers also comes in handy and we've already established that you're good at math.

Me: Yes, I am.

> *Court*: I have the sudden urge to type 80085 on a calculator right now.
>
> *Me*: BOOBS, seriously? How old are you again?
>
> *Court*: Some things never get old. Sweet dreams, Bianca.
>
> *Me*: Night, Court.

As I started to set my phone on the night stand I thought of an earlier conversation we'd had tonight and quickly typed out another text.

> *Me*: You never said whether or not your parents ever call you Courtney?
>
> *Court*: Don't know. I never met them.

My fingers stilled over the keys and I squeezed my eyes shut as if I could erase the words I'd written with telekinetic power. Leave it to me to put my foot in my mouth after such a great night. I wanted to know more, but it didn't feel like a texting conversation. Besides, I needed to think on how to broach the topic.

> *Me*: Well, I like Court – it suits you, very royal and distinguished sounding.
>
> *Court*: You're still drunk.
>
> *Me*: Yes, but it's still true.
>
> *Court*: Get some sleep sweet girl.

And I did.

CHAPTER FIFTEEN

Court

I woke up excited about the day – a surprising reaction considering where I was and what I was going to be doing. I didn't mind travel in general, but this town had never been the highlight of my travel destinations. And under normal circumstances I'd have preferred slamming my head into the wall as opposed to interviewing college kids.

Shit, some of these interviewees could be mine in another month or two. I'd been so excited about the promotion I hadn't really thought about what it was going to be like to try and manage a fresh faced, wide-eyed graduate.

None the less I jumped out of bed, showered, and dressed in my favorite suit while I whistled softly.

As I sat in the back seat of the cab, I shuffled through the resumes for today. I was interviewing ten people over the course of nine hours. A fancy luncheon put on by the college thrown in the middle and a social mixer tonight.

Edward Stanton III, Joseph Michael Stronghold (yeah, the dude put his middle name on his resume – that alone should have discounted him), and on and on the list went with third and fourth generation names. Throwing the resumes back on top of my laptop bag, I pulled out my phone.

> **Me**: Ready to kill it on those interviews?
>
> **Bianca**: Ugh, no. Do you think I can wear sweatpants?
>
> **Me**: Not unless they're phone interviews.
>
> **Bianca**: Boo.
>
> **Me**: Knock'em dead. See you at eleven.
>
> **Bianca**: You too.
>
> **Bianca**: Actually, no – be nice!

Her last demand came as the cab pulled up to the university building where the interviews would take place and I chuckled as I paid and thanked the driver. I found the small conference room I'd been assigned for the day and set up for my first interview.

I wasn't entirely sure what it was I was looking for in an employee. Obviously, I wanted someone intelligent, well spoken, and I guess if I was being honest I wanted someone with the same sort of work ethic and dedication that I had – or at least as most I could hope for.

At five 'til eight, a young man in an ill-fitting three-piece suit stood nervously in the door.

"Hi, are you Joseph?" I asked, moving to the door in

an attempt to make this kid relax a little. Nothing sounded worse than sitting through an interview while the person across the table stuttered out short answers and avoided eye contact.

When he nodded, I extended a hand and then motioned for him to have a seat.

"Thanks for coming out today, Joseph." Taking a seat across from him I slid him the packet HR had sent with me. "You can take these with you. It's a little about the company, the office in New York, and our benefits package."

"Thank you," he fumbled with the papers before tucking them into his portfolio.

I leaned back in my chair hoping my relaxed posture would put him at ease. "I took a look at your resume last night and I have to tell you, it looks great. I think you have a lot of the skills and experience we're looking for in an entry-level analyst."

Okay, maybe I was stretching the truth a little, but the way his face softened, and his shoulders relaxed, I knew it had been the right thing to say.

"Why don't I tell you a little about Harrison and Mac and then we can ask each other some questions and see if this is something you might be interested in. Sound good?"

By the end of the interview, I liked Joseph Michael Stronghold way more than I'd anticipated. I'd even forgiven him for using his middle name on his resume – almost. He'd need some confidence behind the scenes before I could take him to a client site, but I put him in the "keep" file and actually meant it when I told him that it had been a pleasure talking to him.

The next two interviews were flops. Edward Stanton III either had no idea what my company did when he signed up for the interview or he'd wanted to waste my time. And Natasha Lamoure had spent more time pushing out her breasts and posing for me than she had thinking about the answers that were coming out of her boldly painted lips.

When I ushered Natasha out of the room, I spotted Bianca making her way across the empty space between the conference rooms. The rooms ran along the far wall, each boasting a magnificent view of the campus. But my view – damn, 8B looked all grown up. The tap of her black heels echoed in the otherwise quiet space and her uneasy smile, aimed right at me, made this whole day – the whole trip seem worth it.

"Hi," she said when she got within speaking distance.

"Miss Winters," I said and waved her into the room, closing the door behind her. "You look great."

She smoothed her hand down her black skirt. "You're the first interviewer to ever tell me that."

A deep chuckle escaped from my upturned lips. "Yeah, I think my HR director's ears are probably ringing."

I moved toward the chair I'd been using for the interviews and paused. I looked down at my watch. I already knew the time, but I needed something to do with my eyes that didn't involve mentally undressing the woman in front of me. Being here with her felt all kinds of fucked up. We were playing some twisted mentor/mentee game that looked harmless but felt like it could slice me wide open.

In this small conference room standing behind a thick, oak desk that had been designed for intimidation, I only wanted to make her feel equal. "I've got about twenty minutes until the next roman numeral shows up. Do you still want to do a mock interview, or do you want to go grab a cup of coffee or something?"

"Please," she sat down and slumped into the seat. "I'm really regretting my decision to blow off preparing last night."

Taking my seat, I ran my hand down my tie. "Alright, Miss Winters, why don't you start by telling me a little about yourself."

Her eyes widened in panic, but she took a deep breath and nodded. "Okay, I'm in my last semester and will graduate with a B.S. in Electrical Engineering. My interest is in signal processing, specifically machine learning."

"Very good and do you have any experience – internships or co-ops?"

"I had an internship with Mollie Engineering last summer where I was able to contribute to their machine learning team."

"You spent your summers in New York?"

She broke character for a moment, her face lighting up. "Yeah, call me crazy but I love New York in the summer. Everyone else is hurrying off to their beach homes and the streets are quieter."

"Quieter because everyone is trying to escape the heat," I said thinking about the sticky hotness that soaked into the concrete and set the city ablaze during the month of July.

"I don't mind it," she said, shaking her head and a wistful look overtaking her face. "My parents have an outdoor patio where we plant a little garden every year and there's a mister out there with these big, ugly lounge chairs with mismatched cushions where my mom and I sit with a book or an iced tea. It's my favorite place in the whole world."

"You miss New York?" I asked, but I already knew the answer. I could tell she did by the way she talked about it and the look that crossed her face every damn time.

She nodded, her smile falling. "I miss my family."

"Siblings?"

"Two brothers. Leo and Donnie. They're seventeen."

"Twins?"

"Yep, never a dull moment with those two around."

The way she said it made me picture her sitting quietly in a noisy house just taking it all in. I had never been able to do that – stand on the sidelines when things around me escalated into anarchy. When things got out of hand, I either became louder and more obnoxious to drown out the noise or I'd run.

That's who Bianca was, she was the silence – still and unmoving, barely noticeable at all until it was gone. But I'd lived my life in the chaos and noise and had strived for nothing but peace and quiet since I'd been on my own. I had learned to appreciate the silence. I needed it. I craved it.

"What does your family think of you staying for grad school?"

The way she instantly worried at her lip gave her away. "You haven't told them."

"I will if and when I decide to stay, but the twins will be graduating high school soon and preparing to do their own thing anyway and mom and dad are probably counting down the days until they have an empty house."

"You don't really believe that, or you'd have already told them."

She laughed softly and repeated, "I will tell them if and when I decide to stay."

Her posture stiffened, and her face became stoic – a sign she was ready to get back to the interview.

"Where do you see yourself in five years?"

I never planned to ask this question in real interviews. I thought it was a bullshit question. Nobody knew where they'd be in five years' time – not even in a year's time. We rolled with life's punches and adjusted. You could have a hope and a plan, but how often did those work out the way we dreamed it up in our heads? But I was curious about little 8B and what she wanted for herself.

"I'd like to be working for a company that creates products that are cutting edge, but whose core values are still dependable and loyal to its employees and clients."

I appreciated her insight, and I could tell she meant it – every word, but I also knew there was a good chance another interviewer was going to see her answer as a copout.

"What about you specifically, how do you see yourself fitting into a company like that?"

She looked like she was pondering that for a moment. I bet she already knew. Had already considered this question as she'd considered everything.

"I'd like to lead teams or projects. I think I'd be good at managing moving pieces and driving toward a common goal. While I'll be grateful to work my way up and be a member of a team until I'm ready to lead my own, I see myself as a leader."

When she'd stopped speaking the room grew quiet as I let her response hang there. I let it soak in. It was the perfect response, but even better – it was true."

She fidgeted in her chair, obviously waiting for my response. My approval.

"That was beautiful, 8B."

A small, forced laugh left her mouth. "Beautiful?"

I nodded. "It's the best answer to that question I've ever heard."

"Isn't this your first day of doing interviews?"

It was my turn to laugh. "Trust me, that answer is your

golden ticket. It's thoughtful and sincere and says a lot about you knowing your strengths like that."

She nodded and let out a breath. "Any more questions?" she asked tentatively.

"One more." I crossed my ankles and leaned back into the cushioned office chair. "What is your biggest weakness?"

Without hesitation she said, "I am good with numbers and details. I love researching and proving theories. I'm a hard worker and I will put in the time and hours necessary to meet deadlines, but I," she looked down at her laced fingers that laid on her lap. "I can come across as selfish. My focus makes it hard to notice the feelings of those around me. I don't always catch on to subtleties and nuances. I realize this is something I will need to work on."

My throat tightened, and my chest burned. How had this girl, this woman, become so self-aware at such a young age?

"No need to be quite so sacrificial in your answer. Just let them know you are prone to tunnel vision when you're meeting deadlines. They'll appreciate that quality when phrased a way that benefits them."

She nodded again, some of that confidence that had been building since she sat down seemed to chip away and I wanted to help her find it again.

"Just remember, the people interviewing you, no matter their title or merits, have weaknesses too. We all do, none of us are perfect. They aren't looking for perfect." I scrubbed a hand over my jaw. "I'm not looking for perfect."

We stared at each other and it felt like our interview had turned too personal. Like we'd both revealed too much about ourselves. Her more than me, but considering I didn't tell anyone jack shit, I'd given her more than I was comfortable with.

"So, any last words of wisdom?" she asked, standing shakily.

I mirrored her movements and stood, rounding the table. "You could try picturing them naked."

She wrinkled her nose. "Is that what you did when you were interviewing for jobs?"

"Nah," I shook my head. "I went with a slightly different approach."

Her eyebrows drew together, and she waited for me to elaborate.

Leaning in, I brought my lips close to her ear. "I went commando."

"Seriously?" she asked with a nervous laugh as her eyes drifted down to my crotch.

Was she wondering if I was free-balling it right now? My dick stirred at the thought of her considering the underwear situation, or lack thereof, in my pants. "I can't even remember if it was intentional or not. Maybe it was so I'd feel like I'd somehow got the better of them without their knowing or maybe I just hadn't done laundry in a week."

"And that worked?"

"I got a job. I can't speak to whether or not my lack of underwear was the cause or just a lucky coincidence."

Her smile was big and conspiratorial as she leaned in, not as close as I had, but close enough that I was all too aware of her faint floral scent and the light pink gloss that coated her lips. Those full, pink lips parted, and I went rigid. I didn't trust myself to so much as breathe.

"I think I might try that," she said in a husky voice that was flirty and sexy, and maybe I was reading too much into every move she made because she had me so tied up, but I was starting to think 8B might be feeling this thing between us too.

Just maybe Bianca was into me for real. Not because I was helping her and not as a fake anything. In fact, I wasn't even sure my 8B was capable of faking something so good.

As she walked out the door, I was already preparing my next move.

CHAPTER SIXTEEN

Bianca

"Tʜɪs ɪs cᴀᴜsᴇ for a celebration," Tasha exclaimed as she clapped her hands together.

"I don't have the job yet," I said. Again.

JC Engineering had invited me for a second interview in their New York office and I was trying to stay optimistic without getting my hopes up. Tasha was making that difficult with her assumptions that the job was as good as mine.

"I'm sure they've asked a number of candidates to fly out for an onsite interview. Plus, I'm still seriously considering grad school."

"We're celebrating," she said leaving no room to argue. "Unfortunately, all we have on hand is wine."

Tasha got out the wine glasses and two bottles of wine that had been sitting on our kitchen counter top for most of the semester. We made a picnic in the living room – sitting on the floor and using the coffee table to place the array of snacks we'd pulled from the cabinets.

I let her control the music and we sang and danced to Taylor Swift and Ed Sheeran, wine glasses in hand. Singing, dancing, drinking, laughing. The night couldn't get any better. Or so I thought.

A ringing caught my attention. We'd left our phones in our respective bedrooms, so we wouldn't be tempted by the allure of social media or text messages, but the shrill ringtone carried into the living room and we both stopped singing and dancing and stood in the middle of the living room. We stared at each other sharing a look that asked if we should break this moment to find out who it was.

"Let me just make sure it's not my family," I said as I hustled to my bedroom. I unplugged my phone and carried it to the living room as I stared in shock at the screen. "It's Court."

Tasha's eyes lit up and she turned the music down. "Answer it!"

I'd have blamed it on the wine, but my heart pounded with excitement that had nothing to do with the alcohol coursing through my blood.

"Hello?" I answered in a surprised greeting like maybe my phone was playing tricks on me and it wasn't really Court on the other end.

"8B, what are you doing?" his smooth voice had me smiling before he'd finished uttering a complete sentence.

"Tasha and I are hanging out at home," I said.

Tasha spoke louder than necessary and leaned toward the phone. "We're celebrating."

"Celebrating, huh? Sounds like I'm in the right place then."

"In the – what?" I asked, putting a hand to my free ear

and pushing the cell into the other to hear him better.

He chuckled, and I heard the slam of a car door. "I'm outside. You want to tell me which apartment is yours or should I just start shouting until someone points me in the right direction?"

My face must have shown my excitement because Tasha looked at me with an impatient stare and mouthed, "What's going on?"

Ignoring her, I walked to the front door and opened it tentatively. I stepped out, Tasha on my heels, and looked down the stairwell to the parking lot. There he was looking handsome as ever striding toward us with a paper bag tucked neatly under his arm. I waved, having lost the ability to speak, and Court lifted his chin in acknowledgement.

"What is he doing here?" Tasha whispered with bubbly excitement.

I had no idea and I didn't care.

"Can I crash the party?" he asked winking at Tasha.

"Depends on what's in that bag," she said, hands on hips.

She moved allowing him into the apartment and he brushed past me leaving me stunned and still speechless.

He sat the bag on the counter and Tasha greedily examined it pulling out a two liter of diet coke, a bottle of rum, and then every type of candy known to man.

"Did you rob a gas station?" I asked, setting my phone on the counter and picking up a pack of Twizzlers in one hand and powdered donuts in the other.

"I didn't want to come empty handed, but I had no idea what you liked," he admitted.

I laughed and tossed them back on the counter and then stared at him in disbelief. "What are you doing here?"

"It's my last night in Connecticut," he said as if that was

reason enough.

"Oh my God," Tasha squealed as she tore into a Nutty Bar. Her eyes rolled back as she bit into the sugary delight.

Court's fingers lightly brushed mine. "I just wanted to see you again before I leave. I'll go if you want."

"Stay," I said softly at the same time Tasha called out. "Oh my gosh, B, he got pop rocks!"

Court moved his hand and a chill ran through my body. I missed the warmth of his light touch and I wanted more of it. And I wanted it everywhere.

In that moment, I finally stopped fighting the constant buzz of electricity between us. It wasn't his wit or his knowledge on life and the male mind that I wanted. It was him. For reasons I didn't understand and couldn't twist into logic, I felt a connection with Court that I'd never had before.

A friendship and a mutual respect. And a desire. *Current.*

While Court and I made our way to the living room, drinks and junk food in tow, Tasha skipped off to her room, pop rocks and nutty bar in hand, as she sing-songed something about checking her phone.

Court's presence in my apartment had disarmed me.

"I can't believe you're really here in my apartment," I said and shook my head as if the movement would focus my eyes and I'd discover he wasn't really here at all.

He shrugged. "I know it was probably presumptuous to just show up, but it felt too impersonal to send a congratulations text. When do you go to New York for the second interview?"

"In two weeks. The interview is on Friday and then I'm going to stay the weekend, so I can see my family while I'm there."

"That'll be nice," he said, and his tone had a rough edge

to it that I couldn't understand.

We talked about New York – about the location of his office and apartment and I told him more about my family and where they worked and lived in the city. He was tight lipped about his past and his family. I didn't pry – something about the way Aaron had mentioned Court "going through shit" made me hold back.

Tasha never reappeared and from the one-sided conversation I could just barely hear coming from her bedroom, I assumed she was having a marathon phone conversation with Lance. They were adorable like that – they both put on a good show of having nights out with their friends, but it always ends up like this, the two of them on the phone or, more often than not, them calling the night early so they could be together.

I'd have found it frustrating how often she dodged out on me if I didn't also find it hopelessly romantic. I knew she didn't do it to hurt me. I truly believed she just couldn't help the need to be near him.

There was a lull in conversation and I heard the music for the first time in at least an hour, maybe longer. Big Pun played and as if Court was just hearing it now too he laughed. "You do know your old school rap."

"Tasha's playlists are always an eclectic mix. I made her add this one."

"You did not," he said with an unbelieving smile.

I lip synced to the chorus. "I'm not a player, I just crush a lot."

I pointed to him as I sang, and he shook his head. "I am not a player."

"Hey, they were your words, not mine."

"Fair point," he conceded. "What else you got on here?"

he asked.

"Well, Tasha likes everything so some current hits and the classics like Destiny's Child and Tupac."

"Classics? God, I'm old," he muttered. "So, this is Tasha's playlist," he placed a thumb in the air at the direction of the speaker, "but what do you listen to?"

"I like older stuff – Fleetwood Mac, for example. I'm into covers of older songs that my parents listened to."

"You really do miss them, New York, all of it huh?"

"I thought it'd go away," I said. "First semester all I wanted to do was run home, but my parents were so proud that I was out on my own. And it has been great here, don't get me wrong, but I still miss my family and New York every single day."

He nodded, and I thought he might ask more about my family or why I was considering staying when it was so clear I wanted to be with them. He didn't.

"What's your favorite cover song?"

I responded automatically. "Adele, *I Can't Make You Love Me*."

The look on his face was sad and his eyes looked at me with… pity. "Or the Thirty Seconds to Mars' cover of *Stay*, that one is really good, too," I added and stood under the guise of switching the music off.

"Play it for me," he said.

"I –" my protest was cut short as Tasha strolled into the room.

"Play what?" she asked, turning the music off and then plopping into a chair in the living room.

Neither of us spoke for a moment and Tasha looked between us impatiently.

"Bianca is going to play me her favorite cover song."

"Oh, God, not that sad song again."

"It's not sad, it's beautiful," I said with not enough gumption because it *was* sad.

"Oh, whatever, B," Tasha said and turned her attention to Court. "Tell me this isn't sad." Phone in hand, she made a show of pressing play and then setting the phone down on the coffee table as Adele's voice filled the apartment.

With nowhere else to go, I sat back on the couch and pulled my feet underneath me. When I peeked up at Court, he was looking at me – that stupid look of pity stamped all over his face. Tears pricked at the back of my eyes and I didn't even know why except this song and Court's face. And God I was pathetic.

As the chorus started, Court grabbed my hand. The familiar heat from where he touched me earlier returned and I inhaled. It felt too intimate and awkward to have him holding my hand like this, but just when I thought I might rather pull away than have his pity, he started singing along.

"And I can't make you love meeeeeeeeeeeee," he sang off key, voice wavering between octaves. I laughed and grabbed Tasha's phone.

"Alright, alright, it's a sappy song," I said as I paused the music. "What's your favorite song?" I tossed the phone at Court.

He clutched the phone with a grin. Holding it in one hand, he brought his other up to his chin. "I can never pick a favorite. I listen to songs on repeat until I can hardly stand them and then I move on."

I rolled my eyes. "Oh my God, you can't even be faithful to a song."

"Okay, gun to head it's this song."

It took Tasha and I a minute to figure out the familiar

intro – she recognized it first.

"*Glycerine* by Bush?" she asked with a laugh.

"Hey, Gavin was big at an important time in my life."

I smiled because I thought it fit him, but I didn't say that aloud.

"What about love songs?" Tasha asked.

He thought for another minute and then gave us a warning as the music started. "If you ever tell anyone I like this song, I'll deny it."

It was Brett Michaels voice that crooned out and Tasha and I both burst into a fit of giggles as *Every Rose Has a Thorn* played. When I recovered, I started to listen to the lyrics. Really hearing them for the first time. It was a sad song, really – an unrequited love, a man that thinks he's not good enough.

The expression on Court's face was open, like the lyrics had transported him and I could almost see the uneasy teenage boy who listened to this song and felt unworthy or unloved. I grabbed his hand, intent on singing like he'd done for me. I broke whatever trip down memory lane he was having and the taunting grin that was all confident man was back. Still, I forced myself to give him something, just as he'd given me. So, I sang – terribly, but as I should have guessed he'd do – he didn't mock me, but instead he joined me, and we sang – *terribly* - together as we linked hands. Tasha took turns singing and laughing at us.

The song ended, and I found my face hurting from smiling so much.

Tasha yawned loudly. "I'm going to bed," she announced. "Will you be back before graduation?" she asked looking to Court.

"I'll be back in a couple weeks, but I'm not sure how

much free time I'll have."

"Well, I hope you'll stop by if you can."

"I'd like that."

"Night, B."

"So, back in a couple weeks, huh?" I asked a moment later. I was nervous now that we were alone again, and everything started to feel too small, too charged. The apartment, the couch, the space between us.

"Yeah, actually I was going to ask you if –" he cleared his throat and suddenly I was excited. I couldn't explain it, but whatever he was about to ask I already, unequivocally knew I wanted.

CHAPTER SEVENTEEN

Court

"I<small>F</small>..."

Bianca looked up at me with big doe eyes. The want and need practically pouring out of her was my undoing.

I cleared my throat as I ran a hand behind my neck. "If I could use your bathroom before I head out?"

Awkward silence hung in the air while my words registered. Slowly she blinked. Once and then twice.

"Yeah, sure. Of course. First door on the left." Her voice wavered.

I bolted for the bathroom, holding my breath until the door was closed and locked behind me.

Resting both hands on the sink, I looked at myself in the mirror.

"What the fuck?" I hissed at my reflection. "Chicken shit."

I'd just had the best night that I could ever remember

having with a woman. I'd let my guard down, just been myself and we'd connected. I'd felt it. *She'd* felt it.

Pushing off the sink, I looked around the small but tidy space. It was too organized to be shared by two women, but it smelled like Bianca. A small, open makeup bag rested on the counter next to the sink and I hooked one finger inside to pull it open wider. It all looked like basic girly toiletries that could have belonged to any woman except for one item. The blue eyeliner.

I smiled as I picked it up and read the label – electric blue. Fitting. She'd zapped me into another dimension with those eyes of hers.

Replaying the night as I rolled the blue pencil-like tube in my hand, I almost felt like laughing if it weren't so messed up. I'd wanted to ask her to be my plus one for the Sterling's wedding reception. I'm not even sure why. I couldn't get her involved in all that. And even if I were going as just a friendly client, she was twenty-two.

Twenty-two.

Christ, when I was her age, the idea of being a plus one with a thirty-four-year-old would have made me curl my lip. Even if the invite had been to the fucking moon.

I'd been just about to ask her and then she'd looked up at me with big, wanting eyes. Those blue irises the color at the bottom of a flame. Electric blue. I'd never think of them any other way now. They had disarmed me. I had no idea what I was doing with Bianca and it was starting to seriously mess with my head.

Inviting her into my life – on a freaking date - would have ended one of two ways.

Scenario one, awkward laughter from her followed by a quick cover up on my part. She'd do that nervous, strained laugh I heard from her so often and then I'd say something like "Just kidding, 8B. I just wanted to see how you respond when asked out on a date." Yeah, I'd probably have turned it into a fucking teaching moment because wasn't that what this still was?

Scenario two, she said yes way too excitedly and then by the time the reception rolled around she'd be dating Todd and I'd have to spend the evening pretending I wasn't interested in being more than a mentor. Or worse, listening to her go on and on about the prick.

I groaned. I needed to get back out there and out the front door before I made a bigger ass of myself. I uncapped the blue eye makeup pencil and wrote her a note on the mirror. I smiled at my messy blue writing. Hopefully I'd redeem myself in the gesture. It didn't feel like it could get worse.

I returned the eyeliner to the bag and gave myself a silent pep talk as I walked back to the living room where Bianca was busy cleaning up empty candy wrappers and dirty glasses.

"Guess I should get going. I've got an early flight out tomorrow." I shoved my hands in my pockets but then thought better of it. "Here let me help."

"Oh no, it's not necessary. I've got it."

She waved me off, but I stepped forward and reached for the glasses she had tucked between her arm and side.

"Thanks," she said as I took them from her. Her eyes flitted up to meet mine and quickly away. I'd made her unsure and apprehensive and I fucking hated that.

After we'd tossed the trash and put the glasses in the dishwasher, Bianca walked me to the door. I hovered just outside of the doorway feeling like a coward. I had to give her something. I couldn't leave here tonight without her knowing it had meant something to me.

I reached for her hand and clasped our fingers together. Her breath hitched, but she didn't make a move toward me. Our hands bridged the gap that neither of us was brave enough to cross on our own.

Fuck it.

I pulled her to me and leaned down so that my lips were at her ear. She went still as I sang the opening to *Glycerine*. I was no Gavin, but as she turned her head to meet my gaze it didn't matter. Fuck, Rossdale. He didn't have her. And the look she gave me told me I did.

I stepped back before I did anything stupid like push her into the apartment with me on top of her.

Without looking back, I called out into the night like I was a rockstar dropping the mic and rushing off stage. "Sweet dreams, 8B."

After I returned to New York, Bianca and I continued talking every day. Most days we texted all day long. I woke up to good morning and have a good day greetings. She filled me in on her days – how class went, what she had for lunch – it sounded lame, I know, but I loved every second of it. I couldn't wait to see what she'd type next. She didn't mention Todd outright anymore and I certainly didn't ask or try and keep up the rouse that my interest was purely in helping her win him over.

As I got to know Bianca more and she talked more of her family and friends, I realized how big her circle was. It stung when she talked about the happy memories of her childhood.

I'd avoided friends or women with happy families. It wasn't a conscious decision, at least not at first. At first it was by chance.

When you're fifteen years old hanging on the streets past dark with no one checking in on you or yelling at you to get your ass home, it makes sense that your closest friends were going to be people in the same situation.

I'd once had a friend, Ray, who I'd really liked quite a bit. We had a lot in common – even the large chip that we carried around on our shoulders, but when Ray invited me over to play Xbox for the first time I'd arrived at his very upper class, Brady Bunch house, and realized the chip on his shoulder was fake. It was just something he was trying on for size, like playing a broody Heathcliff because it felt cool. After I'd wiped the drool off my face when I got a look at his very nice, very big house I thought surely his parents must be grade A assholes, but when I asked him about his family, he just shrugged a shoulder and said, "Eh, they're alright just always getting on my case about trying harder in school."

That was his biggest fucking problem? It was unbelievable and cruel, and I never went back.

Suffice to say, it may not have been a conscious decision, but my small circle of friends were from backgrounds as fucked up as mine. We weren't playing a part or doing it to piss off our parents – we wished. We were the real deal. The sad sops whose stories made others uncomfortable.

Bianca was the first person I'd ever connected with who had a happy, functioning family life and that part of her made my dark feel darker, but all the good, all the light she brought outweighed the dark and I found it was worth it to be uncomfortable when I was near her.

However, I was seriously second guessing if she was

worth it as I walked up to the Winters' family home for the first time. Bianca had flown into town for her in-person interview tomorrow with JC Engineering and like a fool who couldn't stay away I'd come straight from work when she'd texted and asked if I had plans.

"You made it," Bianca said as she opened the door wide. There was a moment hesitation where it looked like she might throw her arms around me and pull me into a hug. And man, I wanted that. I wanted to feel her arms wrapped around my neck and her body flush up against mine. Instead, I stutter stepped into the house with my hands shoved in my pockets.

She wore a nervous smile and another one of her oversized dresses – this one in a light orange with big pink flowers. It seemed fitting, her old dresses and funky eye makeup, when placed against the backdrop of her family home. Mismatched furniture, shelves of knick-knacks, sketches pinned to the wall with tacks, framed pictures on nearly every surface – it wasn't stylish, but it was lovely. And it was clear even without insider knowledge that this was a home filled with love.

"You too. What time did your flight get in?"

"Around noon," she said as she shut the door behind me and led me through the house. "Everyone is out. My parents are at work until this evening and the twins should be home anytime, I think. They're hard to keep track of."

I nodded to indicate I was listening to her, even though she wasn't looking at me, as I took in every detail of the house. Eight by eleven posed school pictures hung in cheap golden frames in the hallway. Bianca's picture caught my attention first. Her hair was shorter and her face a little softer and younger, but the same blue eyes and reserved smile stared back at me.

On either side of her, matching frames held photos of her brothers. Despite the fact I knew they were twins, it was obvious from the pictures that their style and looks were different. One brother had shaggy blond hair and wore a graphic tee that I couldn't quite make out the design of from the small portion not cut off in the frame. The second brother had shorter hair, worn longer on top but styled in a clean-cut way. He was wearing a black polo shirt that completed the preppy look that was such a weird contradiction to his brother. The one thing that there was no mistaking was they were related.

All three Winters children had the same blue eyes that burned into your soul. It was hard to look at those eyes on the face of her brothers when I'd started to associate them with being purely Bianca.

"That's Leo," she said pointing to the one with shaggy hair. "And that's Donnie." She swept her hand in the direction of the preppy twin.

I didn't have time to do much more than nod before she was moving down to another framed photo, this one of a bride and groom circa the late eighties if the big hair and poufy dress were any indication. "My parents. Obviously, they don't look much like that anymore."

I peeled my eyes from the photos to Bianca standing beside me. She shuffled her feet and fidgeted with her hands clasped together in front of her stomach. She was nervous. What about, I wasn't sure, but it comforted me somehow. Her insecurities brought out the same protective male instinct that her simple and honest reactions did. I wanted to comfort her and be someone that made her feel secure and confident to be herself.

"It looks like you have a really nice family," I stated, and

I meant it. This was not a home of pretention or overtures. The house was small, and the furnishings were out dated, but it was clean and organized and the feat that alone must have been with two teenage boys at home didn't go unnoticed by me.

"Do you want something to drink?" she motioned toward the small kitchen.

I surprised myself by answering, "Actually, there's somewhere I'd like to take you."

I'd caught her off guard, too, by the look on her face. "Okay, let me just grab my purse and leave a note for my family."

"I'll get you back early," I promised after she'd scribbled out something on a piece of paper.

"Where are we going?" she asked once we were outside.

I grabbed her hand and brought it up to my lips and placed a soft kiss to the back. "You'll see."

I knew Leika would be surprised at my willingly bringing a girl to our spot. Neither of us ever brought dates with us unless it was serious. Leika had brought a few others before Jeff, but I'd never brought anyone. And no, I wasn't counting the numerous women Leika has blindsided me with by inviting them to "drop by" so she could introduce us.

I knew Leika would be surprised but the look on her face as I introduced her to Bianca was priceless. Her dark eyes widened and if her lips pulled her smile any bigger her face would split in two.

"Court didn't tell me he was seeing anyone." She gave me a look of approval even though her words hinted at a betrayal.

Bianca blushed, but I didn't contradict Leika. She wouldn't believe me even if I told her Bianca and I were just friends. "Bianca is just in town for an interview. She goes to school in Connecticut."

"Oooh." A million questions flashed by on her face, but Leika turned all her attention to Bianca and the two of them sat side by side like old friends as Leika gushed over her and peppered her with questions.

"I'm gonna get drinks," I said to no one because neither was paying me any attention. It appeared that Bianca didn't mind the way Leika was fawning over her because she was smiling and singularly focused on whatever they were talking about.

From the bar I continued to watch them and a weight I didn't realize I was carrying lifted. Leika was important. She was the closest thing I had to family and I wanted her to approve of Bianca – even to like her. I hadn't realized I needed that so much before I could situate my feelings for Bianca, but now that my mind was at ease, I let my gaze slide to the young woman and something stirred in my chest. I wanted her. Not in the one night, maybe see where things go kind of way. I wanted her to be something more. When was the last time I wanted anyone like that? Had there ever been a time?

As I got back to the table, Leika finally took a breath and the women looked at me as I slid in across from them. Bianca's phone started ringing and she fished through her purse, pulling out the device and waving it as she said, "It's my mom. I'll be right back."

After she was out of ear shot, Leika leaned across the table and whisper-yelled, "Oh my God, why didn't you tell me you were dating? And a college girl? How long has this been going on?"

"We're not dating. I met her on a flight to Connecticut

and we've kept in touch."

"This just gets better and better."

"What?"

"You haven't slept with her." It was a statement and not a question, so I didn't bother confirming it.

"Court, this is huge. I know saying I'm proud of you sounds condescending but screw it – I'm proud of you. She seems smart and level headed and the way she talks about you with stars in her eyes it's obvious she's smitten too."

"I –" Fuck, I didn't know what to say.

"Sorry," Bianca said as she slid back in beside Leika. "No matter how long I'm gone, as soon as I come back to New York my mother needs a play by play of my whereabouts."

Leika and I shared a quick look. I didn't have to be a mind reader to know she was thinking how nice that would be to have a family that cared so much. We didn't often talk about our childhood, but it was a wound that hadn't healed for either of us.

"So how long are you in town?" Leika asked Bianca.

"Through the weekend. I head back to Connecticut on Sunday afternoon."

"We have to have a party at your place tomorrow night, Court. It's been months since you've had people over and Bianca has to have a proper send off. Maybe it'll help seal the deal, so we can convince her to take the job and move here." She linked her arm through Bianca's.

"I have to get the job first."

We sat like that, Bianca and Leika across from me, chatting and drinking until Bianca began checking the time on her phone.

"I should get Bianca home. She has to be bright eyed and bushy tailed in the morning for her interview."

"Aww, I'm sad to see you go, but I just know you're gonna kill it and we're gonna be seeing a lot more of each other." She wrapped her arms around a surprised Bianca and I chuckled under my breath.

"Alright, alright, let the poor girl go."

Reluctantly, Leika let Bianca go and then proceeded to throw herself onto me next. "You did good, bro," she whispered quietly before giving me a light squeeze and pulling back.

The trip back to her parents' house was quieter and our strides slower.

"Leika's nice."

"Nice," I chuckled. "Yeah, she's nice."

"Are you two –" the unasked question hung in the air and I suddenly felt like an idiot for not making it clear earlier.

"Leika's like a sister to me. We've known each other since we were kids."

"Oh. I see."

From her tone, I could tell that no she didn't see, and I let out a deep breath before divulging more personal information than I ever dreamed of telling her.

"Leika and I lived with the same foster family for a few years before I turned eighteen and was no longer a ward of the state."

I waited for the canned pity statement or look, but Bianca surprised me by not doing either.

"It's cool that you've kept in touch."

"She's the closest thing to family I have." I shrugged.

And then little 8B took my hand. "Seems like a pretty good person to have as family."

We shuffled outside her parents' house. I was reluctant to let the night end and Bianca seemed like there was more she wanted to say but didn't know how.

I finally broke the ice. "Good luck on your interview tomorrow. Will you let me know how it goes?"

She nodded and wrapped her arms around herself. "Do you want to come in and meet my family?"

"Another time," I promised and wondered if I'd make good on it. If she'd ever ask again.

"Alright, well..." she dropped her hands in front of her and fidgeted, still not moving.

"Sweet dreams, Bianca," I said softly, and I stepped forward and brushed my lips against the corner of hers for just a second before turning away. I didn't look back, but as I walked I felt lighter and younger and on top of the fucking world. She seemed to have that effect on me.

CHAPTER EIGHTEEN

Bianca

"My baby got her first job," my mother had tears in her eyes as she placed both shaky hands on my face.

"I haven't taken the job yet, Ma. There are still other options – other companies, graduate school even. They said if I decided to go to grad school to call them when I was done, and they'd still be interested if they had openings to fill."

"I thought you said this company was your top pick," my dad interjected. He moved casually in front of us to the stove, taking over the chopping my mother had been doing.

"They are. I just want to think it through before I make any big decisions. Another couple of years of school and there will be more opportunities available for me and a better salary, too. With a better salary I could help out more, pay for some of Donnie and Leo's college tuition. The odds of them both getting scholarships for all four years is unlikely and –"

"No." My father stopped chopping. "The boys are not your responsibility. We'll help them as much as we can, and they'll have to apply for loans or get jobs to cover the rest. You worked hard for your scholarship and they can do the same."

"But I want to help."

"They'll be just fine. We'll be just fine," my father said as he dropped the knife down on the cutting board and walked over to me. He wrapped me into a big hug. "We're proud of you. You've worked hard and it's paying off."

My mother wiped tears quickly from her face but didn't interject. I wasn't sure if it was guilt she was feeling for not being able to help me and the twins more or if she was silently wishing she could do the unthinkable mom move and accept my offer to help. I would regardless, but I knew my telling them that would be met with resistance.

"Are you staying for dinner?" she asked instead as she moved toward the stove and stirred the soup simmering in a big pot. Turning the burner off, she lifted the pot and began walking toward the opposite counter where she'd sat out plates and silverware. I shared a worried look with my father, but he shook his head, silently communicating not to say anything to my mother. He could read the concern on my face. I bit back the words to tell her to sit down and let someone else worry about dinner for a change. She worked too hard.

"No, Court's having people over to his house."

"Are we going to get to meet this Court you've mentioned?" My father asked as he placed a kiss on my mother's cheek and suavely took the pot from her hands.

"I'm not sure," I called as I slipped on my jacket and

smoothed my dress down.

I didn't think Court was too eager to meet my family. I wasn't sure if it was uncomfortable for him because I was a girl and we had this weird friendship or if it was the family dynamic that bothered him, but I had seen it in his eyes yesterday when he had looked at our pictures in the hallway. He didn't want to be here.

I gave them both a kiss on the cheek and I moved toward the front door. "I'll see you guys in the morning."

I took the subway from my parents' house and as we drew closer to Court's apartment I started to sweat with nervousness. I ran my hands down the front of my new dress. I'd bought it after my interview specifically for the party. It was the first piece of clothing I'd bought for myself in years and I was anxious that it was all wrong for whatever was going on tonight. The light pink sundress wasn't overly revealing, but it was nice enough that I knew Court would notice the change in my wardrobe. I'd considered texting him earlier to ask what I should wear, but it had felt important to do it on my own.

When I was finally standing in front of his apartment door, my heart was beating so fast I nearly turned around and headed home, but before I could chicken out, Leika appeared behind me and a tall man with blonde hair that fell nearly to his shoulders was just a step behind her.

"Bianca!" she called out and stepped to me wrapping me in a big hug like she'd done the night before. "I'm so glad you came. How'd the interview go?"

"Good. It went really well. They offered me the job," I said with enthusiasm and it was the first time I'd allowed myself to show any excitement over the news.

"Yay! Then this can be a celebration to many more nights

of hanging out together in New York." She smiled wide as she spoke and then as if just remembering someone else was in the hallway with us, she turned to the man standing behind her. "I'm sorry I forgot you two haven't officially met. Bianca this is my boyfriend Jeff."

"Nice to meet you." He extended a hand and smiled at me while wrapping his free arm around Leika's waist. "Leika's been talking about you nonstop."

She slapped him playfully and his smile widened. "I have not. Don't tell her that. You'll scare her off and I like this one. She's good for Court."

"We're not –"

"Oh. I know." She stepped forward and opened the door without knocking. "He'd never have brought you around if you two were dating – especially so soon, but the fact that he brought you at all says something."

"We're just friends." I tried to sound convincing when I said it – not for her benefit but for mine. Admitting that I felt differently felt like inviting a broken heart.

She stopped and looked back to me, eyes narrowed like she was studying my answer. "You know, I think you both really believe that."

I followed her through the apartment and while I was eager to memorize every word she said about Court so I could dissect it in detail later, my attention was pulled to the open concept apartment. A gray modern looking couch with a matching arm chair faced a mounted TV hanging on the main wall of the living area above a fireplace. It was cozy. Inviting even. So completely opposite of what I'd expected.

Voices drew my attention to the dining area where I could just make out the outlines of people through a large picture window. Leika moved in that direction, Jeff on her heels, and I followed behind them out to a patio like a third wheel, my heart stammering the entire way.

It was larger than I expected, spanning the width of the apartment and several feet deep. String lights hung all around, which surprised me that he'd paid attention to such a detail. There had to have been at least fifteen people already outside, but I found Court immediately. Neither of us moved – just stared. Me taking in the way he leaned casually against the railing, beer in hand. My gaze was drawn to the open collar of his button-down shirt and his tan forearms that were on display thanks to the rolled-up sleeves. He was perfection. Sophisticated elegance even holding a beer bottle.

The air sizzled between us.

Electric potential.

Voltage.

Current.

My feet moved on their own accord and once I'd started walking, Court straightened and met me half way. There was no smile. His face was serious. Hard even.

"Bianca." My name came out in a harsh greeting, but if his eyes could welcome me they'd not only smiled but wrapped me in a hug and kissed me on both cheeks. He scanned me from head to toe, not in a creepy way, but in acknowledgement that I'd put effort into the way I looked, and he appreciated it. He was recognizing that I did this for *him*. There was no Todd tonight.

"Hi."

He leaned down and wrapped an arm around my waist in a half hug. The movement brought his lips to the top of my head and the heat that hummed off his body pulled at me to sway into his touch.

"You look beautiful. Too beautiful. I'm not letting you

out of my sight tonight," he whispered. He dropped a kiss so quick and light to my temple that I couldn't be sure I didn't imagine it before he pulled me around the patio, introducing me as we came to groups of people.

Everyone was beyond nice and there was no awkward talk about who I was and how Court met me. My fears about coming here and meeting his friends were completely unwarranted. No one cared that I was twenty-two or still in college. No one even asked.

More surprising was the people Court associated with were so… normal. Somehow, I'd expected to walk out into a group of tense middle-aged men and women who were too mature to associate with someone like me. Court had never made me feel that way, so I knew it was my own insecurities, but these people were so much like my own friends that I felt at ease.

And Court… he was the most surprising. While he'd always been closed off when it came to personal details about his life, he'd always been affectionate and charismatic toward me. With the people he'd invited to his home, his friends, he was more of a fixture than a contributor to their conversations. I always pictured him as being this dominant force in every circle, but it was clear when seeing him surrounded by friends that I'd projected how I saw him as a personality instead of who he was to me.

"Your friends are nice," I said once we'd found ourselves alone in conversation. The party was in full swing and the laughter and loud conversation filled the night around us.

He nodded and looked over me to the people on his patio. There was a sort of a sad, removed glint to his gaze and I worried for a moment that he resented my being here and keeping him from his friends.

"If I'm honest, these are mostly Leika's friends. Don't get me wrong, they're great, but outside of my buddies from college and Leika I don't have a lot of friends."

My face must have shown my sadness at his words because he grinned as he said, "Don't go feeling all sorry for me now, 8B."

"You don't want friends?"

As if he could read the hidden meaning behind my question, he dipped his head closer to mine. "You want to be my friend, Bianca?"

The zap that blasted through my body screamed no, but my brain was sold on being whatever I could to Court. Being near him set my body on fire and I could no more deny myself that than I could cut off my own air supply.

Court had become important. Vital.

And I thought I was important to him, too. Although, I still didn't know why. Why did he let me in when he guarded his life and his affection so closely?

"Yes," I muttered and the look in his eye darkened as if I've told him I wanted to be more than friends. I wanted to be everything.

Maybe that was exactly what I'd done. He always seemed to know the things I couldn't bring myself to say.

"Come on, let me show you the apartment."

Court took my hand and led me back into his apartment. He didn't stop when we got into the main living area, but instead took me through a door off the living room and we stepped into darkness. I felt the air change around us as I stared up at his shadow.

"Rule number, whatever number we're on, don't follow men into dark rooms unless you're prepared to get kissed."

And then his lips crashed to mine. I opened my mouth

to let him deepen the kiss and his tongue swept in, warm and soft. His hands found my waist as he guided me closer. Not flush against him, but close enough that I knew if I so much as leaned forward, I'd be met with his hard body. I didn't lean in though. I'd frozen – no, not frozen. I'd become *grounded* to the spot.

Court had kissed me before, a soft brush of his lips on my temple or cheek to say goodbye. They'd always left me feeling shaky and weak kneed – a little pathetic, even, because having that reaction from such a kiss had felt ridiculous.

But this kiss…

This kiss made me feel charged.

Alive.

Hungry.

And his intent was clear.

He ended the kiss but didn't let go of me. He rested his forehead against mine. Our chests heaved together, and our raspy breaths were the only noise.

"I'm sorry. I didn't mean to drag you into a dark room and –" His words trailed off and I could feel his body tense while he struggled to find words. "I think we covered today's lesson."

"What?" I said, still struggling to come down from the high of the kiss.

"Today's lesson on men – if you follow them in dark rooms you're going to get kissed," he said as he pulled back and hauled me out of the bedroom.

I didn't get the proper tour he promised, but I did see more of it as he took me to the kitchen to get himself a fresh beer and pour me a drink. He pulled out a new bottle of rum and a two liter of Diet Coke and mixed me a drink while my head spun from the kiss and the fact I was in his apartment meeting his friends. I didn't ask him if he bought the diet and rum specific for me. I knew he had in the same way that he knew I'd dressed up for him.

"There you two are," Leika stepped in from the patio.

I felt the blush in my cheeks, but Court just wrapped an arm around me casually as she joined us in the kitchen.

"You're hogging, Bianca." She looked at Court with a playful scowl. I was being pulled to her before I realize she'd grabbed my hand. "I'm stealing you."

Court chuckled, and his arm fell away from my hips. "I guess I don't have any say in this."

She didn't respond, but when I looked over my shoulder to Court he had a genuine smile on his face while he watched Leika and I walk away from him.

CHAPTER NINETEEN

Court

Leika monopolized Bianca for most the night. I wanted to not mind because part of me loved that they'd taken to each other, but the irrational part of me wanted Bianca next to me. Her presence made all of this more bearable. Sure, I'd had parties at my house before and, I'd probably even had a woman attached to my hip much the way Bianca had been. But they'd been a nightly stand in.

Jeff cornered me well past midnight when people started to say their goodbyes.

"I, uh, wanted to talk with you without Leika," he said and tucked his hair behind his ear.

I gave him my full attention, noting he was avoiding eye contact and looked nervous as hell. Which made me nervous that he'd done something stupid and I was going to have to kick his ass. I liked Jeff. I'd almost even accepted him as a constant in Leika's life.

"Is everything okay?"

"Yeah, no, it's..." He cleared his throat and finally looked me in the eye. We were about the same height, but the way his shoulders sagged I had to crane my neck down to really look at him.

"What's up man?"

"I want to ask Leika to marry me."

A pit formed in my stomach like he'd punched me in the gut. His answer couldn't have surprised me more and my body was doing all the reacting for me. I couldn't form words, but now that he'd broken the ice he began to ramble.

"I've been thinking about it for a while. We've been together for almost a year. I love her. I want to settle down with her. I was going to ask her just to move in with me but then I realized I want that and more. I want all of it. You're the closest thing she has to a male figure in her life and she'd never do anything without your blessing, so I'm asking for your okay first."

I said the first thing that came to mind. A cheesy line I'd probably heard in a movie or a reality show Leika forced me to watch. "I want Leika to be happy and if marrying you is what she wants, then of course I'm okay with it."

He grinned like he'd won the jackpot and I forced my lips into what I hoped was a smile. Leika. My Leika. He was right, I was her family – brother/father figure – whatever I had to be, but if she said yes, she'd be inheriting a real family. A husband, two brothers-in law, a mother and father-in-law. Probably cousins and aunts and uncles. I wanted to be happy for her. I should have been happy for her. I was an asshole for wanting her to not have a family because it made me feel less alone.

He was taking out the ring when I realized he'd continued

talking and was now telling me how he'd picked it out today. He peeked over his shoulder to make sure Leika wasn't in sight before opening the box. A shiny diamond ring sat in the velvet box and it was then that I realized this was always how it was going to be. I pushed people away or kept them at arm's length, but Leika drew them in. She'd always been that way. Shit, she was off somewhere with Bianca right now welcoming her into our group and making her feel comfortable for no other reason than it was who she was.

"It's beautiful. She's gonna love it," I assured him.

He slid the box back into his pocket. I itched to get away from him, but it was only the two of us now. I could see Bianca and Leika inside, deep in conversation, laughing and smiling and I wanted to be with them. Leika my family and Bianca my... I didn't know yet, but I wanted to find out.

"What do you say we go see what they're up to in there?" I asked and patted him on the shoulder. I didn't wait for his answer because Bianca looked up at that moment and our eyes met and instantly I felt better.

As Leika and Jeff said their goodbyes, Bianca shuffled at my side like she wasn't sure if she should leave or hang around. I'd already decided for her, so I hooked my arm around her as Leika took Bianca's number and the two of them made plans to stay in touch.

"I should probably get home," she said after the door shut behind the couple.

"Let me lock up and I'll see you home."

"Oh no, you don't need to do that."

I grabbed my keys and smiled at her earnest expression. "I know."

I couldn't stop myself from linking hands with her. What I really wanted to do was take her back to my bedroom and kiss her senseless until morning, but Bianca wasn't one of my random hookups. I needed more time with her away from beds and dark corners.

When we slid into the cab, I instructed the driver to her neighborhood and rested my arm behind Bianca's shoulders.

"What are you doing tomorrow?" I asked as I rubbed my thumb against the soft exposed skin of her arm.

"No plans. I thought I'd go to Chelsea Market." She gave me a wry smile. "I go every time I'm in town. It's one of my favorite places in New York."

"With your family?"

"No, my parents are working, and the twins will probably spend most the day sleeping."

"Anything else you want to do tomorrow?"

She turned her head in surprise. "Just walk around New York and soak it all in."

"You say that like you won't be back in a couple months."

Her face fell, and I saw it then that she hadn't decided yet. She was still seriously considering going to grad school. Did that mean she was still considering Todd, too?

Clearing my throat, I pushed back my unease. "So, let's do it then. I'll pick you up at nine and we'll do Chelsea Market, walk around, whatever you want."

"Really?"

"Yeah, let's do it up right with a proper New York outing before you head back to the country."

She nodded with excitement. "Okay, let's do it."

The cab stopped, and I opened the door and helped Bianca out.

"Give me five," I said to the driver and followed my little 8B up the sidewalk.

"Thanks for tonight," she said as she fidgeted with the

small purse clutched in her hands. "Seeing you with your friends peeled back another layer to the mystery that is Court Adams."

"A mystery, huh?" I shook my head. "There's nothing mysterious about me. I'm an open book. You just haven't asked me any questions."

She seemed to consider that for a moment. "Okay, fair enough. Tomorrow – a proper New York outing and the life story of Court Adams."

I couldn't help the laugh that escaped from my lips. Or the tightening in my chest because I knew if she asked me anything I'd tell her whatever she wanted to know, and I wasn't sure I was really ready to drop all that heavy shit on her. I dropped a quick kiss on the top of her head.

"Sweet dreams, Bianca."

CHAPTER TWENTY

Bianca

"F<small>AVORITE MOVIE?</small>"

"Commando," he said instantly. "You?"

"Mean Girls."

"I had you pegged for 10 Things I Hate about You."

"Never seen it?" I shrugged.

"What? That's not right. Heath Ledger and Julia Stiles – classic."

"Favorite food?"

He tapped his empty spoon lightly against his lips. "Lasagna. You?"

"Pizza."

We sat on a bench in Central Park with frozen yogurt. Our third food stop of the day. We started with donuts and coffee while we walked the Chelsea Market. Later we'd stopped for brunch in Hell's Kitchen, and then fro yo as we neared the park because Court drew the line at going into the cute cupcake shop I'd wanted to go in claiming no one should have that much sugar before noon. I didn't agree, but I figured I'd make him eat his words after lunch and after his noon time constraint.

"What were you like in high school?"

He shrugged. "I wasn't really interested in high school or any of the cliques. I did my own thing."

"And what was your own thing? What did you do after school or on weekends?"

"I had a buddy whose uncle owned a mechanic shop, we hung there doing odd jobs for cash."

I could sense his childhood was a tough topic and I'd danced around the real questions burning the back of my throat as long as I could. I could either not ask at all and wish I had or bite the bullet. I spooned a large glob of strawberry goodness into my mouth and waited for it to melt as I summoned the courage.

"You said you didn't know your parents and I know you were in foster care with Leika. How many homes did you live in?"

He looked up and met my gaze. He hadn't expected me to ask a specific question and I couldn't tell if it put him at ease or made him more jittery.

"Five or six. I stopped keeping track. The last one was the longest – mostly because of Leika. She covered for me a lot to keep me from getting the boot when I was acting like a shithead – her words -and she was the first person I wanted to keep around, so I was a little better to tolerate knowing if I got booted we'd probably lose touch."

"What was Leika like back then?"

He smiled, his face softening. "Exactly the damn same. That girl's been a ball buster since birth, I think. She was put into the system when her parents were killed in a robbery gone wrong. She was in the store with them when they were killed. She doesn't talk about it much."

My mouth went dry and my heart squeezed for the happy, bubbly woman I'd started to like. "Understandable. Is that what happened to yours?" I shook my head. That was extremely unlikely and not what I'd meant, but God I was too much of a coward to just come out and ask directly. "I mean did something happen to your parents? Is that why you were in foster care?"

"No, my parents just bailed. Couldn't deal with being parents I guess."

"So, they are still alive?"

His face was unreadable but the tone he spoke with was grave and dismissive. "Does it matter? They didn't want me." His tone was harsh. Understandably.

"I'm sorry."

"Not your fault."

"I can still be sorry. It couldn't have been easy growing up the way you did."

He tossed his spoon into the empty container and sat it next to him. "When you don't know any other way it's just normal. Just life."

"Do you ever think about looking them up?"

"No." His answer was immediate and definitive. "They peaced out on me. Blood and genetics don't give them a pass for –" He paused and then shook his head. "No."

I nodded and bit down on my bottom lip instead of throwing my arms around his body and hugging him. I knew he didn't want my pity. "It could give you closure just knowing. Information is powerful."

"Power isn't always for the good."

I'd have been inclined to believe him if it weren't for the way his body hummed with nervous energy. Foot tapping, mouth pulled into a thin line – he was wound tight.

Standing, I tossed our empty containers in the nearest trash bin and then stood in front of him with what I hoped was a charming grin. "I have an idea."

He raised an eyebrow, but his body language relaxed. "That sounds like trouble."

I nodded. Yep, it was definitely trouble and probably a huge mistake that was going to leave me with a shattered heart, but right now I wanted nothing more than to take just a little of the baggage he carried around off his shoulders. I'd trade a piece of my heart if it patched his even a tiny bit.

It took more convincing than I imagined getting Court to agree to go back to his apartment. He'd been handsy and checking me out all day, so I knew it wasn't because he didn't want to kiss me. I thought he was probably worried he was short changing me on the day we had planned. New York was New York, though. No matter where I lived, it would always be home and there would still be lots of visits to do all the things that made me love this city.

With two grocery bags and a box of cupcakes I finagled into the deal, we were set for cooking at Court's place. When I said, we – I meant him. I was going to watch. I told him outright I had no intention of helping and so I'd plopped myself down on a stool on the opposite side of the kitchen counter while Court minced onions. I was mesmerized by the way his long fingers wrapped around the knife and sliced in quick, precise movements.

"You look good in the kitchen," I admitted taking a small drink of the wine he picked out at the store. "And you're right, I like the wine."

I'd been adamant that I wasn't a wine person, but apparently, I wasn't a *cheap* wine person.

He nodded, still paying attention to his task. "That Malbec will go well with the steak."

"Where did you learn to cook?" I asked while I twirled the stem of the glass.

"Mostly self-taught."

"Mostly?"

"I took a cooking class last year." He gave me a sheepish grin before adding. "If you tell anyone I'll deny, deny, deny."

"Finally, some leverage over mister perfect."

He raised an eyebrow and paused over the cutting board. "I'm flattered, but perfect I am not. Far from it."

"Are you kidding? Perfect home," I raised my arms up to motion to the living room so perfectly put in place with what he'd admitted was a designer's touch. "Great job in the most amazing city ever, you're good looking and charming and can get any woman you want. Maybe not perfect, but you look pretty good on paper."

He set the knife down and rounded the counter, spinning me around on the bar stool and invading my space.

"On paper is bullshit. I know... I mean, I remember what it was like just getting out of college, the whole world seems to only view you as a checklist – your degrees, your GPA, your job, your apartment - but it's all bullshit, 8B. Ten years from now I promise you'll look around your life and you'd trade any of that for the things that truly matter."

"Which are?" I asked and swallowed hard, not able to look away from his hazel eyes that swirled with grit and maturity.

"Who you are inside, your values, being able to look yourself in the mirror."

"And you think you've failed?"

He withdrew, stepping away from me and running a hand through his dark hair.

"Shit, Bianca, isn't it obvious by now? I look good on paper because my life is devoid of the things everyone else holds close. When you don't have family or friends, then work and appearances are easy."

"You have Leika. And there are lots of people who are just waiting for you to let them in. All those people that were here last night were here because you mean something to them. That's not nothing."

He dropped his hand but the haunted look on his face didn't disappear.

"And you have me."

The look on his face was almost painful and I stood and walked to him. "Maybe you aren't perfect, but you make me feel…" I worried at my bottom lip as I searched for the right words. The way he so intently watched me and hung on my words told me that I needed to find the right ones. "You make me feel special."

"You are special." His voice was low and full of gravel.

I grinned because it was the perfect response and the idea that he was being perfect even as we had a conversation about him not being perfect was funny to me.

"Special to you?"

"Yes, but special in general, too. The kind of special that any man would be lucky to have – even just for a little while."

It hurt in a way I knew he didn't intend. He'd lumped me into a category that he placed all his women. Temporary one-night indulgences. Okay, I wasn't a one-night indulgence, we'd been coming to this point for weeks. But I was temporary. That was the deal, I knew this.

I *knew* this.

He'd signed up to be a dating coach, nothing more. That was our only thread of connection. It wasn't supposed to get this complicated.

I wasn't supposed to get attached.

I wasn't supposed to want him instead of Todd.

Mustering all the courage I could find, I stepped forward closing the remaining distance between us and ran my hands from his stomach up to rest on his chest. I could feel his shallow breathing under my palms.

"You don't give yourself enough credit. You're allowed to have special things."

I felt the sharp inhale and I knew I'd hit the real issue. He wasn't keeping himself distant from people because he was afraid of hurting them or even because he didn't want them around. He'd constructed a life surrounded by people he kept from getting too close. He wanted them around, but he kept them at arm's length because he was afraid of getting hurt. Of not being good enough to deserve them.

My heart ached for him and still it was so mind boggling ridiculous as I stared up at this beautiful man who made me, a dorky college student, feel sexier and more confident than was probably merited.

I ran my hands back down slowly. I watched his face morph – so many emotions flashed across his hard, chiseled features and I wanted to make him feel how deserving he was. I wanted to somehow make him feel as good as he made me feel. I reached the top of his jeans and hooked a finger under the denim material. His dark eyes were hooded and intense. It was powerful the way he looked at me and I wondered if my desire for him made him feel this way. I felt like I could fly or run a marathon. Slay a dragon. Slay *his* dragons.

As I tugged the material away from his body, he captured my wrist in a movement so quick I didn't see it coming.

"Whatcha doing little 8B?" he asked in a voice dripping with lust and a splash of humor.

"I'm giving you something special."

He smirked at that before using my captured wrist to haul me against him. His lips crashed down on mine hard and wanting. There was no hesitating this time. I gave right back – pushing against his mouth and meeting his tongue before it could invade my mouth.

He groaned, leaned me backward without breaking contact as he slid his hands down under my butt. In one swift, totally suave motion, he lifted me, using a strong hand to wrap my legs around him. My dress was bunched up around my hips and for a brief second I wished that I'd worn something sexier than the cotton panties now on display, but as his hands gripped my skin through the thin material all I could focus on was the hum of my body and the need to be closer.

He walked us through the living area and into another room – the bedroom. I didn't bother to look at the room as he dropped me on the bed. I was only interested in him. His chest lifted and fell as he stared down at me, but he didn't join me.

I patted the bed next to me playfully and a little impatiently.

"You sure you want to do this 8B?" he asked, voice gruff and quiet. The confliction and desire swirled in his multi-colored eyes.

"Yes," I stated, but the confidence I'd had out in the living room was starting to wane.

"Take off your dress," he ordered as he backed up another

step and leaned against a dresser. I took this moment to get a quick look at the room. It wasn't big– gray walls, metal frame bed, black dresser and matching night stand. No photos or personal details in sight. I was stalling, and he knew it because he stepped forward and lifted my chin with a finger forcing me to look up at him.

"You're beautiful and sexy and if you didn't already feel how much I want you –" he took my hand and placed it against the bulge in his pants. "Now you have. If you want to do this – and know that we don't have to – we can go back out there and forget this happened." He motioned with his head toward the living area. "But if you do want this then undress for me, Bianca."

Dropping my hand, he brought his fingers back to my face. Staring into my eyes, he brushed the pad of his thumb against my lower lip and then returned to his spot against the dresser. I stayed seated. My dress was already around my hips so there was no need to stand or maneuver to lift it. Bringing the material up and over my head, I never took my eyes from his. They gave me the reassurance I needed to continue. I unclasped my bra next and with thin, shallow breaths I let it fall.

A low groan came from the man in front of me. My eyes fell to his grip on the dresser. White knuckles grasped the edge of the black wood and I kept my eyes there, transfixed by the strong, sexy sight while I stood and pushed the last scrap of material covering me down my legs.

When I stood upright, I tried my best not to fidget. I just stood there with no freaking idea what to do next. He decided for me, for us, as he lunged at me. He cupped my face with both hands and kissed me softly. Sweetly. He kissed me like we were standing in front of a room full of people, fully clothed instead of inches from his bed, me completely naked.

I brought my hands up to his waist and slid them under his shirt. I needed to touch him. To ground myself to him.

He took a step forward, forcing me backward until the back of my legs touched the bed. With a light touch, he set me on the comforter as his lips moved from mine to my neck and down to my collarbone. A bolt of electricity flashed when his warm tongue glided over my skin. My body arched of its own accord and Court leaned into me until I fell back on the bed. I wanted to protest that he was still clothed, but my brain had short circuited.

Warmth radiated off him as he worshiped my body. No spot went untouched or un-kissed as he moved down, across, up – there seemed to be no rhyme or reason to the way he moved from hip to neck to navel to breast, but each spot was equally attended to. His lips found mine again, the kiss deeper, hungrier. I got lost in the way our tongues stroked and when he pulled away I let out a whimper at the loss of him. Opening my eyes, I found him hovering over me with hooded eyes. "You're gorgeous, sweetheart."

With that, he slid down to my hips and hooked one arm under a knee and forced it up, exposing me. His other hand slid down my body. He cupped my sex before inserting one finger inside me. My body shook at finally being touched where I throbbed.

"So wet. So gorgeous," he muttered.

Another finger joined, and I moaned at the way he filled me. With a sexy chuckle, he planted a kiss on my hip bone.

"Are you ready to give me something special?" he asked, and my eyes opened and moved to his in confusion.

Was that my cue to undress him? Before I could decide

anything, his mouth joined his fingers and I cried out because damn that mouth and those fingers – it was like nothing I'd ever experienced. Granted, my experience was marked more by *in*experience than anything else, but I was certain this moment would have been better regardless. Because Court and I weren't just this. I felt his soul with every kiss and I'd all but gift wrapped my own as I prepared to give it to him.

His tongue worked in slow deep licks and his fingers pumped in and out faster and rougher. The contradiction had my world spinning. I laced my fingers through his hair, pulling at the thick tresses. I wanted him to stop and I didn't. It was ecstasy and agony. He seemed to sense my hesitation and his fingers moved faster, his thumb moved to circle my clit.

"Come for me sweet girl," he said and the way his breath whispered against the tender flesh was almost more erotic than the licking. And I did come.

Hard.

Explosive.

Electric.

CHAPTER
TWENTY-ONE

Court

"T HAT WAS..." HER words trailed off and I couldn't help but laugh. Leave it to my 8B to need to fill the silence after an orgasm.

"Special," I whispered in her ear before placing a kiss on her lips and standing. My cock strained against my pants and pleaded with me to bury myself in her.

I offered her a hand instead and she placed hers in it hesitantly. When she was standing in front of me, I smiled down at her mussed hair and flushed face. She wrapped an arm around herself and I knew the after-glow was fading and she was beginning to become self-conscious again.

"That wasn't what I meant when I said you deserved something special."

"I know," I said as I tucked a piece of hair behind her ear. "But don't I get a say in what's special to me?"

She didn't respond, and I knew I needed to get out of the

small room with her before I changed my mind and said or did something stupid.

"The bathroom is behind you if you want to freshen up, get dressed, or you could stay like this but fair warning I'll probably just stare at your breasts all day if you choose to eat naked."

"You're – we're…" She bit her lip and I saved her the trouble saying it aloud.

"We've got all day together, 8B. Let me feed you then we can go back out and explore the rest of the places on your list, whatever you want. Today is about you."

She nodded, and I forced myself to leave the room.

The kitchen seemed lonely without her and I tried to go about cutting and preparing like I always did – by myself, but my eyes were constantly moving to the bedroom door where I waited for her to appear.

I had the potatoes and steak in the oven and I was re-filling the wine glasses when she showed. A tentative smile and rosy cheeks made her look like an angel. My angel.

"Smells delicious," she said as I handed her a glass.

"Twenty minutes 'til food." With a tilt of my head, I motioned to the patio and we walked out the sliding door to the outdoor space.

"Oh, God," she said, and I watched as she closed her eyes and inhaled deeply. "It smells even better out here."

"I'm pretty sure that's an insult to my cooking."

"I miss New York. Even the smell of it."

Looking out over the balcony, I tried to imagine my life outside of New York. My job gave me the opportunity to travel all over the country, so it wasn't like I thought New York was the end all be all, but she was right. New York was something special. Like her.

"You look good in New York. You'd look good anywhere, but you smile more in New York."

She rested her elbows on the balcony and the sight of her, all innocence and sweetness against the backdrop of this tough city was breathtaking.

"Are you really going to give all this up to stay in Connecticut for another couple of years?" I stifled a groan instantly because I swore I wouldn't go there.

Bianca had made her goal, Todd, very clear from the beginning. And if I were talking as her coach right now instead of a guy who couldn't bear the thought of being a plane ride away from her, I'd be telling her staying was a good move for their relationship. Christ, was she in a relationship with Todd? I'd been careful to avoid any conversation that might lead to her talking about him, afraid it'd break the spell between us.

The look on her face told me I was right to keep it in and that I was a jackass for bringing it up now.

"I don't know. JC Engineering is giving me until the end of next week to decide. I'm going to meet with my advisor next week and try and decide what's best."

"What's best for you or…" I didn't finish the sentence, but she knew.

"There are things you don't understand," she started. "My family needs the help. I have two brothers who are going to want to go to college and move out and I've seen the starting salary for someone with a master's degree. It's a lot more than what I'm being offered now – it more than makes up for an extra few semesters of school if I can continue to keep my scholarship. The boys may have to wait a year to start college, but I can help them this way."

I didn't know what to say to that. I didn't even know

money was a consideration. I wanted to kiss her for being the kind of person who worried about things like taking care of her family and shake her for always putting other people's happiness in front of her own.

"I told you before. This isn't just about Todd," she said quietly.

Just.

Not *just* about him. Which meant part of the reason was him.

"So," I plastered on a smile. "Tell me about your brothers."

"What do you want to know?"

"Anything."

Everything. I wanted to know everything about her and her life, which included her brothers.

"Donnie is quiet. Not shy, just reserved and serious. He's protective and loyal even though I'm the oldest," she smiled shyly. "Leo is the most outgoing of the three of us. He's an artist – sketching and painting mostly. He's practical, too, though, so I have no idea what he'll end up doing. He'll be great at whatever he decides," she said in a proud voice.

"Have they started looking at colleges?"

"No, they're both adamant about staying in New York and going to NYU. They don't run in the same circles all the time, but I think they want to stay together as much as possible."

"Sounds nice. They sound nice," I added.

"You could meet them for yourself. They are hard to pin down while I'm in town, but we have a standing Sunday morning breakfast at a little diner by our house any time I visit. Nine tomorrow – you could join us."

"I don't want to intrude on your family time."

"It's no intrusion. The more the merrier."

The look on my face must have given away my discomfort at the thought of having breakfast with her family. I was sure they were great, really, but sitting around the table with a big, happy family like Bianca's sounded as torturous as it did tempting.

"Just, don't answer now. If you show up, you show up. If not, I get it."

But she didn't get it. Not really. I wasn't even sure I understood why I was hardwired the way I was. I had abandonment issues, blah blah. I heard the diagnosis the therapist said so blandly to my then foster parents and I wanted to roll my eyes exactly like I'd done then. I'd wanted to argue then that just because my shitty birth parents bailed didn't mean I had to carry around their mistakes like some sort of illness. Yet, here I was all sorts of fucked up about having breakfast with Bianca's family.

I wondered if I'd been any better off if I'd actually listened to the therapists who'd tried to help. Was that kind of early betrayal something you could really move on from? The timer from the kitchen saved me from having to delve too deep in that dark corner of my mind.

"Ready to eat?"

She nodded. "Ready."

It was beautiful outside, a clear sunny spring day that deserved to be soaked up, but I steered Bianca to the living room with our plates.

"We're eating in the living room?"

"Rectifying a gaping hole in your education," I said as I turned the TV on and navigated to *10 Things I Hate About You*.

"Oh my gosh, I'm so excited." She practically bounced

onto the couch and her unbridled excitement made me feel like a fucking hero. While I worked to get the movie started she bit into the potatoes and the moan that escaped her lips made her cover her mouth in embarrassment and her face turn a lovely shade of red.

"Good?"

"So good," she mumbled around the food.

We ate and watched the movie in silence, save the occasional moan of appreciation that came from Bianca. Each little moan made me more acutely aware that I hadn't gotten laid in... shit, weeks? Since before I'd met Bianca. That thought caused me to pause and I took a long drink of wine lost in that realization and trying to figure out what it meant.

Bianca's laugh brought me to the present and I forced myself to relax into the couch and enjoy this time with her, knowing it might be the last time we'd do this. If she went back to school and things with Todd progressed, she wasn't going to need me and even with the best of intentions to stay in touch, we were bound to drift apart without something linking us together.

When she finished her food, she grabbed her wine glass and tucked her feet under her on the couch and nuzzled into me. I stiffened without meaning to.

"Oh, sorry did I elbow you in the side or something?" she asked leaning away from me.

I missed the way her body felt pressed up against me immediately – more than I hated the way I was falling for a girl I couldn't have and didn't deserve. I wrapped my arm around her and pulled her back into me. "You're dangerous, 8B."

And she was, but not the way she thought.

After the movie, Bianca dove right back into her quest to find out everything about me. I'd just confessed my first kiss was on the playground behind the art building sometime during third grade.

"Nine, seriously? I don't think I would have let a boy anywhere close enough to kiss me when I was that age."

We were still on the couch, TV off, wine glasses re-filled.

"How old were you when you had your first kiss?" I asked as I played with a piece of her blonde hair watching the way it coiled around my finger.

"No, it's too embarrassing." She covered her face with an arm.

"Come on. Tell me." I tugged on the piece of hair I was holding.

She let out a sigh and moved her arm. "I was seventeen. It was at a party and I think the guy that kissed me was so drunk he thought I was someone else."

"Always selling yourself short, 8B."

"Seriously, about an hour later he was passed out on the bathroom floor."

"Maybe it just took a little liquid courage for him to work up the nerve to kiss you. Ever think of that?"

"No," she laughed. "I never thought of that."

"And was this cowboy your first everything or just kiss?"

She took a sip of wine and when she finally comprehended my question, the look of horror and shyness played equal parts on her expression. "No, definitely not. I – he – no, he wasn't my first."

"No need to be shy. You've already admitted the men you were with failed to get you off, so whenever and whoever they were hardly matters."

"Not men. Man."

My hand stilled around the lock of hair.

"I've only slept with one person. My first semester of college. I met a nice guy during freshmen orientation. We hung out, dated I guess – although mostly it was hanging out on campus and dorm rooms. Anyway, I knew it wasn't going anywhere but I was tired of being a virgin. I wanted to know what the big deal was. Ironic, huh, since he failed to show me what the big deal was."

My throat was so thick, the fact that I managed to speak was no small miracle. A mixture of jealousy, rage, sadness, lust – to name a few, cycled through me. I was all over the fucking place and she was looking at me like my response, my reaction, meant something to her.

"Have to say, I'm sad you thought it was something you needed to throw away just because. And I'm pissed as hell that it went down like that for you - orgasm or no, your first time should have been something worth remembering."

"Was yours?" she asked.

"Sure. I was young and wild and so was she. There was a lot of sneaking around to be together, which of course made it that much better somehow to my twisted teenage mind."

Bianca looked down at her wine glass as she asked the next question. "Did you love her?"

"I loved the escape she gave me. I loved how I was able to forget about everything else and just feel when I was with her, but no, Bianca, I didn't love her."

The air had become charged and I just kept getting myself in this situation where my self-control was pulled so tight I felt like I would break.

"What do you say we get out of the apartment for a while, see some more of New York before you have to head back."

She nodded, but she looked as reluctant to move as I felt. With a groan, I stood and pulled her to her feet.

"Last night in New York, where do you want to go? Anywhere you want in the whole damn city."

She worried at her bottom lip and I ran my thumb over it until she released it and I slid the pad over her full, wet mouth.

"Here. I want to stay right here," she said quietly.

The implication of those words hit hard, and my chest tightened. "You're sure?"

Staying here could only end one way. I knew it. She knew it.

"Yes." Her voice was more assured this time and she moved a hand to the waist of my jeans.

I grasped her hand and kicked myself before I even spoke the words, but I needed her decision to be her own. I might not be a knight in shining armor but taking advantage of women had no appeal.

"Bianca, we don't have to do anything. Today, this," I motioned between us and the TV. "This was great. It doesn't have to go any further. Earlier was –" but I didn't know how to finish that sentence, so I backtracked. "I didn't ask you to spend the day with me so I could get you into bed."

"If you remember, I was the one who asked to come back to your apartment," she said with a shy grin.

"Yes, I know. But –"

"I want to." The soft tone was back, but she continued confidently. The look on her face was vulnerable but undeterred. "I want to know what it's supposed to feel like. What it feels like with you."

I let out a breath and stared at her beautiful face because what the hell was I supposed to say to that? It was more of an invitation than I'd ever been given. Yet still I hesitated. And hated myself every time I opened my mouth to protest. Why was I trying to convince her not to?

Because you know it's not a good idea for either of you. A niggling voice mocked in the back of my mind.

Mostly I thought it wasn't a good idea for me. Bianca wasn't just some woman I'd brought home. Sleeping with her would end us and I didn't want to give her up.

I made a decision and pushed every red flag waving manically in my brain to one of the many dark corners. 8B had asked very little of me. She'd let me call the shots, even when it was her life we'd been playing with. I'd give her this - give her me. For tonight.

Before I could make my limbs work, she reached out a small hand to me. I never imagined little Bianca would be the one seducing me. Let me be clear, I never planned to seduce her, either. Sure, I'd thought about it. Wanted it. Kissed her with promises of more, but if I'd really thought we were going to come to this I would have played the whole thing differently. That annoying voice in my brain said, *You would never have let her get this close.*

Sad, but true. I'd always drawn a very thick line between women I was fucking and any personal or emotional connection. That may have made me sound like an asshole, but I didn't think I had been. I didn't exactly have women banging down the door or lighting up my phone asking me to meet their friends or to go away for a weekend. I suppose I'd done a good job of picking women who were looking for the same thing that I was.

Not Bianca. She'd skidded so far past that line I usually drew. Everything about our time together had been personal and emotional.

I moved quickly, using her hand as leverage as I swooped her up and placed her over my shoulder. She let out a shriek of surprise and excitement.

"You have no idea what you've gotten yourself into," I said as I walked into the bedroom and set her down in front of me.

Her eyes widened and I watched her swallow down the trepidation. I crouched down in front of her and her hands found my shoulder. Running both hands up the back of her legs, I trailed kisses as I went, and she swayed into me. I leaned back to watch her face as my hands disappeared under her dress and pulled her panties down. Her lip quivered as she stepped out of them. I stood, pulling the hem of her skirt up.

"Raise your arms, 8B."

She did, and her body was uncovered as the material lifted and discarded with her panties. I bit one breast through the lace of her bra and I was rewarded with a sharp inhale of breath. I gave the other the same treatment before I slipped my hands behind her and unhooked the clasp. It was almost painful to step back from her, but I did and let the bra fall away from her perfect breasts.

"So perfect," I muttered. "Just like the rest of you."

A slow blush crept up her neck and into her cheeks. "Take my shirt off."

She nodded, and I worked to steady my own uneven breathing while she fumbled with my shirt. She moved closer and went up on her tiptoes as she pushed the fabric over my shoulders and down my arms. The smell of her want invaded my nostrils as her breasts brushed up against my now bare chest. It was almost too much, the connection – the spark that jolted through me as our naked bodies joined. Fuck, we'd barely started and I was already in danger of losing it.

With my shirt in her hands, she brought it up to her nose and inhaled – her eyes fluttered closed as she did. It was so adorably Bianca.

"You smell good," she said after she tossed the shirt to join her clothes on the floor.

I couldn't help but grin.

"Can I –" her words trailed off and her eyes went to my pants. Or more specifically the rather obvious bulge in said pants.

I gave her a slight nod and tried to focus on anything but the slow and unsteady way her fingers unbuttoned and unzipped my jeans before hooking her hands under the waist and pushing down. Her inexperience shouldn't have been so hot, but it was because she was giving me something – a piece of herself she hadn't felt comfortable enough to give anyone else. Maybe her reasons were selfish – maybe I was just practice so she could get it right with fucking Todd. Right now, I couldn't bring myself to care. Right now, she was mine.

I helped her get my jeans and boxers down my legs and when the material was free she finally looked at me. All of me.

"Wow," she said breathlessly, and I swear I grew bigger and harder everywhere, ego included. "You're kind of beautiful, Court."

I quirked an eyebrow.

"You know what I mean. I never thought of a man being beautiful, but you are." She finally reached a hand out and touched me – lightly, not sexual exactly, more exploring.

"I'd like to be offended," I gritted out. "But my penis doesn't care what you say as long as you stand there naked touching me."

Her touch became bolder and I ground my teeth and squeezed my hands into fists in an attempt to force some feeling anywhere but my dick. When I couldn't take it any longer, which was an embarrassingly short amount of time, I wrapped an arm around her waist and tumbled back onto the bed with her. I circled a nipple with my thumb and dropped my mouth to the other. I felt her body stiffen under me.

"Relax, sweetheart. Let me make you feel good. Let me show you what it can be like."

I wanted this to live up to every single ridiculous, unrealistic expectation she had. I wanted to worship her body in a way that ruined her. I wanted to set the bar so high that no man, least of all fucking Todd, could compare.

I moved up, taking her mouth and caressing her face. I reminded myself that she needed the personal connection to hand over her body. I couldn't check out emotionally, and I couldn't let her either, if I wanted her to let go.

I kept kissing her as I allowed my hands to roam down her body. She arched off the mattress and ran her fingernails lightly down my back. It wasn't an 'I want to mark you because I've seen it done in movies' way, it was tender with just enough pressure that I knew she was exploring me – my body, my muscles. She was cataloging every inch of me the same way I was memorizing her.

We stayed like that for a while, hands roaming, and lips fused together until Bianca began to move beneath me. Small motions, wriggling to force my attention to where she wanted me most. I didn't deny her. Wouldn't have dreamt of it.

I pressed one finger inside, curling it and feeling her clench around me. She was so tight and wet, and my dick was jumping to get inside of her. Not yet. I wanted her so close to the edge that she couldn't see straight. She made the tiniest of bucks into my hand, fucking herself with my finger when I inserted another. And then another because I wanted to see how far I could push her. Her eyes opened and widened, locking into mine. She looked at me with lust and frantic energy. Wild. My little 8B looked wild but somehow, I knew this was how she'd be. So perfect and tentative on the outside, but just waiting to be set free.

"I'm gonna... I'm close," she said in a husky voice that I wanted to record and play back every time I touched myself.

I rolled on top of her, holding my weight off her but letting her feel how our bodies molded together. I bent my head down to kiss her neck and while she was busy reeling in the sensation, I opened the nightstand drawer and pulled out a condom.

The sounds coming from her were breathy and loud, moans that shook my body with a carnal desire so strong I quivered when I pulled back and slid the condom down over me.

"You're sure this is what you want?"

I was half afraid she'd say no – that she'd been waiting for an out and now that I'd given her one was about to flee from my apartment and my life. She was quiet for a moment and I searched her eyes for any hint of what was going on inside her pretty little head.

"I'm positive. I've never wanted anything more."

Thank fuck for that.

I nudged at her entrance, locking my eyes with hers. She smiled as if giving me the go ahead and when I moved in an inch her smile disappeared. I stilled, letting her adjust to the intrusion before I moved farther in. She was like a vise around my dick and I was sweating to keep my shit together.

"You're so fucking tight," I muttered as I buried myself completely.

"I think you're just so fucking big," she breathed out.

I certainly wasn't going to correct her there because, hell, those words made me feel like a king. Our bodies joined like this was perfection in a way I didn't know existed. Maybe it was just her – because her body was perfection all on its own. She was perfection.

I moved slowly. Carefully. I never took my eyes off hers.

I knew when she started to acclimate, and the sensation turned to pure pleasure because she met my thrusts, lifting her hips off the bed. I let her dictate the pace and I returned to worshipping her body – licking each breast, teasing her clit, and kissing that sweet mouth.

When her orgasm was close she began to say my name quietly. Almost a chant. "Court, Court, ooooh Court."

I watched as she came undone, clenching me so tightly I followed in an instant.

I wanted to set the bar to an unobtainable level for her. Destroy every other experience -past and future. The way she looked at me, I thought I'd succeeded. A lazy smile on her face spread across her face, like I'd hung the moon and all the stars.

Maybe I'd given her exactly what I aimed for, but she gave it right back and looking down at my sweet, perfect 8B I was pretty sure I'd stumbled over a line where no one else could compare to *her*. I was a mother fucking idiot.

CHAPTER TWENTY-TWO

Bianca

"Oh my God, is it always that…" I struggled to find the right word.

Awesome.

Amazing.

Intense.

Court chuckled and dropped a kiss on my temple.

"Good?" I settled on the word hoping it didn't give away how euphoric I felt right now.

He slid out of me and I already hated how empty I felt without him. I watched with fascination as Court removed the condom and threw it in a trash can just inside the bathroom. He swaggered back to the bed all easy confidence and laid down beside me with his head propped up on a crooked elbow.

"It's different with everyone. Just like kissing, some people are better at it and sometimes the chemistry is just better."

I slipped my bottom lip between my teeth and considered that. Chemistry. Is that why things with Court always felt so much better or had he just had more practice? A jealous heat bloomed in my face. No doubt the women before me had been more experienced and I didn't know if I was more upset that he'd slept with a whole slew of women better than me or if I was angry that I'd probably not even registered on his radar. Because my mind and body were completely blown.

"Get that worried look off your face," he instructed as he ran the pad of his thumb over my bottom lip coaxing me to free it from my teeth. "You were perfect."

"But can you tell I didn't know what I was doing? I mean, of course you could, you knew, but will other men be able to tell??"

Court's expression darkened and hardened almost as if the idea of me sleeping with someone else made him want to murder someone, but then that slow charming smile played on his lips.

"First of all, I promise you no man is going to think that – you are perfection. And secondly, we've got all night to give you as much experience as you want."

It was past midnight when we tore ourselves from the bed. My whole body tingled with a Jell-O-y tingly sensation. Court started the coffee pot as I slid onto the bar stool and watched. He'd pulled on the jeans he'd worn earlier, but left his shirt off – well, in fairness I'd stolen the shirt to wear over my dress, but he hadn't protested, and I was rewarded with a view of denim slung low on his hips and bare feet that made him look domestic and sinful.

My phone sat on the counter in front of me and I snapped a picture of Court just like this. Partly for photographic evidence tomorrow morning when I'd need to prove to myself that this really happened and in part because as amazing as today had been, it felt a little like goodbye.

"Whatcha doing, 8B," he said catching me staring down at the photo on my phone.

"I'm capturing you at your finest."

He quirked an eyebrow.

"Should I remove my pants then?" he asked as he playfully moved his hands to the button on his pants.

"Isn't there some sort of rule against vag shots – I can only assume that goes both ways."

"I think we're done with the rules," he said. "You've officially graduated."

"Do I get a diploma?" I teased.

"Oh yeah." he rounded the counter and pushed between my legs as he wrapped both arms around my waist. "Maybe we'll even get you one of those cute cap and gowns to wear while I give you your graduation gift." He nipped at my ear lobe and then whispered, "Spoiler alert it involves me taking that sweet ass of yours."

I gasped at the thought and my body hummed at the dirty and totally hot picture it painted in my mind.

"It's an advanced course," he said while he trailed feather light kisses down my neck.

I had no words and Court must have taken my silence as hesitation. "Don't worry, 8B. It's not the kind of thing you do on a whim – we'll work up to that."

I wanted to ask when, and how, and could we start now? He talked like whatever this was between us was going to continue and my heart raced, and my stomach flipped because nothing sounded better. Like a semi-truck hitting a median, my heart screeched to a halt as I remembered that

Court and I weren't real. Sure, he'd said we were done with rules, but it had been his idea to pretend this was real. Was he still pretending? Was he still doing this as a service project?

"Are you okay?"

My eyes landed on Court and he tilted my chin up to meet his gaze head on. "Where'd you go, 8B?"

I shook my head. "I'm sorry. I just realized how late it is. I really should get home before my parents worry."

He nodded, but his eyebrows drew together, and he looked like he wanted to interject or stop me.

"Sure, let's get dressed and I'll ride with you back to your place."

I pushed past him, already on my feet and gathering my purse, before he could finish the sentence. "No, that's silly. It's late. I'll be fine. I've taken cabs by myself in New York hundreds of times."

His hands were shoved deep in his pockets as he regarded me carefully, scrutinizing me like he could see every thought as clearly as I they raced through my mind.

"Did I do something wrong?"

My stomach dropped because I knew asking cost him a piece of his pride. I was running just like he was afraid everyone he let close would do, but I couldn't explain the reasons I needed to be alone anymore than I could explain the way my heart was breaking as I crossed his apartment and opened the door.

"Of course not. Today was perfection," I said stealing his word. I blew him a kiss, memorized him with the New York city skyline behind him and I left.

His first text came as the cab pulled up in front of my house.

Court: Let me know when you make it home.

Me: Just got here. Safe and sound!

Court's next response wasn't immediate. I was washing my face in the hall bathroom when I heard my phone ding from my bedroom. I scrubbed my face with the washcloth quickly and padded down the hallway with my heart in my throat. The time since I'd left Court's apartment hadn't made this twisted fake relationship any clearer, but if my eager response to read a text message was any indication of how I felt – I wasn't ready to say goodbye to Court.

Court: How do you feel? You're not too sore I hope.

Me: A little sore.

I pressed send and then added.

Me: Totally worth it.

Court: Take some Tylenol or Ibuprofen before you go to bed sweet girl. Breakfast or lunch before you head back tomorrow?

Me: I can't. I have the breakfast with my family to-morrow.

I tapped my fingers nervously on the side of the phone while I waited for his response. Thirty seconds. A minute. Two.

"Ugh," I groaned out loud into the empty room as I waited for him to respond. To say anything. I didn't want this to be the end, but breakfast with my family was non-negotiable. I'd barely seen my brothers this trip.

Me: *The invitation to come with us is still on the table.*

Court: *What time and where?*

I texted directions and switched my phone to silent. I didn't wait for Court to text back. Couldn't take any lame excuses why he couldn't or didn't want to go. Instead, I laid my head down on the pillow in my childhood bedroom and forced myself not to worry about graduation, my family, or a future without Court.

"WHERE'S MOM?" I asked, when I emerged from the haven of my bedroom the next morning. The twins were at the kitchen table with large bowls of cereal like we weren't going to breakfast in ten minutes.

The smile on my dad's face was tired and regretful. "She picked up a shift at the diner."

"What? No, we were supposed to have breakfast together this morning."

"She'll be there."

"It's not the same," I pouted and crossed my arms across my chest.

The twins stood, nearly in unison, and put their bowls in the sink. The three men of my family walked from the kitchen toward me.

"We just have to make the most of it, huh?" he said with a smile. A smile that didn't meet his eyes and didn't crinkle the smile lines around his mouth. A smile meant for my benefit only – to assure me everything was peachy keen.

The weight of my life and my responsibilities settled back on my shoulders with that fragile smile. We would make the best of it. It's what we did. We stuck together, we had each other's backs, and I'd never resented it until now.

CHAPTER TWENTY-THREE

Court

A CHILL HUNG in the air. The wind whipped around the buildings and the clouds drew together blocking out the sun overhead.

Bianca sat inside the diner with her back to the door. An older man with thinning gray hair sat across from her, a folded newspaper in front of him. In the middle of the horseshoe booth were the twins. They were easily recognizable from the photos, if not from the striking resemblance to Bianca. One brother stared down at a cell phone in his hands and the other moved a pencil over a pad of paper in front of him. Bianca twirled the straw of her drink and even without seeing her face I knew she was nervous.

Nervous I wouldn't show or nervous for me to meet her family? After the way she'd run out of my apartment last night I was guessing both. My palms were sweaty as I reached for the diner door and I tried to trick myself by telling my brain this was just a breakfast with a friend and her family. No big deal.

But it was a very fucking big deal.

I didn't do parents or families. Hell, I barely did people outside of the strict columns I kept. Work, gym, Leika, college buddies, clients. I'd put Bianca in a column, but nothing about her was that tidy and neat. She bled from column to column and outside of the lines in a way that I didn't know where to place her or how to categorize her.

Her father spotted me first over the top of his glasses, looking me over in that way that dads do – measuring and judging if I was good enough for his daughter. I'd like to save him the trouble and let him know up front that I wasn't, but instead I placed my hand on the back of Bianca's chair and smiled politely at the man in front of her.

"You made it." Bianca stood and hugged me. A surprising gesture, but one that put me more at ease. She pulled back and looked to the other members at the table who were now all openly assessing me. "This is Court. Court this is my dad, Glenn, and my brothers Leo and Donnie."

I offered a hand to Mr. Winters which he accepted and pumped once firmly.

"We're glad you could join us," he said and motioned to an empty spot next to Bianca.

There was a noticeable absence to the group, but I didn't ask where Bianca's mom was.

"Coffee?" Bianca asked too cheery as she moved for the pot sitting in the middle of the table.

"That'd be great."

I was grateful for something to do while the awkward silence hung in the air. I was sweating and miserable and wondering why I'd thought there was any way I could do this. Then my gaze slid to Bianca.

Her.

Her.

"So, Court, Bianca says you two met on a flight. You travel back and forth pretty often?" her father asked, and I was thankful he'd thrown me a softball.

"I do quite a bit of travel, but I've just got the one client in Connecticut, so I only get out that way about once a month."

He nodded and looked like he might say more when the waitress stepped up to the table. The woman had an obvious shake to her hands even as she just stood there. I forced my gaze to her eyes in that way we all do when we're trying not to make someone with an illness or deformity feel uncomfortable by staring at the root of their discomfort. I dismissed the idea it was drug related, she looked fragile but not strung out. MS, maybe?

I prepared to give her a polite smile and wait for her to take our orders, but when I met her eyes I froze. Bianca's mom. I knew it even before I heard Bianca make the introduction.

She wore a nametag that said Lucy and an anxious, tired smile. All of this I noted, but what made my mouth go dry was the blue eye makeup. Less obvious than the heavy hand Bianca put hers on with, Mrs. Winters's makeup had a more outdated feel. It was the type of look that said I've been doing this for thirty years and no one is going to tell me it's not in style anymore. Everything clicked into place for me. Everything Bianca had hinted at but not said. Bianca adored her mother – she loved her fiercely and protectively. And her mother was sick.

I looked to Bianca and instead of the fun and playful

look I'd always associated with her blue rimmed eyes, I now saw a girl who dared anyone to harm the people she loved. Electric blue armor.

I stood and took Mrs. Winters's hand gently. A gesture I could tell took her by surprise in the best of ways.

"It's great to meet you Mrs. Winters. You've raised a really lovely daughter," I said, and peered down at Bianca, suddenly afraid I'd said or done all the wrong things, but her smile was reassuring.

Bianca's mom grinned too and then shooed me back to my seat.

"Bianca is lovely all on her own. Always has been." She cast a quick loving look down at her daughter and my insides actually hurt at the familial love at the table. What would it have been like to be part of a family like this? It was a question I hadn't allowed myself to ask. Ever.

"I'm sorry I can't join you for breakfast. We're short staffed this morning." She pointed with a pen around the busy diner.

"I want pancakes," Leo spoke without looking up from his sketch pad.

"Me too," Donnie said, pulling his gaze from his cell but only for a quick glance at his mother.

"Me three," Bianca said looking young and shy as she glanced to me. "Their pancakes are the best."

"I guess me four then."

"Just wheat toast and fruit for me," her father said with a grimace.

"Doctor told him he has high cholesterol," Bianca whispered in my ear as she handed her mom our menus. With a conspiratorial smile, she scooted closer to me.

I watched Mrs. Winters out of the corner of my eye. Her

gait was off, not slow but unsteady. Why hadn't Bianca told me? And immediately I resented all the things I didn't know. The things I hadn't thought to ask because I was a selfish prick who didn't ask the type of questions that invited others to share about their families.

"Leo, what's the name of that band you like, The Black something or other – six letters." Mr. Winters stared down at his crossword puzzle, pencil in hand.

Leo looked up from his sketch. "The Black Crowes."

"That's not it. Crows is only five letters."

"It's The Black Crowes," he said again in that teenage way that pushed he was right without further explanation.

"There's an e in it – C-R-O-W-E-S," I said as I lifted the coffee mug to my lips.

Leo really looked at me for the first time, studying me. "*You're* a fan of The Black Crowes?"

I could hear his accusation that it wasn't possible I had any clue about a band as deep and dark as The Black Crowes. I guessed looking at me today it'd be hard to read beyond the nice clothes and practiced demeanor, so I didn't flinch too much at his reaction.

"Sure, I saw their Say Goodnight to the Bad Guys show in electric and acoustic."

"Bad ass. Did they do any Beatles covers?"

"Yeah a couple."

"God, that had to have been nuts."

I thought back to not only the concert, but also that time in my life. I'd been a train wreck. I guess most people probably looked back at their twenties with some sort of mature cringing. "Yeah, it was pretty insane. Are you into other early nineties bands?"

Bianca groaned loudly.

"Oh no, you didn't?" She shook her head playfully and I looked from her to Leo who just smirked. "You had to ask didn't you." She stood and motioned for me to get up. "We might as well switch spots so you two can go all fanboy."

I didn't miss the pleased smile she gave me. A thousand things communicated between us.

Her: Thank you for coming.

Me: Thank you for inviting me.

Me: I like your family.

Her: I appreciate your trying to talk to my brother.

It turned out Leo and I had a similar taste in lots of things from music to movies to video games. The pancakes came, and I dug in with the rest of the family.

Bianca and her father poured over the crossword between bites, Donnie bounced between the puzzle and mine and Leo's conversation. He was more reserved with his words than Leo, but he hadn't made me feel like an outsider, giving me the same courtesies he gave everyone else at the table, so I guessed that was something.

What I didn't miss was the way Bianca stole glances at me. Her face was so full of love for her family and happiness just sitting around a table with them barely talking. The only time I noticed a crack in her happiness was when her mom came to the table. It was a sort of sad, resigned look that she peered up at her mother with and I'd have loved nothing more than to stand up and tell Mrs. Winters to take my seat and let me be the one to wait on them. I didn't because one, that would be weird as shit and two, I'd have made for a lousy server, but it seemed all wrong sitting and enjoying the morning when she should have been in my spot.

"How were the pancakes?" she asked me as she cleared the plates.

I patted my stomach in response. "Best pancakes I've ever had."

She shot me a delighted smile and then fixed her stare on the twins. "Boys, did you finish your resumes so your sister could take a look before she leaves?"

A murmur of groans were the only responses from beside me. I interjected, hoping to ease some of the heat it looked like they were about to take. "What kind of jobs are you looking for?"

Leo shrugged. "Mom thinks we need a summer job to keep us busy."

"You do," she stated sternly. "and it'll look good on your college applications next year, too."

"My company is looking for interns. It's mostly cold calling and data entry, but the company is great, and the office is down near Bryant Park." I gave a small shrug to let them know I wouldn't be offended if they weren't interested.

"That's really nice of you," Bianca's mom said and gave the boys a pointed stare.

Bianca raised her eyebrows and narrowed her eyes slightly. "Yes, it is nice of you."

The boys murmured some mild interest in the idea and I opened my wallet and gave them my card with instructions to email me their resumes if they were interested, if not, no big deal.

I insisted on paying, which appeared to cause some annoyance to Mr. Winters, but it felt like the least I could do. Bianca's mom returned with my card and a receipt and handed it to me with an embarrassed smile. "I get a discount for family."

I smiled and nodded as I slipped the card back into my wallet. I scribbled out my signature after providing what I hoped was a generous tip without coming across as outrageous.

"It was real nice to meet you Court," Bianca's mother said as we all stood from the table to leave.

"You too, Mrs. Winters."

"We'll hope to see more of you when Bianca moves back," her father surprised me by saying.

I swallowed a lump in my throat. "I'd like that."

As the odd man out, I shuffled awkwardly toward the door. I flipped my hand up in a small wave and met Bianca's piercing blues. "See ya later?"

She nodded. "I'll walk with you."

When we were outside, she linked her arm with mine. "Thank you for coming. I'm sorry if –"

"No, don't be sorry." I turned to face her. "Don't be sorry about them. Ever."

We continued walking a slow pace to the curb, stopping when we were at the corner. I wanted to ask about her mother, about Todd, about everything – I'd let too many opportunities go by without letting her in and now I wanted to open her wide and spill every detail no matter how small and insignificant to her. None of it was insignificant to me.

"Your mom –" I stopped, not sure how to ask, but she understood.

"She has Parkinson's disease. She was diagnosed about four years ago, but it's progressing faster now. We're not sure how much longer she'll be able to work or…" her voice trailed off.

"I'm sorry."

She shrugged, and my emotions moved up and down like her shoulders. What would it be like to have an amazing family and watch the people you love crumble before you? I didn't know, but I could see it took a toll on my 8B.

"They liked you," she said and brushed her windblown hair out of her face.

"I liked them, too," I admitted.

"Bianca, we're leaving," Donnie called from down the sidewalk and she turned and held up a finger that she'd be there in one minute before turning back to me.

"I gotta go, but I'll talk to you later?"

"Yeah. You've got my number." I cringed at the way it sounded.

I'd come here to make sure we were on the same page. That page being that I wanted to repeat the last couple days over and over. I'd come here to tell her our story was just starting and to slam shut the chapters of Todd for good. But I didn't know how to get all that out standing on the curb while her family watched on and waited impatiently for her to join them.

I leaned forward, planted a kiss on her temple and gave her side a squeeze. As I did, I inhaled her scent and had to resist the urge to wrap my arms around her and kiss her the way I wanted to. The way I'd come here to do.

"Later, 8B."

She took a few steps backward, watching me with a coy smile before she turned and hurried to catch up with her family.

CHAPTER TWENTY-FOUR

Bianca

I SAT ON my bed replaying the whole weekend to Tasha when my phone lit up with a text from Court. The gleam in her eyes and wide smile rivaled mine and that was saying something.

"What's it say?"

> *Court: Did you make it back safe, 8B?*

"So, are you two like dating now? How did you leave it?"

I groaned. "We didn't talk about it. I have no idea how to act, what to say. Am I supposed to go on pretending like this is all part of a game to get Todd?"

I hadn't even thought of Todd while I'd been gone. He hadn't reached out and I'd been too preoccupied to lament about it. I suppose it was just par for the course. That was always how our relationship had been. A few sparse texts, mostly on the weekends. It wasn't unusual for us to go days or even weeks without talking.

Also, if I was honest, time in New York had given me time to distance myself from Todd and the up and down guessing games, outright exhaustion that our whatever friendship/relationship was. Maybe there'd been a reason we hadn't come together on our own. Something that had nothing to do with my not putting myself out there and everything to do with me forcing something that just wasn't meant to be.

"I think that ship has sailed. Just talk to him." She stood to leave, stopping at the door and turning back. "It sounds like a pretty nice weekend. Any chance it helped sway your decision to move to New York?"

"Yeah," I said thinking back to the way Court looked shirtless and cooking in his kitchen. "It really was, but I don't think it's going anywhere. He doesn't do relationships and besides I really want to make this decision for me – for my family. Court, Todd, men – they aren't certain, but my family has always been there for me."

She nodded. "Do me a favor?"

"Anything."

My phone beeped with another text message.

As if on cue, she pointed to the phone at the end of my bed. "Don't be so quick to discount this one. I like Court. Maybe he's the guy for you, maybe he's not, but at least communicate with him and hear what he has to say before you write him off. Even if you stay, maybe it could work. I mean it's worked for you two so far."

I nodded, and she gave me a small smile before closing the door behind her.

Court: I'll be up until I know you're safe so just text me whenever you can.

Me: I'm back, safe and sound. Thanks for this weekend. It was special.

Court: I'm not sure anyone has ever thanked me for sex before. Saying you're welcome makes me feel like a giant douche.

Court: You're welcome

Me: What's your week like? Traveling?

Court: Actually, I have to come back to CT at the end of the week. Can I see you?

Me: Yeah, I'd like that.

The week passed in a blur. I'd dialed back the number of texts I sent Court each day and he didn't try to compensate or push me for more. I'd like to say I didn't fixate over this because I was so busy, but that would have been a lie. Not that I wasn't busy. Classes were insane, I'd met with my advisor twice about graduate school, and there'd been the obsessing over my decision for next year. Every spare second, though? Those seconds, minutes, and hours between sleep and activities? Those had been filled with Court. I was so keyed up by Thursday that Tasha forced me out of the house for a senior party. Todd texted to see if I'd be coming, but I couldn't work up the same excitement about seeing him as I'd felt just two weeks before.

"I'm gonna go find Lance. You okay?" Tasha asked as

we made a lap at the off-campus house party. Music blared from the speakers set up next to a window in the kitchen and people floated through the old home with plastic cups in their hands. Spring had finally made its way to Connecticut and the backyard was where everyone congregated.

"Yep," I said finding Todd across the yard. He spotted me at the same time and we moved toward each other.

He smiled, big and cocky like he was genuinely happy to see me. I tried to force the same type of smile back at him, but it felt brittle and small.

"Hey, you look great," he said letting his gaze fall over the pale-yellow dress and down to the flat sandals I wore. I'd forgone the attempt to dress like someone I thought he'd want and dressed in what I'd wanted. It felt good to have him like what he saw when it was just me, but his approval didn't make my body hum like it did when Court complimented me.

"Thanks, you too."

Grabbing my hand, he led me over to the keg and poured me a drink. We circled the party together and I tried to relax – enjoy the moment and not compare it – *him* to Court.

"Hey, Todd wanna play beer pong? We're one short." I recognized the girl as the same one he'd ditched me for only a few weeks ago and the snarky look she gave me told me that she remembered me too and didn't see me as anymore of a threat now than she did that night.

Todd surprised me, though. And her.

"Nah, gonna hang with B."

Her mouth dropped open and it was the best thing I'd seen all week. My spirits lifted, and I let Todd tug me away as I gave her a small wave with my free hand.

"It's fine if you want to go play," I said when he stopped

and pulled me into a quiet corner near the edge of the yard.

"Nah, I just want to hang with you. I feel like we haven't had a chance to talk lately."

I wanted to laugh because I'd been trying to get his attention for years and now that I had it... it felt like too little too late. But I liked and respected Todd in spite of his fickle behavior.

"How was New York, the interview, tell me everything," Todd relayed the questions in steady succession like he couldn't wait to hear the answers to all of them.

"New York was great. The interview went well, they offered me a job."

He gave me a playful frown, lifting his eyebrows and sticking out his bottom lip in a pout. "Aww, man does that mean you're leaving me?"

I shook my head. "I don't know yet. I haven't decided. Part of me wants to go back to be closer to my family and help out more with my mom and the boys, but I just don't know."

"I get that. How is your mom?" he asked as he lifted the cup to his mouth.

"She's getting worse," I told him and let my shoulders sag. "I don't know how much longer she's going to be able to work." A piece of the weight I'd been carrying around lifted as I said the words aloud. It felt good to tell someone that knew the history.

"Has she called my uncle yet?"

I shook my head. "No, she's still carrying on like things aren't changing. She's not ready to accept it."

"Are they coming for graduation?"

"Yeah, I think so." Actually, I wasn't sure they could afford it and I hadn't asked them outright for that very reason, but I wasn't about to admit that to Todd. He wouldn't understand. Couldn't possibly understand.

"So, let's have lunch with both our families while they're here. Maybe once your mom meets my uncle she'll feel more comfortable. He's amazing. I can't wait for you to meet him."

"Thank you," I said, feeling shame for using his connections and gratitude that he was so generous with it.

Todd's uncle was a neurologist who specialized in treating patients with Parkinson's. I'd learned that about him freshman year, but it wasn't until last year when my mother's symptoms had become more pronounced – the situation seeming imminently dire - that I'd confided in him all my worries about my mom and family. It had been something real we'd shared, and I think it was what had bound us together. So much of college was fake – a life without a lot of rules or responsibilities. Parties on weeknights, days of doing absolutely nothing if that's what you wanted, and relationships that sometimes only lasted a night. But when I'd opened up, we'd shared something that went beyond our small world here.

"Hey, I told you I'd help, and I will. I got you." Todd lifted my chin and looked into my eyes.

I gave him a small smile and he grinned down at me. "What are you doing tomorrow night?"

"I'm not sure."

"I have a family thing, my uncle will be there, come with me?"

"I – I'm sort of seeing someone." It was a lie. A sort of lie. I *wanted* to be seeing Court. It felt like we already were. Maybe that was just the fake relationship we'd created, but it didn't feel fake anymore.

He tucked a piece of hair behind my ear and nodded

solemnly. "I see."

Was the disappointment on his face real? I'd never been completely sure of Todd's feelings. Sometimes he acted like we were more than friends, sometimes not. He was so lackadaisical about the whole thing leaving me to second-guess him at every turn. He was lukewarm, and I wanted passion. I wanted the person I was with to love me in a way that left no doubt. Electric. Passionate. The way that Court made me feel, probably without even trying. It struck me then – maybe it had never been Todd's feelings that were the problem, but my own.

"I'm sorry. I should have told you sooner, but it just happened. It's new."

"I get it," he said. "Guess I drug my feet a little too long, huh?"

I smiled up at him, but I didn't respond. For better or worse, my whatever-relationship with Todd was what brought me to Court. And the idea that I might not have met Court if Todd hadn't been so back and forth filled me with sadness. It had been worth it.

"I'll understand if you don't want to introduce my –"

"Give me some credit," he interrupted. "We're friends. We'll be friends no matter what. So, Friday night? No pressure, you can just come as my friend. There'll be free food and booze," he added.

I hesitated, and Todd grabbed my hand, swinging it between us. "Just friends."

"Alright. Yeah, that sounds nice."

In the course of an hour I'd managed to get Todd to choose me over the allure of party games and girls vying for his attention, invite me off campus to meet his family, and all of this would have made me elated just a month ago. But now it didn't. I wasn't elated. I was sure we'd have a good time together and I was excited to meet his family, but my heart and my mind wandered to New York and to Court. I knew what I wanted.

I cut out early under the guise of an early morning meeting, which was true. I needed to call JC Engineering and give them my decision tomorrow. Back at home, I made myself a bowl of Capt'n Crunch and sat on the couch flipping through channels. When I'd watched an entire episode of The Golden Girls without remembering a single thing, I gave up and pulled out my notebook. It was time for a good ole pros and cons list before I was sold on my decision. But when I flipped open the book, I found the rules I'd written. The ones Court had taught me.

1. There is no such thing as the friend zone.
2. Men just want to have fun. Invite him to play drinking games, etc.
3. Dress in trendy but conservative dresses or skirts, heels, hair down, just a touch of makeup.
4. No sleeping with his friends.
5. Spend time where he is and stay in his line of vision
6. Have something prepared to say when you see him – mention his hobbies and ask about his future plans
7. Light touching is good
8. Don't overthink things
9. Leave him wanting more
10. No vag shots – keep texting classy

I'd scribbled notes in the margins and written Court's name and number for safekeeping. It was almost laughable as I read through the list. I'd done exactly what Court had said and he had gotten me the boy and now all my heart seemed to want was him. I gave in and texted him.

> **Me**: *When do you fly out?*
>
> **Court**: *Tomorrow morning, but I don't think I'll be free until late tomorrow night. I arranged my flight so I don't go back until Sunday afternoon, can we spend Saturday together?*
>
> **Me**: *I don't know. I might be busy washing my hair.*
>
> **Court**: *Is that an invitation for shower sex? If so, kudos for stepping up your sexting game.*

I blushed, but the idea wasn't unwelcome.

> **Me**: *Lol. Only you could turn a brush off into an invitation*
>
> **Court**: *Aww you trying to get rid of me sweet girl?*

As if. I huffed with a dramatic eyeroll that would have made Cher from *Clueless* proud.

> **Me**: *No, definitely not*

Definitely, definitely not.

CHAPTER TWENTY-FIVE

Court

Knocking on Mr. Harrison's door, I held up the resumes. "You want to take a look at these before I give them to Nancy?"

He motioned for me to come in and I did, placing the papers in his outstretched hand. "Finally picked your team?"

"I think so."

He shuffled through them quickly, barely scanning them. "It's your team. I won't interfere with who you hire unless it becomes a problem down the line."

"Speaking of, I wanted to ask about a summer intern. I know Nancy usually assigns them based on skills and need, but I had someone specific in mind from the pool. I've already run it by her and she says I'm on the list to be assigned one."

"Fine by me," he said as he passed the resumes back. "Headed to Connecticut tomorrow?"

"Yeah, I'm going to check in with Mr. Sterling tomorrow afternoon before the reception."

"Good for him," he said on a laugh. Mr. Harrison was well aware of Allen's turnover rate with wives. "And good for you. Maybe a forced night out will be good for you. Have a little fun and cause a little trouble."

I left his office without another word, pondering the kind of fun and trouble I was looking to get into this weekend. All my ideas were 8B-specific.

As I was packing up my office, Leika sent a text.

Leika: *Drinks? I'm already at our usual spot.*

Me: *Be there in twenty.*

As I walked to the bar my mind drifted to Bianca, as it had all week. I hadn't heard from her much since Sunday. I'd been trying to give her space to make up her own mind on what she wanted, but I knew she had to give JC Engineering an answer, maybe already had, and that made me anxious beyond words. Had I factored into her decision at all? Maybe it was selfish to hope that I was at least a consideration. I hadn't given her much of a reason to and I understood her desire to help her family. But Bianca belonged in New York. To New York. She lit it up and it lit *her* up.

Leika waited at our usual bar. Same booth, same drinks, but Leika didn't wear her usual bubbly, happy smile.

"Court," she said sternly by way of greeting.

She stood, and I gave her a hug. "Uh-oh. What did I do?"

"I was about to ask you the same thing."

We sat, and I poured a drink and eyed her warily over the pitcher.

"Bianca," she finally said throwing her arms up. "She hasn't returned any of my texts since Friday night. What. did.you.do?"

I was sure the culpability was written all over my face. Confirmed when Leika shrieked, "Oh my God, tell me you didn't sleep with her?!"

"What? I thought you liked Bianca?" I'd been expecting Leika to be thrilled when or if she found out that Bianca and I were more than friends. I thought she'd be ecstatic that I'd finally found someone decent. She'd been after me about settling down with a nice girl for as long as I could remember.

"I do and so do you, which is exactly the problem."

Trying to wrap my brain around her logic, I scrunched my eyes together and took a long pull from the glass.

"You're gonna have to explain that to me because I'm not getting it," I finally said after I swallowed down the light beer Leika always insisted on ordering.

She let out a sigh like it was beyond obvious and I was being thick-headed. Maybe she was right, but I was still lost.

"You're treating her just like all the others you disposed of so quickly. Bianca is not a wham-bam-thank you ma'am girl."

Laughter exploded from my chest. "Seriously?"

She rolled her eyes and took a drink from her glass.

"I'm not treating her like the others. I brought her here, I introduced her to you, I spent an entire day with her. When's the last time I went on a day date?"

When was the last time I'd been on any date that wasn't solely a payment for sex later?

Her posture relaxed, but a sad expression crossed Leika's face. "I know. I know you're trying, but you need to get yourself together first. You're barreling down head first without any consideration for how your shit is going to impact her. Are you still going to Connecticut this weekend? Does she know?"

My chest tightened and the darkness that had lifted since I'd met Bianca descended on me. "Some of it."

"She needs to know. All of it. All of you. You can't start a relationship with someone like Bianca until she understands your past and the impacts it has on you now. Doing it this way where you let her fall in love with you and then she finds out pieces of the story later is going to end terribly for both of you. She'll feel betrayed that you weren't open and honest and then when she runs scared you'll feel aban..." Her words trailed off, but the blow didn't hurt any less.

Abandoned. She was going to say abandoned.

Leika and I didn't talk much about our shit. I didn't mention her fear of just about everything – walking the streets of New York after dark, convenience stores, being home alone. They stemmed from a place of excruciating pain that she wouldn't let herself go back to. The night her parents died in front of her. And she didn't mention my inability to let people in for fear of them leaving me. Abandoning me like my parents and every foster parent after them.

Leika let out a deep breath. "Look, I get it. You think telling Jeff my childhood sad story was easy or that it was something I wanted to do? Hell no. But he had to know in order to truly understand me. And your shit is way more fucked up than mine," she added with a smile trying to lighten the mood.

I gave her a solemn nod.

"Bianca is good and understanding. She deserves to know, and I promise you telling her will lift a weight off you."

"Hmpf," I mumbled, as I drained the glass.

I was still chewing over Leika's words as the plane made its final descent into Connecticut the next morning. The ride had been bumpy, turbulence making the plane rattle and shake, and I couldn't help but wonder if it was a sign of what was to come.

I took a cab straight to Mr. Sterling's office and straight into the chaos. Everyone stood around chatting and laughing. No one even pretended to work. It seemed Allen's excitement for tonight had the whole office in a celebratory mood. There was cake in the break room and Allen Sterling himself was in the center of it all. Big, boisterous laugher erupted from him and filled the room. I couldn't help but be jealous of him. Despite my certainty that this relationship would end like all the others, he seemed so purely, blissfully happy.

When he spotted me standing in the doorway, he beckoned to me. "Court, come in, come in. The office threw me a little pre-reception celebration. Have a piece of cake."

Shrugging my laptop bag higher on my shoulder, I hung in the doorway. "No, thanks. I was just gonna set up in the conference room. Will you have time to go over the latest reports?"

He waved me off like work was the last thing on his mind. "It can wait. Put your stuff down in the conference room and come join us."

Forcing a smile and reminding myself that he was paying

me to be here, I did as he said. When I rejoined him, Margaret had also appeared, hanging on one side and standing on the other a young man that looked less than thrilled to be there.

"Court, you remember Margaret. And this is my son Theodore."

Something pushed in the back of my brain. Some sort of awareness or memory, but it was quickly forgotten as Theodore stepped forward. "Nice to meet you, sir."

Great, I was a sir. I took a closer look at the young man in front of me. His dress pants and button up shirt were pressed neatly, and he had the defiant, chiseled chin of a kid that had lived a posh life but still thought he could relate to people.

"You too."

Theodore gave me a polite nod and then turned back to his dad. "I gotta get going. I'll see you tonight."

With that he left, and Allen moved his attention to me. "They're always coming and going at that age. Speaking of going, I know you just got here but I need to see Margaret home so she can get ready for tonight." He glanced at his watch. "Why don't you go check into the hotel and we'll meet back here in an hour to go over the reports?"

Running a palm over my chin, I gave a small nod. "Great, see you then."

I swallowed, my throat thick with tension. I knew exactly what I needed to do with my sudden free time, but when I arrived at Bianca's apartment I paced outside in the parking lot so long people started to stare at me like I was cracked out. That was exactly how I felt. Or what I assumed it felt like.

Me: *You home? I'm outside.*

207

Instead of responding by text, she opened the door and waved. I walked to her trying to piece together what I needed to say. How I could possibly say any of it without scaring her away for good.

I took in her standard uniform – floral dress and leggings and the familiarity of it, moved me forward.

"Hey, I didn't think I'd see you until tomorrow," she said as she held the door wide for me to enter.

There was a pause and it looked like she wanted to embrace me, but I couldn't allow her to touch me before I'd unloaded.

"Sorry, I should have called but I needed to see you."

By the concern on her face I knew she'd read the worry and trouble in my words and demeanor.

"Is everything okay?"

I motioned for her to sit in the living room and I followed her to the couch. I drummed my fingers nervously on my thigh as I started speaking. Rip it off like a Band-aid – just tell her everything.

"I wasn't completely honest with you in New York."

Her hackles went up – back stiff and hands nervously clutched in her lap.

"You asked about my parents." I cleared my throat and asked myself for the trillionth time why I was here? Why was I telling her this? The answers were all the same.

I wanted a future with my 8B.

"The truth is, I did look them up. About a year ago, I hired someone to do some digging. Leika thought it might help give me some sort of closure and I guess I was curious, too."

I watched sadness and nervousness pinch her features, but she didn't speak.

"My parents were young when I was born. Fifteen. They were from a place not far from here in Connecticut. On top of getting knocked up that young, my mother was an addict. The best I could find out she was sent away to stay with some relatives in New York City. When I was born, the state took me from her – because of the addiction. She OD'ed a few months later.

"Oh my God," she said and covered her mouth with both hands. "Court –" she moved to scoot closer to me, but I raised a hand.

"Let me finish." I needed to get it all out. I'd held it in too long. I hadn't even been this forthcoming with Leika. She'd had to pry information from me bit by bit over months. But I needed Bianca to know. And if I didn't tell her now I didn't think I ever would.

"Most babies get adopted – it's the older kids that have a harder time being placed, but my mother had used during the pregnancy and so I," my voice broke. "I was born dependent on opioids. Drug babies aren't quite as easy to love – we scream for the first few months of our lives and some end up with a whole slew of medical issues. I guess I was lucky in that regard, I was healthy. But I wasn't a baby anyone wanted because of it so I bounced around foster homes. I did that most my life. I never stayed in the same place more than a few years. Some of the foster parents had good intentions, some of them just did it for the paycheck, but it didn't matter. I was too angry at the world for it to matter who they put me with. I refused to talk or cooperate, I was a complete asshole if I did speak to them. As I got older and people stopped trying to connect with me, I found trouble in other ways. I did shit I'm not proud of – stealing, vandalism, basically I was a punk."

"You were acting out," she added.

I nodded. "Maybe. I was bitter and pissed at the world. Anybody that tried to get close I ran off and eventually people stopped trying. I was just biding my time until I could be on my own."

"What about your father?" Bianca looked pale like it was her past we were uncovering instead of mine. "You said your mother died, but what happened to your father?"

I let out a breath. "He stayed in Connecticut. Went on to finish high school, college, got married, had more kids. I never heard from him or my mother's family. It's like after she died they all just forgot about me too."

"Are you sure he even knows about you. If her family sent her away…"

I nodded solemnly. "His signature was on the paperwork. He signed away his rights."

"I'm so sorry Court."

We sat in silence for a few moments and Bianca wrung her hands nervously while I worked up the courage to continue.

"That's not all." I scrubbed a hand over my chin. "He's still here. In Connecticut. In this damn city."

She looked up, wide eyes and mouth parted. "Are you going to reach out to him?"

I looked at her sweet unassuming innocence so excited at the possibility of me finally finding a family and I'd never felt so hard and dark by comparison.

"Yes, but not in the way you think." I sighed. "This isn't about reconnecting with my father, so he can wrap me in his arms and tell me how much he thought of me over the years." Even as I said the words I couldn't keep the tiniest bit of hope from taking purchase. Hope was dangerous, and I needed to keep it carefully in check. "But I do want to move on and I think telling him what an asshole I think he is might be the only way I can do that."

"But, what if –"

"What if he wants to be a father to a thirty-four-year-old man he never met?" I laughed. "He's a big shot in the community. He's not going to want some drug baby secret to come out and tarnish his reputation."

"You don't know that," she insisted.

I scoffed. "If he'd wanted to find me he could have. He had the means and plenty of opportunity. Anyway, that is why I'm here. Why I took a client here and why I'm here now. Ten months I've been sitting on this information. Waiting, trying to decide if I really wanted to come face to face with him, but now I've practically been gift-wrapped an opportunity and it feels like the right time. I can speak my peace and be done with him."

Bianca scrunched up her face like she was trying to understand.

"He watched her get sent away and just wiped his hands of both of us."

"Court you don't know that."

"I know enough. I just want to look him in the eye once and demand he face the consequences of his actions."

It sounded so much more callous when I said it out loud. But he'd built a whole life pretending I didn't exist. Like my mother had been nothing. I wanted to be rid of him the same way – erase him from my life forever.

Her blue eyes turned the shade of a country love song – sad but mesmerizing.

"What?" I finally asked and hated the way my voice cracked. Hated that I was still affected by the shit that happened to me before I was even born.

"I'm so sorry for what you went through, but are you sure you want to do this? You have a father that's alive and he's here. Can't you give him the benefit of the doubt? There are a million reasons why he might have stayed away," Bianca pleaded.

I'd waited patiently for this moment. The time I could look my father in the eyes and remind him that no matter how rich or successful he was, no matter how picture perfect his life looked from the outside, I would always be around as a permanent reminder of the shitty person he really was. He was good on paper, but a mother fucking failure in my eyes.

I scoffed. He wasn't getting the benefit of anything from me.

"Please don't try and talk me out of it. I care about you and your opinion means a lot to me, but I need to do this."

"I agree." She nodded. "You should connect with him if that's what you want, but don't walk in there guns blazing, talk to him – ask him the questions so you know. If you're already assuming the worst, what can it hurt?"

Bianca scooted closer and took my hand. Warmth and contentment spread through me.

"Do you know why I majored in electrical engineering?"

I shrugged, thrown by the change of topic. I knew Bianca loved math and problem solving, but I guess I never thought about what led her to electrical engineering.

"When I was a kid we lived in this dumpy apartment in the lower east side. It was gross and just dirty," she shuddered as if remembering the place. "Among its many charms was shotty wiring. Anyway, the maintenance guy was nice, and he didn't mind too awfully much when I tagged along. He let me hold the flashlight and he talked to me as he fixed electrical issues in the building. Which by the way, turns out he knew very little – I guess that sorta explains why there was always a new issue. Anyway, the problem solving, and the intricacies of the wires were cool, but it was the excitement on people's faces when we fixed the problem that I loved. No matter how many times the lights went off, when we flipped a switch on a blackened apartment and light flooded the darkened space, their faces literally lit up with the room."

Her face was happy and free in remembrance.

"You brought them light," I said more to myself than her. I did understand because it was exactly how she made me feel. Being around Bianca brought a lightness to my life. A blazing white heat to the darkness I carried with me.

"I know it's incredibly cliché, but I believe that good overcomes evil. That when things seem impossible, there is a way to solve it if you just look at it from another angle. And that light will always return."

"I don't expect you to understand," I muttered quietly. How could she possibly? Her with a loving family. She couldn't fathom a world where people didn't cherish and protect their children.

"I do," she said and laced her fingers with mine. "I understand you. I see you and I see light."

My face twisted with pain and resignation.

"Why are you telling me all of this now?"

Instead of answering her, I leaned forward to brush my lips against hers. I soaked up all of her. All the goodness and all the hope for the future. Maybe there would be another 8B down the line for me. She wouldn't be as perfect, but I didn't deserve perfection. Didn't deserve her. Couldn't she see that?

"Court," she said when I pulled back.

I looked down at her beautiful face and tried to memorize every detail.

"I want to be there for you. Messy or not. This is what relationships are, letting people be there for you and being there for them. Not just in the good times, but in the bad too. I'm here. Right here," she placed a hand on my chest. "I'm not going anywhere. Do what you need to do. I'll be here. I want to be there when the light floods your face again."

I wanted to laugh off the possibility that was true, but her tone was dead serious and so I let her words take purchase just a tiny bit. Was it possible she still wanted me? Why would anyone want any part of my fucked-up life? I wasn't good for anyone. Never had been. Wasn't the story I just told her evidence of that?

CHAPTER TWENTY-SIX

Bianca

"Are you sure it's okay I'm here?" I fidgeted with the neckline of my dress as Todd and I made our way up to the front of the hotel. I knew that this was important, but my heart and my mind weren't in it.

"It's fine, I promise. There's no reason to be nervous." He stopped and grabbed my hand, looking down at me with his smiling brown eyes. This was the Todd I had fallen for. The one that had made my stomach flutter and my heart race. Charming, sweet, reassuring. But my body was completely unaffected by him now.

I nodded, but the truth was I was less nervous about meeting Todd's family than I was about Court – wherever he was. I'd been tempted to stay home until he called, but the logical side of me knew I needed to take this opportunity to meet Todd's uncle. And it wasn't like I could do anything pacing the floor of my apartment. Still, I clutched my handbag to my side and willed it to vibrate with a call or text from Court.

This afternoon had felt like him saying goodbye, but I wasn't going to let him push me away so easily. I was prepared to show him that I would stand beside him through good and bad. He was important to me and I was confident that I was important to him too.

I pushed away the guilt about being out with Todd. I should have told Court, explained the entire situation while he was sharing his truths, but there hadn't been a moment that felt right to bring it up. And I guess I was scared. Would he understand why I needed to be friends with Todd? Or that despite not wanting to be with him that I wanted to be his friend – even without his connections. Todd was someone that had been there for me when I'd needed someone to talk to and that meant something to me.

"It's really just a party," Todd said as we walked through the lobby to the ballroom. "This is his fifth wife and they already did a big wedding with reception. This is just an excuse to throw another big shindig."

Sadness for Todd's life, however perfectly-packaged, stung as I pictured what his life had been like growing up. His mother had died when he was young, and his father had been inserting new stepmothers into his life in rapid fire succession. That couldn't have been easy.

"Come on, let's get a drink before we say hello to my dad and new mommy dearest."

"Okay," I laughed, and he shot me a wink and a smile as he pulled me inside the ballroom.

The affair was elaborate and over the top like nothing I'd seen before. The room stretched out in all directions. Instead of the usual reception setup of round tables for guests and the bride and groom sitting stiffly at a head table at the front of the room, couches and chairs were placed in groups all around. A band was set up in one corner. Not a DJ - a full band who sounded good enough to be on the radio. Maybe they were. I took it all in feeling more like I was in a posh night club than a hotel ballroom as Todd pulled me toward one of the many bars set up around the room.

"This is incredible," I said and let the soft music relax me.

Todd looked around with a dismissive glance. Was he really so unaffected by the money and class of a party like this? I wanted to ask if the previous four had been like this, but instead I accepted the champagne glass he handed me and sipped carefully.

The bride was easy to spot, despite her lack of white and veil. She stood in the center of the room wearing a red dress that dipped low in the front, a middle-aged man I knew immediately was Todd's father thanks to the matching build and stature stood hoveringly to the side. They clung to one another in that newlywed fashion. Maybe this marriage would be different – maybe it would last. I hoped so for Todd's sake.

"You want to dance?" Todd motioned with his head to where a few couples had gathered in front of the band.

Fear made my eyes go wide. I didn't know how to dance the way people here were dancing. Unless it was shuffling side to side and swaying my hips I was useless on a dance floor. "You know how to dance like that?"

"Sure."

"I think I'll pass."

I shook my head. I'd thought I had a clear picture of just how different Todd and my life had been growing up, but this night was taking it to a whole new level. I felt a sudden relief that we'd classified our relationship to the friend zone because not only did I not feel comfortable surrounded by this much money, I didn't think I ever would. And I was okay with that. Money was a means to an end for me, not something to be paraded around. I didn't judge them for their over the top spending, but I couldn't imagine a time it would feel normal either.

"Alright, well, let's get the social obligations over with and we can hang in the corner by the bar. I don't see my uncle yet, but he'll be here."

I followed behind Todd, his warm hand cupping mine, as he made his way through the crowd to the happy couple. They stood in the middle of a circle of sharply dressed men in suits and beautiful women. Todd's father, Mr. Sterling, tilted his head back and laughed as we approached the group and he looked so much like his son I had a sudden image of what Todd might be like in twenty years. The thought that Todd might end up with a slew of ex-wives and a child that resented him for it, made me depressed.

My thoughts were cut short when a voice cut through all the others, striking me with force and voltage so powerful I stopped, rooted to the spot.

No, no, no.

Todd, unaware that I'd stopped, continued pulling me behind him and the sudden momentum had me off balance and tripping. I gasped as I rammed into his shoulder, gaining the attention of the group in front of us. All eyes were on us, but I felt *his* bore into me. I was vaguely aware of Todd introducing me to his father and the new wife. I shook their hands and mumbled my greetings, but the hurt and confusion I felt from the man to my left overpowered it all.

"And this is – I'm sorry, I forgot your name," Todd said,

and I finally forced my eyes to Court.

"Court," he responded in a rough voice and reached his hand out to me like we'd never met. I took his hand, the jolt of his touch nearly breaking me.

"I thought your name was Theodore?" Court asked Todd like he was trying to catch up to what was going on as well.

"I go by Todd. Something my dad never adjusted to," he said simply.

I was still lost in a million possibilities and scenarios and feeling like I was going to throw up when another man joined us. I felt Court's demeanor change immediately and when I looked up, the hard lines of his perfect, beautiful jaw were clenched so tightly I nearly didn't recognize him. I followed his hard gaze to the man who had joined us.

"Uncle Cal," Todd said, his face beaming with pride. He looked to me with stars in his eyes. "I'd like you to meet my uncle Dr. Callahan Sterling."

The man gave me a friendly smile and pulled Todd into an affectionate hug. I struggled to return the smile. I could feel the hatred radiating off Court.

"You must be the lovely young woman my nephew has told me so much about."

"B-bianca," I said with a quivering voice and extended a hand. He shook it once, a genuine warmth to his smile.

I pulled my hand back first and stole a look at Court whose eyes were wild as he looked from me to Dr. Sterling. He looked so young and fragile and utterly confused as he tried to make out what was happening. I didn't want to be right, but it fell together like a math problem I'd been studying for hours. The man I'd hoped would be a hero to my family, to my mother, was the person responsible for all the walls Court built around himself. The person who had left him to the mercy of the system.

The doctor spoke as my mind raced through all the implications of this discovery, and I forced my attention back to him.

"I am so very sorry to hear about your mother's diagnosis. I work with a lot of people living with Parkinson's. I'm sure Todd has told you, but I'd be happy to look over her case and meet with her if she's interested. We're doing some clinical trials now that have been encouraging with preventing dementia and some of the more progressive symptoms." He spoke quietly so as not to be heard by the people next to us, but Court hovered at my side and I knew he was hanging on every word.

"Thank you. That's very generous of you."

I forced myself to meet Court's eyes. Pain and hopelessness etched in stone. My heart broke for him, for the boy who'd spent his whole life not feeling good enough, and for myself because how did this change things? Was this man as good as Todd said or as bad as Court thought? Was it possible to be both?

Court finally stepped forward, placing a hand at my back protectively but I felt the intensity in the angle and tone of his voice. "Dr. Callahan Sterling?"

Holding my breath, I watched the doctor's face carefully. Would he recognize Court? Would Court call him out right here in front of everyone? I couldn't venture a guess and I didn't know which way I hoped it'd go.

"Nice to meet you. I didn't catch your name," Dr. Sterling said with an easy smile and extended a hand.

The faintest smile played on Court's lips. "Courtney Adams."

If I hadn't been so carefully watching the exchange I

might have missed the way Court held onto the shake too long or the way Dr. Sterling paled and stilled as the name registered.

"And how do you know these two?" He asked Court but looked to his brother.

Allen Sterling placed a hand on Court's shoulder. "Court here is the best damn risk analyst I've worked with in the past twenty years. Sharp as nails and dedicated to his work. All work and no play. Sort of like you, brother."

I whimpered at the statement, no longer able to bear witness to whatever was going to go down. I accepted two things. One, Dr. Sterling was Court's father and he knew exactly who Court was. And two, Allen and Todd were completely oblivious, confirming something I'd hoped wasn't true – that his father had kept him a secret.

I turned to Todd and quietly muttered, "I'm sorry, I need to…" I trailed off, no excuse seemed fitting. "Please excuse me."

I didn't look back to see Todd's reaction at my brash departure, I just hurried out of the ballroom looking for a place to hide. I found the restroom first and hustled through the large oak door to a thankfully empty room.

I slunk against the wall and let a tear fall. For what I wasn't even sure. For Court? For my mom? For everything?

The creak of the door opening alerted me that someone had entered, but it was his presence I felt. Current flowed between us.

"Is *he* why getting Todd was so important to you?" His words were mean and accusing.

"No," I pushed away from the wall ready to defend my intentions. "I never expected this. Todd wanted to help so he invited me here to introduce me to his uncle… your father."

"Why didn't you tell me about Todd and Uncle Cal?" he said the last part in a mocking voice and it rankled me that he was mocking my friend who had done nothing to him.

"I don't know. I wasn't sure how to bring it up and then today…"

He paced the white tiles of the ladies' room. "Fuck, Bianca. I'm having a hard time wrapping my brain around this. Are you with Todd? Was everything between us really just about getting him… about his connections?"

"What? No, of course not. You can't really believe that."

"I don't know what I'm supposed to do or believe. You show up here tonight with him and now I find out he's related to my father? That's some shit."

"He recognized you," I said quietly.

He nodded. "Yep. His reaction is about what I expected."

"Are you going to talk to him here tonight?"

"I don't know. Yes. Maybe. I don't know," he repeated.

"Look, Court, Todd speaks so highly of his uncle. Go talk to him. I know it won't be easy, but…"

His eyes darkened, and his hands balled into fists at his side. "That man —"

"Is a world-renowned doctor. A respected member of the community. I know what he did thirty-five years ago was crappy, but it doesn't mean he's all bad. I need him. He is the best shot my mother has. Her bullshit doctors in New York sure as hell aren't going to give her the same level of care."

A pained expression pinched up his face. "He abandoned me. He abandoned my mother."

I nodded because I guess I knew as soon as I'd put it together that I'd made a decision. It was why it hurt so damn much. "And I hate him for that, but I need him more than I hate him. And I think you need him to – if only to get some closure."

"So that's it? You're choosing Todd and my deadbeat dad over me?"

"No, this has nothing to do with Todd or you. It's not even about me. My mother needs him."

A strangled groan erupted as he shoved both hands through his hair. I shook my head and placed a hand on his face.

"This is silly. We're talking in hypotheticals and you haven't even given him a chance."

"And hypothetically if I told you the thought of him helping you makes me see red? That I'd do everything in my power to bring him down with a scandal of a drug baby he abandoned as a teenager just so he could go nowhere near you or your family? What then? Would you still want to be there for me? You said this is what a relationship was – being there for each other when it was messy – well, 8B, this is about as messy as it gets."

"Is that what you want? A relationship with me?"

"I care about you. A lot. I want to be with you," he said, but visibly stiffened. I believed in his feelings for me, but he'd said time and again, in so many different ways, that he wasn't capable of committing.

"We can figure this out together. You don't need him."

"That's not fair. You're asking me to choose between what's best for my mother and what's best for you. You can't ask me to make that kind of choice."

"Life isn't fair."

He looked at me expectantly, waiting for my answer.

"It goes both ways. You have to be there for me, too. And if you can't understand why I need him..."

"No, I don't understand. You're hiding behind your

mother's illness like it excuses you for hurting me. It doesn't, and you are. There are other doctors."

"That is not what I'm doing. God, how can you be so dense? My mother is sick. Maybe you don't want family, friends, or people in your life, but I do. I hold on to mine tightly and I'll do whatever I need to help my mom get a few more good years before she can't live a normal life. No one that truly cared about me would ask me to make a choice that would hurt my family."

I looked down at my feet and summoned all the courage I could as I imagined my mother and the carefree smile that used to play on her face. "If you can't stand by me that's on you, but it doesn't change anything. I need him."

He shook his head, eyes wild. "You're choosing to need him."

Exasperated, heart shattering in my chest, I exhaled a breath and stood straight, confident in what was necessary. "I guess it's on you to decide what you want then. Talk to him, don't talk to him. Be there for me or not… I can't force you to be in this with me. I can't make you…"

My voice trailed off. I couldn't make him love me. I felt the current between us, but did he? Was I shuffling my feet and forcing a spark?

"I can't make you want me as much as I want you."

He growled like a wild beast and slammed a fist down on to the marble counter top. The dragons were back. I hadn't slayed them. I hadn't brought him light.

And the worst part is my own light had dimmed. I'd had a glimpse of how perfect things could be between us, and now it was gone.

Knowing we were at a stalemate, I slipped out of the ladies' room wanting my mom and New York liked I'd never wanted either before. I wanted to hear her voice, see her smile, and wrap myself into her arms. I longed for her soothing pats while she comforted me humming softly under her breath. The best parts of sickness and heartbreak were the moments spent with my mom while she put my broken pieces back together.

Todd leaned against the wall just outside the ball room. He pushed off the wall and met me halfway, giving me a confused and worried glance. I gave him a brittle smile.

"He said to give this to you." Todd handed me over his uncle's business card with a grin. "He's pretty great, huh?"

My smile and hands felt shaky.

"Thank you, Todd," I said as I slipped it into my purse. "I'm actually not feeling very well. I think I'm gonna head home."

"Bummer. Let me tell my dad and we'll get out of here."

"No, stay. It's your dad's fifth wedding reception. How often do those come around?" I joked as my heart broke a little more. "I'll be fine."

He put his hands in his pockets and smiled at me. "You'll be okay?"

"I'll be fine. Thank you for tonight. It was really decent of you."

He shrugged as if it had been no big deal and I guess it wasn't to him. I wondered if things had been different would I have been happy with him? Would he have ever really been happy with me? I couldn't place my feelings anymore. How much of my attraction for Todd was tied to his connections and the desperation I felt to get my mother help? I wanted to think I was able to separate the two, but the guilt that nagged at me wasn't so sure.

After Todd went back inside I marched around the

entrance. I'd half convinced myself to go back inside and find Court, but a small part of me – mostly my pride – cowered. God, I didn't know if I could stand to see the hurt in his eyes again, but I wanted him to know that I loved him. Maybe that was selfish because it probably didn't matter at this point, but I wanted to tell him. I wanted to scream it because he was so deserving of love and I didn't think he'd been told near enough.

Was he in there right now talking to his father? Maybe there was still a chance they'd talk, and everything would work out okay.

I steeled my nerves and prepared myself to run through that door, find Court and love him like he'd never been loved before when my phone rang, and hope bubbled in my chest. I answered without reading the screen so anxious to hear Court's voice nothing else mattered. Instead, Leo's voice spoke in my ear.

"Bianca," his voice was broken, and dread washed over me. Tears pricked at my eyes and I knew. I knew before he even said another word. "It's mom."

CHAPTER TWENTY-SEVEN

Court

I watched him through narrowed eyes as he worked the room. He smiled, shook hands and patted backs, he laughed heartily and drank slowly.

Confidence and easy-going charm oozed from his open suit jacket and loosened tie. Every few minutes he glanced around the room warily. Was he looking for me? I tried to push back the comparison – the way we'd stood eye to eye, the same dark hair and hazel eyes. I'd waited for this day – the day I could finally look him in the face. To remind him that his mistakes weren't buried with her. And I had dreamed of the way the color would drain from his face as he was forced to acknowledge my existence. His son. No, he didn't deserve that kind of claim on someone he so easily discarded. His punisher. I was set to right a wrong. No one got to erase their past. No one.

Funny, I always imagined that I'd feel like a weight had

been lifted when I'd finally confronted him. Finally, being free of a piece of my past, but instead I felt like I was trading a piece of my past for a piece of my future.

My heart pounded against my chest as I watched him say his goodbyes to Allen and his new bride. There was a genuine affection between the brothers and I wondered if my father had ever wanted to confide in him. It was obvious he hadn't shared my name because Allen had never shown any glimmer of recognition toward me outside of our working relationship. Hell, to me, the resemblance seemed obvious. Much as I hated to admit it. Amazing what people could overlook if they wanted to. No one would suspect that the good doctor had a son my age or that he'd left that son to be raised by someone else. In my case, lots of someones.

Tossing back the last of my scotch, I decided to forgo my own goodbye to the happy couple. After tonight, it probably wasn't going to matter anyway. My pulse beat rapidly, and I took in deep, raspy breaths as I waited in the shadows just outside the hotel waiting for him to emerge from the party. A cool acceptance of what I had to do settled over me.

The sliding glass doors opened, and he stepped outside into the early spring evening, whistling lightly under his breath. A chilled breeze whipped through the night, but he didn't seem to notice as he pulled his keys out and spun them around his finger, still whistling a happy, carefree tune. What kind of man knows his son is right in front of him and just leaves? The kind that never wanted you.

I emerged from my spot in the shadows and he paused. While I remained partially hidden he gave off an air of suspicion, but not concern. Fuel to my already raging fire, the way he dismissed me as a threat because what I was dressed nice? Because he was above the dangers lurking in the shadows? He of all people should've known that a wolf disguised as a sheep was still a wolf. When he finally got a good look at me he stopped, a myriad of emotions taking over his expression. Guilt. Shame. Dread. I noted that happiness wasn't among the many reactions as my father got a good look at his son.

"Dr. Sterling," I taunted, my voice laced with ironic respect.

He flashed me a speculative smile. "Yes. Courtney Adams, the young man working for my brother?"

Was he serious? We were playing it like that? Whatever hope I'd had for this moment was gone. Extinguished. He wasn't a good man who'd made a choice to give his son a better life, he was a coward. He hadn't wanted me. Still didn't want me. And nothing beyond that mattered.

I laughed a bitter sound as I locked eyes with him. "Yeah, that's me. Courtney Roosevelt Adams. Quite a mouthful, right? I used to hate my name. Who names a kid – a boy – Courtney? Don't even get me started on the middle name. Guess my mother just liked the name, hard to say, since she died."

I'd been named for his mother. Courtney Roosevelt – her maiden name. He knew it. I knew it. And now he knew that I knew exactly who he was.

He studied me hard, openly assessing me as if he might have some idea what a son he hadn't seen or talked to was supposed to look like. He nodded as his gaze landed back on my face. "You have her nose and mouth."

The words pissed me off mostly because they also dislodged something inside of me. Did he mean his mother or mine? I hadn't known either of them and wouldn't ever get that chance. He said it like he was remembering one of them fondly and there was no place for his happy stroll down memory lane.

"Maybe I do. I guess I'll have to take your word on that," I spat.

"I can't believe it's really you. I used to wonder if I passed you on the street, or in a busy airport if I'd know you. If I'd see you and just know. I guess not," he said and frowned like he was disappointed that he hadn't been able to place me immediately.

"You gave up the right to have such delusional fantasies a long time ago."

He nodded again. "I suppose I did. How did you find me?"

I stepped forward, lifting my chin so I was just the tiniest bit taller. "It wasn't that hard. You know, I've been waiting for this day since I was a kid. I'd lay my head down on whatever shitty pillow or floor I was currently sleeping on and I'd imagine all the things I'd say to you. When I was younger, I thought this moment would be filled with happy tears and hugs and you'd whisk me away to a better place. I believed that there had to be some mistake or logical reason you'd left me. Don't worry I gave up on fairy tales a long time ago."

"Courtney – "

"No, you don't get to talk. I came here tonight to get some sort of closure. I actually thought seeing you might be cathartic or some shit, but you've just managed to piss me off even more. I want nothing more than to expose you for the heartless prick you are and then watch you squirm as your country club buddies start giving you the cold shoulder. Treating you like the piece of trash you are. All this," I circled my hand in the air, satisfied to see his smug look disappear. "Society, community. You think they'll still be bowing at your feet when they find out about me?"

I could smell it. Fear. The threat of loss. I had his full attention. I stepped back and pictured Bianca's face. Those electric blue eyes that paved a path to goodness and light.

"Lucky for you, I can't do that." I swallowed the bile threatening in my throat. "Someone I care about needs you. So instead I'm going to offer you a choice. You met a young woman earlier tonight, Bianca Winters. Her mom has Parkinson's."

He nodded.

"Help her mother and you're off the hook. I'll go away, and you can keep pretending I don't exist."

He looked confused by my threat. "You want me to help her mom or you're going to tell people I'm your father? What proof do you have?"

"I don't need proof. This isn't the Jerry Springer show. All I have to do is help the information get in the right hands. That, along with my very long rap sheet, should be enough to get people talking. It may not be enough to take you down completely, you're too respected and good at what you do, but maybe it'll cause you enough grief to give you a glimmer of what my life has been like."

He ran a hand through his hair. "And if I don't agree to your terms?"

"So, you won't help Bianca's mother?"

"Todd's girlfriend? That's who you want me to help?"

I nodded and ground my back teeth.

He let out a long sigh. "What reassurances do I have you won't do it anyway?"

"I guess you'll just have to trust that I grew up to be a more honest man than you," I muttered.

"How much do you want for your silence? Perhaps we can

sit down with my lawyer and come up with an agreement."

The insult didn't land right away. He thought this was about a pay day? Why did rich people always think it was about money?

"You're unbelievable. No," I shook my head in disgust. "Fuck no."

I started to walk away but turned back. The questions burned in the back of my throat and I gave in to the temptation. "One question. I get why you didn't want me, but how could you abandon her? She needed you."

The pain on his face twisted and contorted and he nodded solemnly. "She did. I failed her. She was sick. I didn't know how to help her. I wanted to, but I didn't know how."

His pain transferred to me because I saw it now. I saw her through his eyes. And I wanted to ask if it was why he became a doctor and if he loved her. If he loved me, even for a moment. Instead, I gave him a resigned nod and walked away feeling Bianca's lightness fade out completely and the heaviness of my life before her settle back in its place.

CHAPTER TWENTY-EIGHT

Bianca

My phone pinged with an incoming text alert and my heart... my stupid, stupid heart jumped with hope before I looked at the screen.

> *Tasha:* How are you holding up? Anything I can do...
> text you knock knock jokes, fly out to see you?

I smiled at her consideration. Tasha was the only person I'd told, but since it was now Monday and I was missing classes it wasn't going to be a secret for long. Not that many people would care enough to ask. Mostly I felt like I should have at least told Todd, but he'd want to call his uncle and I wasn't ready for that. Todd adored his uncle. When he spoke of Dr. Callahan Sterling, his eyes shone and his face gleamed like being related to the world-renowned doctor made Todd a better person by genetics. As angry as I was at Dr. Sterling,

I wasn't prepared to pull the rug out from under Todd.

And I still hadn't heard from Court. I knew he was hurting and I wondered how he'd left things with his father. Had he worked things out, gotten the closure he needed? The pit in my stomach said otherwise. So did the lack of text messages.

I pulled out the business card Todd had given me and ran my finger along the frayed edges. They were worn where I'd clutched it, agonizing over whether to call him or not. I'd meant what I'd said to Court, I'd always choose my mom but right now I couldn't bring myself to call the doctor that had abandoned a man I cared for deeply. I was at an impasse.

After tucking the card back into my purse, I texted back a response to my best friend.

> **Me**: I'm fine. You just worry about passing your art history final. I'll be back late tomorrow night. Thank your father again for getting me a flight at the last minute.
>
> **Tasha**: I will. Let me know if you need anything else. Xoxo

"Shouldn't the doctor be here by now?" Donnie asked as he paced the tiny hospital room.

I shot him a look of annoyance and stole a peek at my mother. She'd looked sad the first day. A broken hip and a series of bruises along the entirety of her left side from the fall had scared us all into a realization that the time had come. The time where she'd no longer be able to get around like she had fought to for so long – despite all of our insistences that she find a job where she didn't have to be on her feet so much.

Today, three days later, and hopefully the day she'd be released to go home, she just looked defeated. Like she had completely given up hope that she could live a normal life. The doctors had warned us years ago that depression was common, even to be expected, as her symptoms got worse and the disease progressed, but I was not prepared for the light and jubilance that was always present on my mother's face to disappear. It was worse than any medical diagnosis. Her spirit was gone. She hadn't even chastised me for flying home. Or for demanding that I would return to New York for good as soon as finals were over.

A short rap on the door drew my attention to it and the man entering. Dressed in the same white coat the rest of the doctors wore, it was his dark hair and eyes that made my breath catch. All eyes in the room turned to him at my sharp inhale.

"Good afternoon," he said in a friendly tone as he strode to the hospital bed where my mother laid. "I'm Dr. Sterling. How are you?"

She looked first to me as if acknowledging that I had gotten him here and then braved a smile in his direction but spoke truthfully as she responded. "The emotional injuries are far worse than the external ones."

He spoke softly. "Yes, I understand. It's perfectly normal – not that you give a damn what's normal or not."

That pulled a real smile from her and even a bit of life returned to her eyes.

He offered her his hand and held it almost like he was shaking it but without movement. "I'm not sure how much your daughter has told you about me, but I'm a neurologist. I work with a number of people in all stages of the disease. I've had a chance to look over your chart and I think you'd be a great candidate for a new therapy we've been using with limited success. It wouldn't be a cure, you understand, but could give you longer with your current level of motor skills and cognitive function."

"And I could do the therapy here in New York?"

Dr. Sterling looked to me for the first time. His blank expression met the surprise in mine and then glanced back to my mother. "Yes, it's twice a week here at the hospital. I'll get weekly reports and I'll be back at least once a month to see you personally and gauge your progress."

Her hands shook a little more as she considered his offer and asked the next question. "That sounds great, but also expensive. Will our insurance cover the therapy?"

He swallowed, and I could tell he chose his words carefully as he said, "Everything is covered. You'll just need to fill out some paperwork relieving the hospital and myself of any liability, standard forms but I do urge you to read over it all carefully. Especially what will be expected of you and what benefits you may gain. I'm not going to lie to you, it will be hard and frustrating and if you feel like giving up now, well it's just a fraction of what you can expect the first month or two. I will push you to do things you probably haven't tried to do in some time."

He smiled and patted her hand before dropping it back gently onto the bed. He let his gaze roam around the room to each of us. "I'm sure you'll come up with a number of questions after I've left... feel free to call me at any time. Meanwhile, I'll get you on the schedule."

With a curt nod, he turned to leave.

My mother, father, and brothers exchanged hopeful smiles, but the lump in my throat wouldn't allow me to celebrate just yet.

"Be right back," I said to my mother as I dropped a kiss to her temple.

I jogged after him, catching him just as he reached the nurse's station down the hall.

"Dr. Sterling?" I said as I stopped behind him.

He turned and smiled, giving me the polite grin I assumed he used on all patients and families. It wasn't insincere, just reserved. "What can I do for you Miss Winters?"

"I wanted to thank you for coming so soon. I didn't realize Todd even knew of my mother's accident yet. I left in a rush Friday night," I rambled as I wrung my hands in front of me.

He studied me carefully like he was trying to decipher my words. I wished I'd been less adamant to stay offline. For all I knew, Court had gone nuclear and really outed his father's secret creating some sort of smear campaign. For just a moment I was grateful he didn't know my connection to Court, and then ashamed because Court deserved better than that.

"I'm sorry I wasn't able to be here sooner. I called her doctor this morning to get records and he told me of the accident. I flew in as soon as I could."

I balked. He'd flown in specifically for my mother?

"Oh," I said now completely unsure of what to say to this man who I wanted to hate but had dropped everything to come see my mother. "I assumed you'd found out from Todd. I – well, either way, thank you," I stammered out.

"You're welcome."

I walked away in a daze. Confused by how I felt about too many things. Graduation, moving, my mother's worsening condition, Dr. Sterling being Court's father but also getting my mom into a program that I was certain wouldn't be available through any other means – I felt exhausted by the ways my world had been knocked on its axis.

I detoured to the waiting room before going back to my mother's hospital room and pulled out my cell phone. With shaky hands, I typed in Dr. Callahan Sterling and son into the search browser. I held my breath while the search results loaded, but there wasn't anything recent in the news. I clicked on the first link which took me to a bio page where a picture of a model-worthy family stared back at me. Dr. Sterling stood next to a regal looking blonde woman and on the other side of him, a girl about sixteen I'd guess with hair as blonde as her mothers and a young man who looked so much like Court my insides hurt. The boy was probably twelve or thirteen by my best guess, still awkward and gangly but there was no doubt he was going to grow up and be as handsome as his father. As handsome as Court.

My heart ached for Court more than ever. What had it felt like to see this picture after years of wondering about his parents? Somehow, I knew he'd assumed that his parents had given him up with the desire not to have kids or a family, but Dr, Sterling had eventually made a family and a name for himself and seemingly never looked back on the son he'd given up when he was a kid.

I clicked through a few more links, a few more pictures of him and his wife at events and news of numerous awards and honors that had been bestowed upon him. I wanted to throw up or call Court.

I tried another search string, Court Adams and Dr. Callahan Sterling. Nothing. Well, thank God for that anyway. Hope surged in my chest. Hope that Court and his father had been able to have a civilized conversation. Hope for my mother. But just as quickly as I allowed myself to look to a positive future, I remembered even if both those things were true, Court and I were apart. The pain on Court's face had been a white flag. He'd pulled away even as I'd been the one to put the actual distance between us. Still, the ugly truth was that I had walked away. I'd made a stand with confidence that I'd gained from Court himself, but I feared I'd gotten it all terribly wrong. And if I had made the right decision, could my heart ever be pieced back together without Court in my life?

I RETURNED TO school the next day. My mother was settled back at home with my father and brothers to look after her and two weeks' worth of freezer meals friends and neighbors had brought over. It eased some of my guilt for leaving.

My mom assured me she would be fine, that there was no need to hurry back and she'd even pushed me again to reconsider graduate school. I had considered it. I would make more money with a master's degree to add to my resume, but it all seemed so unimportant now that my mother's condition was worsening. How many good years did she have left where she would be able to walk, able to talk, able to get out of bed? My throat tightened at the thought of her dependent on a walker or wheelchair. How far off was that?

No. I would not allow myself to throw a pity party. If I expected my mother to keep a positive outlook, I had to, also.

"Wanna have a study night in front of the TV with *The Walking Dead* as background noise?" Tasha called from the living room.

"Can't," I said from the open bathroom door where I studied my reflection. "I'm meeting Todd at the library. He has notes for our History class."

I re-did my bun and then reached for my eyeliner. I made the blue line thicker on the top and bottom of my eyes. My gaze landed on the note Court had written on the mirror. I hadn't been able to force myself to remove his words, *Sweet dreams.*

Somewhere along the way it had become his signature sign off to me and the words touched something inside of me every time. I shook my head, trying not to dwell on the fact I'd never hear him say those words again. And the blue scrawl on my mirror and the text messages on my phone history were the only proof that it had ever really happened at all. Court had touched so much of my life and yet left so little behind.

I left the bathroom and shoved my textbooks and notebooks into my backpack while avoiding Tasha's disapproving scowl. She raised an eyebrow and crossed her arms waiting for an explanation. I hadn't told her much about what had gone down between Court and me. I didn't know how to explain without telling her everything, and everything felt like too much. Like it was Court's story to share. Leika and I knew, but who else? I frowned as I thought about the people he'd let close to him. Only two. And now only one was still by his side.

"We're friends and we're just studying at the library with lots of people and me with mountains of work to do to catch up," I said as I hefted my bag on to my shoulder.

"Alright," she said by way of concession, but I knew she wasn't going to drop it completely until I told her at least some of what had happened. I just hoped by the time she was done being patient it would hurt a little less to talk about.

Todd was waiting for me upstairs at the library. The same prime study spot as last time, but sans the friends.

"Where is everyone?" I asked as I sat my things down on the coffee table in front of the couch. The whole setting too intimate with just the two of us. Busy library or not.

"They all bailed on me to stay at the house and study."

I moved to grab my bag. "Oh, well you should have called. Tasha was asking if I wanted to study with her anyway."

He stood and lifted a hand in front of his chest in a gesture to stop. "No don't go. Please. I lied. I didn't invite anybody else. I wanted to talk to you."

I sat hesitantly. "Okay."

Todd raked a hand through his hair and took a seat opposite of me. The coffee table was between us, but it didn't seem like a big enough obstacle to keep my heart out of his grasp. He brought both hands together and clasped them almost casually between his knees.

"Look, this is all really shitty timing and I know you're set to move back to New York in a few weeks and I'm staying here for another four years and then who knows where I'll have to go, but I'm not ready to say goodbye to you. I know you said you were sort of seeing someone else and I respect that, but if it's only sort of then maybe there's still a chance for us?"

I opened my mouth to speak and no words came out. He'd stunned me.

"Would you at least consider it – keeping me, or us, as an option. I'll come to New York when I can, and you can visit me, we can talk and text. You're going to be busy with work and your family and me with school so maybe it could work."

"I don't know what to say," I admitted finally when he looked at me expectantly.

"Will you just promise me you'll think about it?"

I nodded and stood with my bag. "I think I should go back to the apartment until –"

I had no idea what I was going to say, but he nodded in understanding and stood. "I'll walk with you."

We walked in silence, me mulling over how quickly things had changed in the last week, and him giving me space, I assumed. When we reached the parking lot where his BMW was parked in a meter spot, he motioned to the shiny, red car. "Can I give you a ride?"

It felt like the least I could do, just a ride, not a promise of anything more, and I slipped into the passenger seat. It was only a few blocks to my apartment and Todd was pulling up outside the complex before I'd had little more time to think about what he'd asked. He put the car in park, but left the engine running. I swallowed hard and looked over at him ready to tell him I didn't think there was any way I could get involved right now, but before the words could leave my mouth he captured my mouth with his. It seemed to be his signature move.

The kiss was soft, and I allowed his lips to guide the pace as he moved slowly. His hand moved to my chin and I stiffened with the additional contact before forcing myself to relax. To explore, to discover, to savor, and ultimately to judge. There was no jolt of electricity like there'd been with Court. His hand felt intrusive and forceful where Court's had always seemed safe and loving. And when Todd finally swept his tongue into my mouth, I didn't have the desire to tangle mine with his. I was analyzing, and I hated myself for it.

He pulled back and smiled at me, a lazy smile like a man who'd just given a girl a kiss she would never forget. And I wouldn't, but for all the wrong reasons.

CHAPTER TWENTY-NINE

Court

May and June went by without Bianca and somehow, I survived despite the ache in my chest. With July came the warm weather, dinners out on the patio, and a new team of wide-eyed and eager recent graduates and college kids to manage all on my own.

I hadn't had to deal much with Allen Sterling. No visits to Connecticut, just a couple conference calls where I waited for him to fire me, his own nephew, but if Dr. Sterling had said a word to him, Allen never let on.

I'd started to prep one of my new team members to take over the account; I was itching to be free from all ties to the Sterling family. I'd never been so grateful that my mother had given me her last name instead of his. Maybe she'd known he'd never accept me as his own. Had that been why she'd named me after his mother? A silent fuck you for abandoning us?

Things marched on exactly like they'd done before, only I wasn't the same. I was now painfully aware of the solitude I'd created for myself. Work didn't satisfy me like it had before, but I threw myself into it anyway desperate to distract myself.

And so, I settled back into things. Almost as if Bianca had never happened. But she had, and it was the little things that hurt the most. The way I checked my phone first thing in the morning waiting for the good morning texts I'd gotten used to her sending. Every woman I saw –sitting across from me on the subway, the barista at the coffee shop, even Nancy in HR – they all wore blue around their eyes and I wanted to wipe it from their faces. It belonged to her and to her mother. Ridiculous, I know, but that's where I was.

And Leo. He'd been hired as an intern, placed on my team as I'd asked, and now I saw him three days a week. It made me feel closer and further from Bianca. A million things rattled around – things I wanted to ask him, about Bianca, about their mom, about him, but I couldn't bring myself to ask. Didn't think I deserved to know any of it.

I was the first one into the conference room for our weekly team meeting, followed by Leo. His hair was a shaggy mess as I'd come to learn was his style, but he wore a nice pressed pair of khakis and an oversized button-down shirt that I guessed was probably his father's.

"Hey, Leo."

He gave a small wave and took a seat a few chairs down from me. "Hi, Court."

"How are things going?" I asked, leaving it purposely vague so maybe he'd tell me about more than just how work was going for him.

He nodded a little too enthusiastically. "Really great. I

can't tell you how much I appreciate your getting me the job."

My face warmed because I hadn't meant to make him feel like he owed me or needed to thank me. Fuck. It was a shit intern job.

"And your brother, what did he end up doing this summer?"

It seemed like a safer question than the one I wanted to ask, but as his face fell serious and grave I wished I had just stuck to the weather or sports.

"He's decided to do his own thing working nights so he could spend days with mom. Ever since the accident, he's been…"

He continued but I only half heard as he went on. Accident?

I don't know why I wanted to act like I knew. Maybe because Leo had assumed I did and I wanted to live in a world where I was still a part of Bianca's life enough that I would be privy to those sorts of details. So instead of asking what happened and admitting I was in the dark, I asked, "How's she doing?"

A few others on the team were entering the room now so Leo's tone lifted, and he gave a nod to those entering as he answered. "Much better. Although, I think that could be more about Bianca moving back than anything else. She always has been mom's favorite."

I gaped, but Leo didn't notice because the room was now filled with the team and the usual greetings and chatter that preempted our meetings was getting underway.

I must have said and looked the part of Court the boss man because no one seemed concerned by the noise in my head or the pounding of my heart as Leo's information tore back open my only half-mended heart.

She was back. Bianca had moved back. I didn't know why or what it meant, but just knowing she was back in the city she loved fed me with happiness. And then that happiness destroyed whatever hope I had left of her ever speaking to me again. She'd come back, but she hadn't called me.

The day was too busy to give into the compulsion to obsess over the new information and figure out what to do with it, and it wasn't until I was walking to the bar to meet Leika for our weekly drink that I could start to mull over what it all meant.

It was only five blocks to the bar, not nearly enough time to run through the million different reasons I thought Bianca might have come back. Was it the accident Leo had referred to? Had she come back for the job at JC Engineering? Was it the allure of New York City?

I really wanted to believe some part of her had at least thought of me as she'd made the decision to come back, but the radio silence for the last nine weeks was hard to get past. It stung that she hadn't contacted me, hadn't thought to call or text to let me know she was back. And it pissed me off that I'd somehow let someone in and gave them the power to hurt me. I didn't even know how it had happened. She'd fused herself to me and I couldn't separate the pieces that belonged to her. Couldn't separate the pieces of my life that didn't feel wrong without her part of it.

Leika was already at our table, as usual, but instead of her wary smirk she wore an all-out smile that was so big and genuine it made my mood feel even darker. Sluggishly I made my way to the table and opened my arms in time for her to throw herself into them.

"I'm engaged!" she squealed happily and squeezed me

tightly.

Shit. I'd completely forgotten about Jeff planning to propose. She pulled back and we scooted into the booth. She made a show of her hand flashing the diamond ring on her finger.

"Congratulations!" I said in a voice that I hoped was cheerier than I felt. "When did he do it?"

"Last weekend," she said smiling in that contented way people looked when they talked about proposals and weddings. "He took me to his parents' house in Jersey and did it in front of the whole family." She paused for dramatic effect. Leika felt the same way I did about big families – they made us uncomfortable. We didn't know what to do or how to act with that many people hovering around us. "Aunts, uncles, cousins, even his great grandma was there," she finished with an eye roll.

"Well you must really love him then since you said yes," I pointed out.

She sighed. "I do, lucky fucker."

"So, are you going to plan some gaudy, awful wedding and make people watch you walk down the aisle and do the cha cha slide?"

"Yep, might as well pick out your cummerbund now." I groaned and Leika laughed. "Also, it's going to be in New Jersey."

"You're killing me," I told her as I spun the drink in front of me in slow circles, two hands wrapped around the glass to keep it steady.

"I know, I know," she said and shot me a small smile. "But you're gonna have to get used to weekends in the garden state because I'm going to need you to visit me occasionally and keep me sane." She bit her bottom lip and waited for my reaction.

When realization finally dawned, I pulled at the collar of my shirt and loosened my tie. Leika was moving. I should have seen it coming sooner, but Leika had always complained about Jeff's big, noisy family and the way they were always getting in their business. I never imagined she'd move away from New York – let alone to Jersey.

"Why? His family makes you crazy?"

Leika studied me for a moment. With a shrug, she said, "I think that's what family is. A bunch of flawed people that you choose to love despite how crazy they make you. Jeff makes me want to scream sometimes but I still love the shit out of him. You too," she kicked me under the table. "And someday I'm going to have kids of my own and I want them to have all of that. A grandma that babysits, cousins to get in trouble with, birthday parties with everyone…" her voice trailed off, but I heard the hope and joy in her words.

She was taking all the bad shit and moving past it toward a future that was everything she'd been denied. I should have been happy for her. I was, deep down somewhere that I couldn't access right now because everything in my own life was so completely fucked.

"I don't know what to say," I admitted as I scrubbed a hand over my face.

A sad look crossed her face. "Say you're happy for me and that even though it'll be inconvenient, and you hate taking the train, that you'll come visit me and still be part of my life."

I nodded. "I am happy for you. It just feels weird, I guess. You're the only family I've ever had and now it's like you're getting adopted and joining this big, happy family and leaving me behind."

"You'll always be my family, Court. If it weren't for you…" her voice broke and I kicked her back under the table.

"I'm excited for you, kid. When's all this happening?"

"Soon. Sometime this month hopefully. We're going back tomorrow to try and nail down dates and find a place to live that isn't his parents' basement."

I let out a chuckle and sat back in the booth trying to relax and enjoy this, knowing soon these types of outings would have to be planned out way in advanced and would probably be weeks or months in between.

"Now, your turn for the hot seat." Leika sat forward and leaned her elbows on the table. "Have you called Bianca?"

I shot her a look of surprise. Leika had treaded carefully around the topic since the confrontation with my father. "No, she made things clear the last time I saw her."

I left out the part about her being back and not having contacted me, but then something struck me… Leika latched on to Bianca right away when they met, in fact I knew that Leika had texted Bianca after she'd gone back to school.

"Did you know she's back?" I accused.

Leika smirked. No hint of apology in her voice when she said, "I wondered when you were going to figure that out."

"How exactly was I supposed to figure that out? It's not like we're still speaking. The only reason I know is because her brother let it slip her mother had an accident. Is she okay?"

"I'm not playing messenger. If you want to know you'll have to call her yourself."

"She made a choice," I said through gritted teeth.

"A choice to get her mother the best doctor she could find. Do you really hold that against her while blackmailing him to help her at the same time?"

"You know it isn't that simple."

"It is to her."

"I just –" my voice cut out and I hesitated, trying to decide if I was really going to admit what Leika already knew but I'd never confirmed with words. I took a deep breath. "I thought she was different. That she would stand by my side and fight with me. Fight for me. I thought she'd stay."

"Her mother is sick, Court. She didn't do it to hurt you. In fact, my guess is it hurt her a great deal to make that choice. The ridiculous thing is that she did exactly what you wished everyone would have done for you – she stood by the people who love and depend on her. It's who she is. She will always stand by the people she loves, you included, but you have to earn that love. Right now, she needs you. It'd be a good time to stop wishing things were different and start showing her how much she means to you. Does she have any clue what you did for her? Why your father is helping them?"

"No." I shot her a warning look. "You didn't tell her, did you?"

"Of course not, but I think she has a right to know."

"All that matters is her mom gets the care she needs."

Leika smirked as she lifted her glass. "You're completely in love with her."

My eyes widened, and a weight settled in my stomach. I didn't bother refuting Leika's words. Maybe I hadn't said it aloud, but I'd been grappling with the same realization for weeks now. I couldn't get her out of my system. Didn't even really want to.

"Can we talk about something else?" I muttered and swallowed the last of my beer.

"Sure," Leika chirped. "Let's talk about the toast you're going to give at my engagement party next weekend."

I shook my head and let out a rough chuckle. "Why don't you just write it for me since I'm sure you have a very specific list of things I can and cannot say."

It was after eight when Leika finally sighed and said she needed to get home to pack for her weekend away. We hugged, both holding on for a little longer than usual. Things were changing, and it seemed we both felt uneasy about that.

"Love ya, kid," I said as I pressed a kiss to her temple. "Make sure your place has a spare bedroom. If I'm visiting freaking New Jersey I don't want to sleep on the couch."

CHAPTER THIRTY

Bianca

I'D JUST SETTLED into bed when the ping of an incoming text set my heart to beating wildly. It didn't matter that it had been months without talking to him – every text still had me hopeful that it was him. And every time I looked at the screen, that hope dissolved into a wave of disappointment.

> *Leika*: I got engaged! Party next Friday at 7pm. Address attached.

I stared at the words for five minutes before I responded. I was happy for her, of course, but how could I possibly go?

> *Me*: Congratulations!

I didn't tell her I'd be there. Even the thought of being in the same place as Court had my stomach flipping.

Leika: Say you'll come. PLEASE? I know things are weird with Court, but I promise to shield you from him if that's what you want.

I sighed. Was it what I wanted? It was what I probably needed. I vividly remembered the hurt and anger in his eyes the night I'd discovered his father was Dr. Sterling. I didn't think that was a pain that I could erase so easily with a casual hello at a mutual friend's party. In truth, I was surprised she'd even invited me. We'd shared a few text messages over the past few months, but I'd known where her loyalty laid. I typed back quickly before I could talk myself out of it. If Leika had invited me, she'd either cleared it with Court or knew he'd be okay. She wouldn't knowingly inflict pain his direction. Maybe he'd moved on. The idea of that was even more depressing.

Me: I'll be there.

And so, it was settled. I was finally going to lay eyes on the man who haunted my dreams.

The next afternoon I still reeled from the idea of seeing Court. I'd been late to work, spilled coffee on my dress, and now I was late again.

"I'm here. I made it. I'm sorry I'm late," I gasped as I jogged up to the front of the hospital, cursing the strappy sandals I'd chosen to wear, where my mom and Donnie stood waiting.

"You're late," Donnie said with an annoyed glare and turned, pulling mom with him to the sliding glass doors that would bring us into the main lobby of the hospital.

"I think we already established that," I grumbled and

pushed my purse strap back up to my shoulder.

I'd been accompanying my mom to her therapy twice a week. Even after it was clear Donnie had it covered.

I wasn't sure what I had expected in terms of therapy, but the exercises were less of the weight machines and yoga I had anticipated from the research I'd done, although she did some of that, but more things like playing ping pong and dancing.

Donnie had taken on the role of my mother's daily guardian and caretaker with a possessive hold and he took that job seriously. And, unlike the rest of us, he'd been able to make it fun. To make mom feel less like a patient and more like she was out doing something fun with her teenage son. I loved him for that, but it made me feel sad and hopeless at the same time. I'd come back to be of help and to spend more time with her, but it felt like all I did was make her sad and remind her that the disease was progressing.

Donnie and I flanked her to the check in desk, but I stayed back as they entered the therapy floor.

"I'll just be over here," I said and pointed to the small waiting area.

My mom gave me a small smile, but Donnie kept his eyes on our mom as he held the door open for her. I watched for a few moments, just let myself see and try and come to grips with what was happening. My mother was sick. The therapy was helping in some ways – she was less stiff, she said she felt more alert, but she wasn't going to ever be able to hold down a waitressing job or hand stitch the hem of my dresses. Her shaking was sometimes subtle and other times so pronounced I wanted to hold her hands as if I could steady them and make it stop.

On a positive note, my work was going well. They'd even

been understanding with my mother's condition and allowed me to work a somewhat flexible schedule so I could attend her therapy sessions. I hadn't regretted coming back, which made me feel confident that I'd made the right decision. A master's degree wasn't off the table, I was planning on applying at NYU next semester and though I knew it would take more time to do it while holding down a full-time job and helping out with mom, I looked forward to the additional work. Busy hands left less time to stare hopelessly at the pictures of Court that I'd been unable to delete.

Just thinking of him made my fingers itch to pull up his contact information and send him a text, but what could I possibly say? To my knowledge, he hadn't exposed his father, at least not publicly. I'd kept an eye on the news waiting for the destruction Court might be able to cause the revered doctor with a bombshell of an abandoned son he'd had over thirty years ago when he was barely a teenager.

Each time I typed in the google search bar I half-hoped and half-dreaded the outcome. I knew it cost Court something to keep the past buried and I wondered if he'd ever truly be able to move on until he felt vindicated somehow. I didn't think exposing his father publicly and putting both their jobs and reputations on the line was the way to go, but I understood the need he felt to right a wrong.

As if I'd materialized him with my thoughts, Dr. Sterling appeared at the reception desk. He spoke quietly with the receptionist as he handed her a stack of papers. When he looked up and caught my stare he gave me a polite nod and a weak smile.

His demeanor toward me had never been as friendly as that first night with Todd. Whether this was just how he was when dealing with a patient's family or not, I couldn't guess. Maybe I wore my barely concealed anger at him more flagrantly that I thought. This man was responsible for hurting someone I loved, but also responsible for helping someone else that I loved, and I didn't know how to wrap my brain around that.

I breathed a sigh of relief when he disappeared from sight only to be taken by surprise when he strode through the door into the waiting area.

"Miss Winters," he said by way of greeting.

I stood because... well, I didn't know why. He'd thrown me and put me at a disadvantage and standing made me feel less like a child.

"Hello, Dr. Sterling."

"I wondered if we could talk for a moment in my office?"

"My mother should be done in about fifteen minutes, should we –"

He shook his head before I could finish. "This isn't about her care."

I nodded and swallowed, hoping to dislodge the lump in my throat as I followed him through the door and down a hallway of offices. He stopped at the last room and motioned for me to go in ahead of him. My mind raced through reasons he might want to talk to me and I worried at my lower lip as I sat and watched him round the large, wooden desk in the corner of the room and sit across from me.

"If this is about payment or insurance," I started thinking back to the mail stack, not able to remember a single bill or insurance claim in the months she'd been under his care.

He lifted a hand. "No, that's not it."

He used that same hand to scrub over his jaw and for the first time, Dr. Sterling looked unsure. It was an odd look for a world-renowned doctor and it immediately put me ill at ease.

"Can you tell me what your relationship is to Courtney Adams?"

My mouth gaped open because this was the absolute last thing I had expected him to ask. What had Court done? Or had Todd somehow figured it out?

When I hadn't spoken, he continued. "I'm sorry to ask, I know it isn't any of my business, but I need to contact him, and I was hoping you could help me."

"I don't understand. Why do you need my help?"

His head bobbed around as if he were settling on how much to tell me. "He didn't give me any contact information and I have a few things I need to settle regarding our business agreement."

Shock turned to anger, and I balled my fists in my lap. And then I laughed because what else could I possibly do? "Business agreement? He's your son."

A pained expression crossed his face, but I didn't have any emotion left to pity him. "So, you do know." He nodded. "I wasn't sure if you were in on it or not. Now that your mother's care is underway I would like to try and talk with him. Try to reason with him. Get our agreement down on paper. A scandal wouldn't be good for anyone. I'm sure you can understand that, but I'm afraid Court's track record isn't something I want to leave to chance."

"In on what?"

He studied me for a moment. "Court threatened to divulge our relationship to the press if I didn't help your mother," he stated plainly.

All the blood rushed from my face and I felt shaky and disoriented as I tried to grapple with this information. Court had used the threat of his relationship to Dr. Sterling to blackmail him into helping my mom? How dare he use my mother's disease as a bargaining chip in his plan to ruin his father.

"You didn't know," he finally said, and I shook my head.

Dr. Sterling sighed, and I finally allowed myself to see the situation through his eyes. God, no wonder he'd treated me so coolly.

"He had no right. I will talk with my family. If you could refer my mother to someone maybe half as good as you it would mean a lot to us. They had no idea about any of this," I said as I stood on shaky legs.

"Please, Bianca," he stood as well and motioned for me to sit. "It's really best for all of us if he contacts me. I'd appreciate your help reasoning with him, so we can come to some sort of agreement, so we can all move on with our lives."

"Move on with our lives?" I balked at him. "You think Court can just move on like none of this ever happened? Like you didn't throw him away like garbage?" My voice rose, and I could feel the anger warming my face. "Did you even try and talk to him? Explain to him why you never contacted him throughout the years?"

I moved to leave, but apparently, I wasn't done saying my peace. I whirled and clenched my hands into fists as I spoke. "Court is the most amazing person I've ever met, but the damage that you caused," my heart squeezed, and tears stung at the corners of my eyes. There was so much more I wanted to say, but I didn't trust myself not to break down.

"I suppose I'm going to need to buy your silence now as well?" he asked but didn't wait for my answer. He opened a desk drawer and pulled out a checkbook.

"You're unbelievable. God, I can't believe I told Court

he should give you the benefit of the doubt. I think he's exceptionally lucky to not have had you for a father. He's good and honest and leaving him alone is probably the most decent thing you've ever done." I marched to the door, tears falling freely now.

I sent Donnie a text to tell him I'd had to return to the office and I did. I buried myself in algorithms for the next six hours, working well past my coworkers and into the early evening. I blocked out everything but numbers and equations until my fingers ached and my stomach rumbled so loudly I finally gave into my body's signs that it was time to go home.

I needed to decide what to do about my mom's care. About Dr. Sterling. About what it meant that Court had used my mom's illness as a bargaining chip. But it wasn't just about me. It was about dad, and Leo and Donnie.

And my mom.

The house sat quiet. Mom and dad were watching *The Voice* and barely pried themselves from the screen long enough to mumble a hello as I entered. Donnie was at work. He'd started a job as a dishwasher at a night club in Hell's Kitchen. My parents hadn't been pleased, but the pay was better than minimum wage and it left Donnie free during the day to be with mom.

Grabbing a plate of leftover meatloaf from the stove, I took it outside on the patio. Leo sat lounged on an easy chair with his sketch pad in his hands.

"Hey," I muttered a greeting as I took a seat next to him.

"Hey," he replied without looking up.

I watched him draw as I ate. The easy way his hands glided over the paper always amazed me, but tonight as he drew a portrait of a woman, I felt the day fall away and I felt truly at peace for the first time maybe since moving home. He shaded around the eyes, creating a dramatic look and then added wisps of hair around the face, giving the woman a carefree elegance. There wasn't a picture attached, but I knew this photo from memory. So did he, apparently.

"She was so beautiful," I said as he smudged strategically with his finger in certain spots.

He gave me a small nod and looked up as if just realizing I was watching him. He put the pencil down and stared over at my food. With an eye roll, I handed over the plate.

He grinned and shoveled the remainder of my late dinner into his mouth in three easy bites.

"You got any more?" I asked, nodding to the paper.

He shrugged, and I took that as an invitation. I grabbed the sketchbook and flipped to the front. Each page was her and there was something almost reverent about the way he'd captured our mom in the various stages of her life. I stopped at one, staring a long moment, before I set it back down in front of him.

"She's even more beautiful now," I said as we both looked on to the picture he'd drawn of mom. An older version of the same woman he'd been drawing – wrinkles around her eyes and mouth in this one, but the same heart-shaped face and big eyes that made you want to stare at her just a little longer.

"How's work?" I'd avoided asking over the last few weeks because I was afraid even the mention of Court's name would splinter my heart, but after today I felt like there wasn't anything my baby brother could say that would make the day worse.

"Good."

I rolled my eyes again because one-word responses were typical of my brothers, but damn did they always have to make me work for every scrap of information?

"What do you do all day? Fetch coffee? Run errands?"

It was his turn to roll his eyes at me. "Court's not that kind of boss. He doesn't make us do stuff like that."

The first slip of his name and I had survived.

"That's good," I said.

"He hooked me up with the marketing team, told them I was thinking about a career in art, so they're letting me work with them a few hours each week to help design their new website," he said and then added. "Pretty cool."

Pretty cool was the teenage boy equivalent of "OMG, that's amazing!" and I felt like an ass for not having asked about his job sooner.

"That's awesome," I told him with a small punch to his upper arm which earned me a small grin. "Congratulations."

He picked the sketch pad back up and I leaned back in the chair content to just sit some more with the quiet sound of his drawing lulling me back to reality – back to what was important, my family.

"I think he misses you or something," he said, not looking up.

I stilled.

"He doesn't ask about you, but he's always asking me how *things* are going, and I don't think he means work. Did you two, like, have a falling out or something?"

"No, we just –" I started and then sighed.

I didn't want to lie to my brother, but I wasn't about to tell him what had gone down. I wasn't even sure how I was going to tell my mom that Dr. Sterling was going to transfer her care. I knew Leo wasn't a child anymore, he'd grown up in the same house I did – with all the same issues that forced us to see things a little differently than our peers. We still got mad at our parents, sure, but we didn't scream "I hate you!" and threaten to run away like our peers had – we'd held on tightly to the good.

But, sick mothers and poor families weren't in the same realm as abandonment and the big sister in me didn't want to put any more negative in his head.

"It's complicated," I finally finished.

"Why do old people always say that when they don't want to say. Why not just say, I don't want to say?"

"I'm old now?" I asked in mock horror.

He grinned, one side of his mouth pulling up.

"Fine. I don't want to say."

"Want me to quit?"

"What? No, of course not."

He shrugged a lanky shoulder. "I don't want to work for someone who treated you badly."

Pride and a strong sense of protectiveness swarmed me. "It's not like that. I'm really excited that you have this opportunity."

Leo nodded and stood. "Cool. I'm gonna go meet up with Donnie. He gets off in a bit. See ya later."

"See ya," I said and watched my baby brother walk toward the door.

"Hey, Leo," I called, and he turned. "Maybe just spit in his coffee once for me if you get the chance?"

He laughed. "Sure thing."

CHAPTER THIRTY-ONE

Court

A KNOCK AT my front door pulled me from Arnold taking down bad guys and winning the girl. It was Sunday, my binge-watch day. The one day of the week I didn't leave the house if I could help it. And I couldn't remember a time anyone had ever shown up without calling. Pressing pause on the movie, I sat forward and waited to see if they'd go away. Maybe it was a wrong door or a solicitor.

Another knock. This time louder and a few raps longer. I stood and moved to the door, more annoyed than curious. I peered out through the peephole. The woman on the other side wore perfectly ironed slacks and a pink cardigan. She bit at her lower lip and shifted uncomfortably, but it didn't distract from the air of money and upper class about her. Cursing under my breath, I opened the door to Mrs. Callahan Sterling.

She gave me a shaky smile when I didn't greet her. "Hi,

I'm –"

"I know who you are," I said.

"Oh," she bit at her lower lip again as if unsure about her decision to come here, but then straightened. "Could I come in for a moment?"

I opened the door wide by way of invitation and she entered the apartment walking straight to the kitchen counter and placing her purse on top of it as if she planned to stay awhile.

"What can I do for you Mrs. Sterling?" I asked, staying close to the door and crossing my arms over my chest.

"Please, call me Mercy. I'm sorry to just drop in, but I was in the city and I wanted to introduce myself."

That struck me as funny and I smirked. "I don't mean to be rude here, but can we just skip to why you're really here?"

She smiled at me and sat on one of the barstools looking far more comfortable than I would have guessed

"Okay, then." She removed a folder from her purse and placed it on the counter with a light slap. "Now that Mrs. Winters is no longer under your father's care he," she paused and corrected, "*we* wanted to see if there was any way we could work out an agreement to keep this all under wraps."

"What do you mean she's no longer under his care?"

"The family requested to be transferred to another doctor located here in New York."

Color me confused. Of all the things I expected her to say, that wasn't even on the radar.

She stood and drew her purse up to the crook of her elbow. "There's a check in the folder, a non-disclosure agreement, as well as some personal affects he thought you might like."

"I don't want his money."

She narrowed her eyes. She couldn't fathom any other reason I'd done this to their perfect family and I just felt sad for her. Money didn't buy happiness or loyalty. People that were easily bought were easily manipulated, too, and I wasn't someone they could play games with.

"I'm sorry for what happened to you."

"But?" I asked because she looked like she wasn't finished.

"I'm just not sorry enough to put my own family through this kind of ordeal."

I nodded. I got that. It made sense. I didn't like her much, but I understood her at least. She was protecting her family. I wasn't hers to protect. But I had been his.

She strode over to me and stopped. "He became the man he is today because of you, because of her. I'm sure that doesn't make you feel better, but you've always been the driving force behind his motivation to do good in the world."

I scoffed because a) the idea that my shitty life made him a better man just straight pissed me off and b) if she thought their life was a penance then she'd never understand a life like I had been dealt.

With that, she left, not even a goodbye as she shut the door behind her. I stared after her for several long minutes feeling so goddamn angry and hurt and angrier that it hurt because fuck this seemed to be a theme with me now – letting down my guard and feeling the ache of disappointment all over again like I was just a kid.

I moved to the kitchen in a haze, opened the fridge and pulled out a bottle of water. The feel of the cool plastic around my fingers and in my mouth eased some of the heat that sat in my chest and radiated through my limbs.

I spotted the folder and moved around it, eyeing it like a

poisonous animal. Curiosity got the better of me. On top was the check. Apparently, Dr. and Mrs. Sterling thought two-hundred thousand dollars was the going rate for a lifetime of neglect. I used the paper underneath the check to move it out of the way, not even wanting to touch the money that was supposed to make up for the fact he hadn't wanted me. *Still* didn't want me.

The non-disclosure had his messy handwriting already scribbled at the bottom and reminded me too much of the way he'd signed me away in the first place.

Moving on, the last thing in the folder was a white envelope, the seal left unglued. Inside were a stack of photos. A young man and woman stared up at me and I flipped over the photo to see the names, but I already knew – it was my mother who stared up at me, a wide smile on her lips as she leaned into Callahan Sterling.

The next several photos were just of her – a school picture where she gave a forced, half-smile, a picture of her in a cheerleading outfit holding red and white pom-poms high over her head, and last, a picture of her with closed eyes and pursed lips tilted up like she'd been about to kiss the person holding the camera.

I wondered, not for the first time, what had happened – what circumstances brought her from a smiling cheerleader to an addict that couldn't stay clean to care for her own child. Was it possible she'd always been both?

I stepped away from the counter and shoved both hands into my hair. My head roared, and I hated that my quest for revenge had turned into something that was twisting and turning my insides. I cared about the answers to the questions screaming in my head. I wanted to know, and man did that fucking sting.

I snatched my cell off the coffee table in the living room and dialed the number – the digits never called but memorized like I'd dialed them a million times. He answered on the third ring, his polite but curt hello only further grating my nerves.

"Why did you abandon her?"

He was quiet for a moment, but I didn't fill the silence to ease the tension.

"She was an addict. She couldn't have been reasoned with. We were young, and it wasn't the kind of thing people did, especially in my family."

I noted his word choice. She couldn't *have been* reasoned with. Not she couldn't be – he hadn't even tried. He was a coward. Had been then and still was. I'd heard everything I needed to know. He couldn't give me any answers that would fill me with peace. I was going to have to find it on my own. Without him. It was time to let go of any hatred or hope toward him because they were hard to separate. The only way to ease my hatred had become to hope for something different. And I didn't want to expect or receive anything from him.

He must have taken my continued silence as my desire for him to tell me more and he spoke again. "Cassie wasn't welcome after my parents found out," his voice cracked, "neither of you would have been welcome. It was better this way."

A heavy silence crackled between us.

"Are you still there?" he asked, and I nodded several times before I answered.

"Yeah, I'm here. I'll sign your agreement, but I don't want a dime of your money."

"I don't understand. What is it that you do want?"

"I want you to help Bianca's mom."

"That's not up to me."

"Why? Why did they request a transfer?"

He let out a long breath. "I asked Bianca to help me find you, so I could reason with you, get you to sign the non-disclosure."

Time stood still as my decisions and their implications flashed before me. Hadn't this been what Bianca wanted? What her whole family wanted? What difference was it how it all came together? The important thing was that she got the care.

Then another thought occurred to me. Had Bianca's family transferred out of loyalty to me? That didn't seem right. Bianca had been very clear that she would do whatever was necessary. Yet, I couldn't come up with another reason she'd give up the very thing she'd wanted more than anything just because I'd had a hand in making sure it happened.

"Are you really as good as everyone says?"

"I'm sorry?" His voice was taken back and confused.

"I've read all the PR bullshit about the *great Dr. Sterling*. World renowned, a pioneer..." my voice trailed off. I sat and let my head fall forward. "I've seen the write ups and the awards, but I'm asking you. Are you really that good or is it all just talk?"

"I'm good. Probably the best. The best on this side of the country anyway. I've devoted everything to my career."

I ran my hand through my hair and tugged at the ends making my scalp tingle. "Then don't transfer her. I'll talk with the Winters family. Don't do anything until I've had a chance to speak with them."

I must have stunned him into silence.

"Do we have a deal?"

"She means that much to you?"

"Do we have a deal?" I gritted out.

"Yes, we have a deal. I'll send over an updated agreement this week."

Of course, he had to get it down on paper.

I hung up the phone and sunk into the cushion, letting my head fall back so that I stared up at the white ceiling.

Fuck it.

I grabbed my wallet and keys and shot out of the apartment. It was only when the cab pulled up in front of the Winters' house did I think about the state of my appearance. At least for once the outside matched the inside. I felt *and* looked like shit.

I knocked on the door and then stepped back and shoved my hands in my pocket. I'd been prepared for someone else to open the door, to need to explain what I was doing there, but instead the door flung open and I was met with a tunnel of electric blue. My stomach dropped and took flight at the same time making me lightheaded and nauseous.

Bianca stepped back when her eyes met mine.

"Hi." I stayed firmly in place willing her not to slam the door in my face. She didn't, but maybe worse, she just stood there waiting for some sort of explanation on why I was standing outside her door. She looked stunned and completely off guard.

"I'm sorry to just drop by like this. Can we talk?"

"Dinner's ready everyone," Mrs. Winters called from inside the house.

"Hungry?" she asked softly – a total contradiction to the outburst I was expecting.

Hell no I wasn't hungry, but I'd eat fried SPAM if it meant she'd talk to me.

I nodded, and Bianca opened the door wide. We entered the dining room just as everyone was sitting down to eat, and all eyes were on me.

I offered a small wave as I greeted them. "Hey everyone. Sorry to drop by so unexpected."

"Court, how lovely to see you," Mrs. Winters said. "Are you joining us for dinner? Bianca put out another place setting."

"We're gonna eat on the patio, Mom."

Bianca grabbed a plate from the table and handed it to me. She motioned with her head to the kitchen and I followed her. She pointed to the counter where several casserole dishes were laid out. I moved toward them in a daze.

My stomach growled despite my disinterest in eating when the lasagna hit my nose. I took a serving and moved to the next dish and then the next. Bianca followed behind me and after our plates were filled, she led me back through the dining room. I exchanged an awkward wave with Mr. Winters who gave me an understanding look. Donnie and Leo were glued to the baseball game on the TV in the living room, which had been turned so they could see it from the dining room table. All of it was so all-American and homey and I felt like an ass for coming in and making it weird.

Bianca strolled out onto the patio and stopped in front of a metal dining table. She put her plate down and then looked to me. "Want something to drink?"

"That'd be great," I said and tried a smile, feeling it fall short. Nothing about this, except being near Bianca, was great.

She disappeared back into the house and I let out a groan and settled into one of the metal chairs across from where Bianca had placed her plate. I remembered she'd called this space her favorite place in the world and I looked around, seeing her in all of it. Twinkling lights, a fountain, the garden she'd mentioned. There were mismatched lounge chairs and wicker furniture with bright colored cushions. Just like the inside of the house, it had a warmth and comfort to it that couldn't have been bought with showroom furniture.

The sound of the sliding door pulled my eyes to Bianca walking toward me with two glasses of what looked like tea.

She put them down in front of us without speaking.

"This is a great space out here. I can see why you love it so much."

She looked around as if she were seeing it for the first time. "It's my favorite place in the whole world. Not that I've been very many places," she added. Her eyes bore back into mine. "What are you doing here? I never thought I'd see you again."

"I'm sorry I didn't come sooner. I was wrong, and I overreacted and made you feel bad about standing by the people you love. I think what you did, who you are, is beautiful. I don't expect your forgiveness or anything like that, I just had to tell you that I was sorry and that you absolutely should make sure your mom gets the very best care possible. I should have seen that sooner and I should have stood by you to help make sure that happened."

"You think I'm upset because you didn't stand beside me while I let your prick of a father near my family?"

"Y-yes," I said slowly.

She shook her head. "You used my family, my mother, as part of your plan against your father. You forced him into our lives after he ruined yours. How could you do that?"

"I —"

But she didn't let me speak.

"You know how much she means to me. I would do anything for her, would trade everything else for more good days with her and you used that for your own personal revenge."

"I just wanted to make sure she got the help she needed."

"It wasn't your place. Do you know what it was like watching him with her? What it was like seeing my family look at him like he was their savior?"

I paused. I didn't understand. She'd told me she'd never forgive me if I ruined him. She'd wanted him to be able to help her. I'd helped make sure that happened.

"You said – "

She cut me off again. "I know what I said. And I meant it, I'll always choose her. She needs me. But I didn't want him to help, not really. Not after I found out what he did to you."

The confidence she'd spoken with melted and she leaned into the table, shoulders hunched, and eyes filled with tears. "You pushed him into our lives and I didn't want him there. I hated him. I still hate him. I'm sorry. I'm so sorry that I hurt you."

She sobbed. Big, fat tears rolling down her cheeks. I moved to the chair beside her and wrapped my arms around her. She mumbled into my chest and between the muffled sound and the sobs it came out in incoherent fragments. "Loved...mom... you... hate what he did... you were right... I'm so scared... my mom... my mom... my mom."

I held her.

I didn't know what else to do.

We sat like that for a long time. Until the front of my shirt was wet from her tears and her sobs turned to sniffles. I let her pull away first. I didn't want to let go, but I didn't have any right to hold her either. She wrapped her arms around herself as if she wanted the comfort of being held but no longer wanted it from me.

With a hesitant hand, I reached for her, the only thing in my life that I was certain of anymore – light and goodness and love. Her eyes closed as my fingers rested on her cheek. She leaned into my touch and it was all the sign I needed from her that we could get through this. I hadn't lost her, and I was going to do everything in my power to hold on before she was gone forever.

"Let him help her. Let me do this for you, for your family."

"I can't. If my mother knew –"

"She doesn't need to know any of that. All she needs to know is that he's the best and he's going to do everything he can to help her."

"At what cost? I don't want to hurt you."

"If he can help your mom then it'll be worth every day I lived hating him."

She started crying again and I felt her need to be close, to feel, and I wrapped an arm around the back of her and pulled her into my chest once again. I circled a thumb lazily over her shoulder. The fountain trickled lightly and the sound of horns and traffic from the street carried into the patio, but it was just background noise. My senses were overwhelmed with her. I couldn't keep my eyes away from her profile – her thin, elegant neck, her black eyelashes fanned out framing her eyes. The warmth of her body pressed against mine and the soft skin under my fingertips. The floral, feminine scent that I'd come to know as hers. And the sound of my heart beat drumming in my ears.

We sat like that until her tears had stopped again. She

sighed and pulled away taking a piece of my solitude with her. It was always like this. She took a little piece of me even without trying. Even without me being aware until it was too late.

The sliding door caught our attention and Leo stuck his head out. "We're gonna cut the pie. Want a piece?"

Bianca looked to me.

"No, thanks. I should get going."

She shook her head and Leo disappeared back into the house.

I stood, wishing I hadn't wasted the last two months without her and already thinking ahead to when I might be able to see her again.

"I meant what I said. I'd rather have him help her than live knowing she didn't have every opportunity possible. Please let him help."

She nodded and crossed her arms over her stomach. We shuffled to the door and I paused before opening it and losing the privacy we had outside.

"Can I call you later? Take you to lunch or –"

Indecision and worry in her eyes, she peered up at me so innocently and guarded.

"I don't know. I've got a lot going on. Between work and my family –"

"Hey, I get it. You don't need to rearrange your life for me."

"It's just." She bit her lip and looked all innocence and uncertainty. "Losing you last time hurt. I don't think I could bare it a second time."

My heart literally squeezed in my chest making it painful to breathe. This girl was going to be the death of me.

"I'm not going anywhere." I pulled her into me and she

wrapped both arms around me and held on tight.

And I wasn't. Couldn't. She was everything. I'd be whatever she needed me to be – friend, boyfriend, shoulder to cry on because giving her up wasn't an option. I was going to be there for her - messy or not. Good times and bad, just like she'd said. I had no idea what any of that meant really, but I'd take cues from my 8B. My perfect little student.

CHAPTER THIRTY-TWO

Bianca

I woke up the next morning to two texts from Court.

> *Court*: Good morning, 8B
>
> *Court*: Can you meet me after work? I need help picking out an engagement gift for Leika. She told me I couldn't give her cash.

I chuckled as I rubbed my swollen eyes and yawned. My face hurt from the sobbing fest I'd had the day before and it was a reminder of how much I'd missed him. Those tears had been in part because I was mad at him, but I'd been mad at him because he hadn't understood how much he meant to me.

> *Me*: Sure. I need to get her something, too. She invited me to come.

Court: Meet you at 6th and 34th at six.

I threw back the covers and shot out of bed more excited for the day than I had been in a while. Yes, I loved my job, but there'd been a sadness that floated over my days when Court and I hadn't been talking. I wasn't sure if it was smart to jump back into allowing him to consume my days, but I hoped there wasn't any harm in us at least being friends. I missed his friendship. I'd missed *him*.

I dressed in a simple blue sun dress and flats and tossed a pair of heels into my purse for after work. I was kind of glad that I would be meeting him straight from work. He wouldn't be expecting me to be dressed up and I wouldn't have to obsess over picking the perfect outfit for later.

My morning commute had become my favorite part of the day. Out in the bustle of the city with all the other people heading to work, heads down, headphones in, made me feel like part of something great. Some of the biggest and best companies were here and when I thought about what the people of New York accomplished from eight to five Monday through Friday it was nothing short of incredible.

I ate a granola bar as I walked the last block to the office building and then took the elevator up to the ninth floor. JC Engineering had the ninth and tenth floors. Executive offices were on tenth and the development teams, including mine, were all on the ninth.

I shared a pod of cubicles with two other new engineers, Robert and Jared. We'd settled into a comfortable routine with each other. We mumbled our good mornings and chatted a bit as our workload and schedules allowed. They'd set up a nerf basketball hoop in our area and people congregated to play and talk. I probably should have been practicing passing and shooting after work so I could join in, but as it was, I wasn't prepared to embarrass myself and make it even more apparent how much I didn't fit in by shooting an air ball.

I was the only woman engineer under the age of forty and I think my presence made my peers a little anxious. They wanted to treat me like one of the guys, but I wasn't. I wasn't even a tomboy – I was all girl. Girly girl. I always had been. Dresses and makeup were part of who I was, and it was even worse now that I'd invested in some of my own clothes and wasn't wearing my mother's hand me down dresses.

I couldn't even imagine their faces if I wore my Court-inspired outfits. I'd worn heels for my first few weeks of work because they felt more professional than my flats, but there'd been a slight change – for the positive – since I'd switched to wearing my flats all the time. In the corporate world of science and engineering, people couldn't seem to make sense of me. Why couldn't I be a girly girl and an engineer without making people uncomfortable?

After our morning stand up where we all went around the room and gave a brief rundown of what we were working on, any roadblocks or areas where we needed help, and what we hoped to accomplish before the next meeting, I buried myself in work. Five of us newbies had each been given the task of writing software for one piece of a larger project and I wanted to finish mine first and I wanted it to blow their minds. If I couldn't fit in by gender, I'd fit in by being so good they couldn't overlook me.

I worked through lunch, nerves about meeting Court later were settling in and my stomach churned with unease. I didn't know where we stood. We each had been hurt by the other and whatever we were then would be different now. A friendship with him wasn't unrecoverable, I didn't think, but there was no guise of mentorship to make our interactions calculated and straightforward. Who we were to each other had changed. Or had it? Maybe it hadn't for me, I'd always wanted Court as he was, but I wasn't sure he could say the same about me.

I pulled my phone out of my purse with the intent of sending a quick text to Court. I thought some sort of messaging now would make tonight less stressful, but I came up short when I saw I'd missed a text from Todd.

> **Todd**: Hey! I'm going to be in town this weekend. Anything going on? Let's hang out!

I let out a long breath as I read it over and over. Todd stayed in Connecticut as planned, and as he'd promised, he'd kept in contact. Some weeks it was a single text to say hi and check in, other weeks nothing, but he hadn't been to the city yet and I'd been grateful. Whether it was fair or not, I couldn't look at him the same way after everything that had gone down with his uncle and even without that barrier, his kiss hadn't made me feel anything. No spark, no tingles. Nothing like Court's. Maybe I wouldn't ever be anything more to Court than a friend, but he'd shown me what it could feel like – how my body could hum under his touch and I wasn't going to settle for anything less than a man who made me feel electrified.

Despite all my anxiousness for our shopping trip, I was running five minutes late to meet Court. When I finally stood before him out of breath and belatedly realizing I still wore my flats, I held up my finger indicating I needed a moment and pulled out my heels. Teetering on one foot, I slipped one of the silver heels on and then switched to put the other on.

"Okay, sorry, ready now."

I waited for him to move, but instead he glanced down at my feet a moment and then back up at my face like he was trying to decide to say whatever was on his mind.

"You really want to wear those while we walk around shopping?"

I shrugged and wrapped my hands tightly around the handle of my purse.

"So, put the others back on," he said motioning toward where I'd stowed them away.

"I'm fine," I said as I took a few steps toward the store as if to demonstrate.

We walked up and down the aisles of kitchen and dining appliances and décor. Court was adamant that he wanted to buy something useful and practical for Leika's new place, but I was drawn to the pretty frames and china place settings. I'd tried to steer him toward serving platters or fancy silverware, but he just scrunched up his face and shook his head at each item.

"What about these then?" I asked, lifting a single crystal wine goblet from the shelf. It was heavy in my hand with intricate details around the base and cup.

"I dunno. Leika is more of a beer drinker. I can't picture her breaking out crystal wine glasses unless it's to mock them."

I placed it back on the shelf. "Okay, then, what about this?" I said jokingly as I pointed to a wooden checkers board with shot glasses instead of checkers. It was too beautifully crafted to be a gag gift and the care and workmanship of the board and glasses were almost comical for such a game.

"That's awesome," he said as he moved past me. I couldn't

help but laugh as he looked it over like it was the greatest invention of all time. "She'd love this."

"What happened to practical and useful?"

He shrugged and grabbed a box of the set from underneath the display. "Your fault."

In the end, I purchased the practical gift, a toaster oven. I didn't know Leika well enough to know what sort of pretty things she might want for a new house, but everyone needed a toaster oven, right?

As we stepped back out into the busy streets, shopping bags in hand, we stood shuffling our feet, neither of us knowing what to do next.

"I, uh, should get home," I said pointing in the opposite direction of his apartment.

He nodded but took my large and quite heavy bag from me. "You can't carry that thing all the way home." He put both bags in one hand effortlessly and hailed a cab.

He opened the door for me and then handed me my bag. I was disappointed that our goodbye had been so rushed, but he was right – there was no way I was going to make it home with this bulky thing.

I leaned forward to give the driver my address, but Court beat me to it as he slid in beside me. I watched with surprise and elation as he instructed the driver to make two stops, dropping me off first and then him.

"You didn't have to do that," I said with a smile big enough that I was sure he knew how glad I was he had.

"It'll give me more time to hear about how your new job is going," he said as he leaned back and adjusted his tie.

"It's good," I said, brushing my hair back behind my ear and wishing for something to do or say that would take the attention off me.

He raised his eyebrows. "That's all I get?"

"I love it, but it's different than I expected."

"How so?"

"Well, the work is great. They really threw us newbies right in. I have a small project that I'm totally responsible for and I love that."

"But?" he asked with a concerned squint.

"I don't really fit in. I mean, I've always been more of a loner than a social butterfly, but I guess I've always had at least one friend that I could count on. But now there are very few women and the men stick together. It's a little lonely," I admitted feeling both ridiculous and sad.

"You should try spending some time with some of them outside of the office. Suggest a happy hour or something. We did that a lot when I first started out at Harrison and Mac. It was easier to let loose and get to know each other with a drink in hand."

"That's a good idea." I nodded letting the idea roll around in my mind and I decided it was worth a shot. I'd overheard my pod mates mention a bar nearby, so it should be easy to convince them to go one night after work. "Thank you," I added.

"Sure."

My feet ached, and I pulled my heels off and groaned louder than I intended as I rubbed at my arches.

"Why do you do that to yourself?" he asked.

"Fashion over function."

He shook his head. "I like your other shoes – the ones you had on before."

"Yeah, I know, they're fun but heels are so much sexier – more eye catching."

His eyebrows shot up and I giggled at the caveman look

on his face.

"What's wrong with wanting to look good?"

"Nothing. Nothing at all. I'm just saying, depending on the kind of guy you're trying to attract, it doesn't matter."

"No?" I asked, crossing my arms over my chest. "I'm pretty sure you're the one who came up with the rule that I should dress a certain way to get a man's attention."

"And are you trying to get a man's attention?"

"I –" I opened and closed my mouth trying to determine just how honest I was willing to be. "I wanted to look nice for our first time hanging out again." My voice was soft, and I bit at the corner of my bottom lip as I waited for his reaction.

He grinned a slow sexy smirk that set my heart racing. "You've never looked sexier than you do right now. No shoes required to get my attention. In fact, no shoes, no shirt – I'm good with any state of undress that might make you more comfortable."

A flush crept up my neck.

Court took my hand and squeezed. "You don't need those rules with me. I see you. The rules, those were meant for idiots who couldn't see what was right in front of them." He leaned in close again, his familiar scent making my heart beat wildly. "I'm a smart man. I don't need ribbons and bows to see what a gift you are in my life."

When we reached my parents' house, Court got out and extended a hand down to me. I awkwardly scooted over in the seat with the toaster oven on my lap, wishing I'd bought the crystal wine glasses, so it was easier to maneuver. I finally gave up and handed him the bag. He laughed but took it and then guided me out of the cab with a hand at my elbow.

"Thanks for seeing me home."

"Thanks for coming with me to shop. To think Leika might have ended up with something useful and practical," he said with a wink as he handed me my bag back.

I rolled my eyes but laughed. "I'm denying that I had any hand in picking that gift," I said and motioned with my head to his bag.

The tension was back as we prepared to say goodbye. Was I supposed to hug him? Kiss him on the cheek? I had no idea what the protocol was here. When I couldn't take the awkward standoff any longer, I moved forward and gave him a weird half hug inadvertently ramming the toaster oven into the back of his legs in the process.

"Oh, God, sorry," I said and stepped away quickly. I held a hand over my face and peeked out to see him slightly buckled over and a grimace on his face. "Alright, I'm going inside now. Night."

I heard him chuckle softly as I backed away from him.

"Night, 8B," he called in a sexy voice filled with humor at my expense.

I hummed lightly as I entered the house. My mother sat at the dining room table, recipe books and cards scattered around her.

"Hello," I called. I dropped the toaster oven on the floor and took a seat across from her.

"You missed dinner, but there's a plate for you in the microwave," she said without looking up.

"Where is everyone?"

"Your father went to pick up my prescriptions and the boys are out with friends."

I watched her in silence for a few minutes. She studied each recipe card, copied the recipe onto a new card, and then filed the old card away in her recipe box and stacked the new recipes. A seemingly easy task was slowed by the tremor of her hands, but she kept at it even when I could tell she was getting frustrated.

"What are you doing?"

She finally looked up, meeting my eyes and placing the pen down. "I'm copying my recipes for you."

"What? For me? Why?"

She smiled. "My mother did the same for me. She copied the recipes her mother had given her and gave them to me."

"Why not just copy them on the printer or scan them to a USB?"

She scoffed. "I know it's hard to believe now, but someday having my handwritten recipes will mean something to you. It'll be like I'm with you every time you bake an apple pie or make grandma's spinach dip," she said holding up the card in front of her.

"Moooom." My eyes filled with tears because she was right. It would mean something. It meant something now.

She waved off my tears and went back to copying the recipes.

I picked up a pen and a fresh card and started to copy the recipes, making my own stack.

"You don't have to do it now," she said.

"Not for me," I said as I printed the ingredients to a chicken pot pie recipe. "For the boys."

We worked in silence for a while. My hand was cramping from holding my hand so stiffly trying to keep my penmanship neat and legible.

"You were with Court tonight?" she said it like it was a question, but she already knew. I'd told her this morning before I'd left that we were going shopping together for Leika's engagement party.

I nodded and focused my attention on the pie dough recipe in front of me.

"Are you two dating?"

I looked up, surprised by her directness. "No."

"Why not? He seems like a nice young man. Leo speaks highly of him as a boss and he's very handsome."

I fought for the right words. I didn't want to lie, but I didn't want to give her the entire story either. "I don't think Court dates much. He's a little leery of people and relationships."

The look on her face showed genuine concern. "How come?"

"He grew up in foster care, got shuffled around quite a bit. I think he got used to people leaving or turning him out so he's not big on putting himself out there."

She nodded, and her face turned pensive. "Except with you."

"How do you mean?"

"Well, he came and met your family. He gave your brother a job. He's certainly put himself out there with you."

I couldn't argue with her logic, but I wasn't ready to hope that it was because I was different to him – more important. Court put people into categories and I wasn't sure what I was or how I fit into his life, but I needed to find out before I let him crush my heart into a million pieces… again.

CHAPTER THIRTY-THREE

Court

I PACED THE apartment making sure everything was perfect. Chinese was on the way, the apartment was clean, and I had all her favorite drinks and snacks stocked just in case. God, why was I so nervous? I ran a hand through my hair and took a pull from my beer hoping it would ease my nerves.

I'd invited Bianca over to help me write my toast for Leika's engagement party. I did need to write the toast, but more importantly I needed to spend more time with Bianca. I couldn't lose her again. I'd survived without her, but I just didn't want to anymore. She was worth the risk. I was through letting the past keep me from having what I wanted. And I wanted Bianca.

A light knock on the door had me rushing to open it.

"Hey," she said breathlessly like she was just as nervous to be here as I was to have her here.

I motioned her inside. "Can I get you something to

drink? Food is on the way."

"Sure," she said as she sat her purse on the counter and perched herself onto the bar stool.

I mixed up the Diet Coke with a splash of rum and handed it to her while I took my place next to her. "How was your day?"

"It was good. I'm actually coming from happy hour with a few of the guys at work so thank you for the suggestion."

I stilled. Maybe I hadn't thought this through. She worked with all men. Men who were not blind.

"How was it?" I asked when I found my voice.

She laughed as if catching on to my discomfort. "It was fine. Apparently, I'm a good wing man. I hooked two of the guys up with girls at the bar in under an hour. I've taken the Court Adams rule book and passed it on to more unfortunate souls."

I chuckled and shook my head, ready to defend the wisdom I'd passed on to her when the doorbell rang. We settled in the living room with takeout boxes.

So, what sort of toast are you going for – sweet, funny, both?"

"Definitely funny. Leika and I don't really do the sappy stuff."

"Yeah, but this is different."

I shook my head. "I'll do sweet and sappy at the wedding."

She nodded. "Alright, so whatcha got?"

I held the fork up to my mouth and motioned with my head to the kitchen. "I wrote down a few things. I'll grab it when we finish eating."

Her eyes widened in excitement and she stood and rushed to the kitchen. I watched her scan the counters and zone in on the folder Mercy Sterling had brought over.

Mouth full of orange chicken, I tried to wave my hands and get her attention, to communicate somehow that it wasn't the right place, but it was too late. The look of excitement fell and in its place was a look of horror, and then sadness as she got to the pictures. She was lost to the contents of the folder, presumably at the check, and I'd crossed the room and was shutting it in her hands before she looked up.

"Is this…" her voice was shaky, and she looked up at me with disbelief. "Did he pay you off? Is that why you didn't out him? Why you are suddenly okay with my mom seeing him?"

"No," I said. My voice came out harsher than I'd intended. "Fuck, no. I never wanted his money. I wanted him to pay with his peace of mind and life of honor. He sent his wife over to make sure I wouldn't go back on my word after your mom switched doctors."

Realization dawned on her features. "I'm sorry, Court. He cornered me at one of my mother's therapy sessions to see if I was in on it. I didn't know what he was talking about of course, I thought Todd was the connection. Once I knew what you'd done, saw how terrible he really was, I couldn't let him treat her anymore. He did treat her well, if that's any consolation."

"I guess it will have to be."

"Why didn't you out him publicly? He didn't know our connection. Todd could have still got my mother in with him. Why did you step in?"

My jaw tensed at Todd's name, but I considered her question. It was so simple, but was she really ready to know all my truths?

"I wanted to be the one to help you. To help your mom and your family. I've spent my whole life resenting dudes like

Todd – like my father. And not just resenting them, wishing I was them. I was pissed off that I didn't have that kind of life – it always seemed like the ones who least deserved it were the ones that ended up with money and power."

"Oh, Court."

"No, I get it now. I know that what he has is a shallow life. I don't know who I'd be if I'd grown up with him as a dad, but I know I wouldn't have met Leika or you – and you two are the best things in my life. I'd do anything for her. I'd do anything for you. I wanted to be the one you counted on. I don't regret what I did. Your mother got what she needed. Maybe I should have told you first, but after you walked away, I didn't know if I'd ever see you again."

"I walked away, and you still put my happiness over yours," she frowned, but placed a hand on my chest.

I shrugged. "That's what you do when you love someone. The same way you put your mom first."

"You loved me?" she asked and pulled her bottom lip behind her front teeth like she was trying to keep from smiling.

"Love, not past tense."

I'd expected her to question me, analyze it like she did everything, or I even hoped she might say it back, but my little 8B took me completely by surprise when she threw herself into my arms. No words. No questions or proclamations, just her body pressed against mine. I took her mouth softly, wanting to give her this. Wanting to give her me. All of me. She reacted with a passion I'd forgotten her capable of. Okay, not forgotten, I'd savored those memories, replaying her kisses and moans so many times they'd become like a highlight reel. But I had pushed them so deep into my memories that it felt more like a dream than reality.

She pulled back and I missed the taste and feel of her immediately. She was lit up and smiling brightly as she took in ragged breaths. Touching her lips, she looked at me like she wanted to go another round and I was ready. So damn ready.

"I should go," she said, and I faltered.

"What? Why?" I could feel my forehead crinkle as I struggled to understand why she was leaving.

"I need to do some extra work tonight and get to the office early tomorrow. It's my dad's birthday tomorrow night so I planned to take off a little early."

"Oh, okay," I shoved my hands into my pockets. "You didn't even hear my toast."

"I'll hear it Friday. You don't need my help. Leika will love whatever you say because it comes from you."

She leaned up on the balls of her feet and gave me a quick kiss on the cheek. "Talk to you tomorrow."

I watched her go, completely dumbfounded. The door closed behind her and I paced. I replayed the entire night. What the fuck?

I tore out of the apartment and skipped the elevator, choosing the stairs instead to get to her faster. I reached her on the sidewalk, her hand lifted to hail a cab. I watched her, so damn beautiful and she looked so young and happy. She smiled as the cab stopped and she slid into the backseat and shut the door. The street was busy, and horns blared as traffic stopped and started all down 42nd street. As the cab driver edged back into traffic her eyes met mine with surprise. I lifted a hand, realizing how ridiculous I probably looked staring after her, but that sweet smile was back, and she lifted her hand to her lips and then blew a kiss in my direction.

I texted her as soon as I got back up to the apartment.

Me: Why'd you run off, 8B?

I tapped my foot waiting for a reply. It came as soon as I'd given up and put the phone on the counter where I couldn't obsessively wait, or worse send a second text.

I dove for the phone, eager for her reply.

Bianca: "Always leave them wanting more"

"Motherf-" I grinned despite myself.

Me: What did I tell you about those rules. Throw them all out. You don't need any of them. I just want you.

Bianca: Maybe that's just because I'm following the rules. Maybe you're unconsciously reacting to them and don't even know it. Who knows what'll happen if I go back to being myself.

She was teasing. I was almost certain, but I couldn't help but wonder if there wasn't some concern and truth to her words.

God, I was an idiot. I'd told her she needed to be someone other than who she was to get the guy and now that guy was me. My chest ached, and I was pissed at myself and at fucking Todd, too.

Those rules had been the best thing that had ever happened to me – it brought me closer to my sweet 8B, but they weren't what held us together now. I was going to prove to her, somehow, someway, that she was perfect just the way she was. The way she'd been the first time I'd met her and that I didn't want her any other way.

Me: Toss the rules and let me prove it to you. Sweet dreams, 8B.

The next day found me tense and grouchy. Bianca would be busy with family stuff tonight and not being able to see her had me irritable. Leo stopped by my office to show me the latest design specs for the new website, but I was only half-listening.

"These look great," I told him sincerely as I scanned the pages of the mock ups. "You've got a really good eye."

"Thanks," he mumbled with an embarrassed grin. "You coming over tonight?" I hesitated, but he continued. "Birthday dinner for my dad."

When it was clear that I hadn't been invited, he gave me a one shoulder shrug. "I'm sure Bianca just thought you wouldn't want to come, but Mom's making enchiladas and you don't want to miss out."

I laughed as he patted his stomach.

"Thanks for the heads up, but I think I'll let you guys have your family time. Sounds like you guys need it with how busy you all have been lately."

He nodded without another word and backed out of the office.

I'd always treaded around people's family time giving it a wide berth. Maybe that had been more about me than them, but wasn't the point of family time for the family to spend time together? I felt uneasy about just showing up. Wouldn't have Bianca invited me if she really wanted me there? Or was Leo right – was she afraid of pushing me to do something I'd made clear was uncomfortable?

Leika called as I was leaving the building.

"Hey, bridezilla," I answered.

"Har, har. What are you doing?"

"Just leaving work. You?"

"Trying to pick out a wedding dress," she answered sounding more than a little defeated.

"By yourself?"

"Well I can't exactly take Jeff."

"What about his mom or one of your girl friends?"

She let out a huff. "His mom would have me covered head to toe in lace, but yeah I should probably ask one of my girlfriends to come with me. I'm way out of my league in these stores. So many white dresses and they all look the exact same to me!"

I laughed. "Anything you need me to do before Friday?"

"Nope, just show up and be your charming self. Preferably with Bianca by your side. Have you talked to her yet?"

I realized for the first time, Leika was out of the loop with my current life. I'd turned to Bianca instead of her. That made me happy and sad. And it also made me realize how little I'd been there for her since she'd started dating Jeff. I didn't think she'd minded or even noticed. He'd become her rock. Her world. The same way Bianca was becoming mine.

"Yeah, we talked. I'll fill you in Friday night."

She squealed happily in my ear and I pulled the phone away with a grin.

"See you Friday," she said merrily.

"Later, kid."

I headed out of the office and grabbed a cab. I stopped by the store Bianca and I had shopped in just two nights ago and picked out the first thing that caught my eye, which was unsurprisingly a crystal platter that Bianca had pointed out as an option for Leika's engagement party. I had no idea what you bought the woman you hoped would be your girlfriend's father for his birthday, but Bianca had assured me then "everyone loves crystal". I wasn't so sure, but I was trusting her advice wouldn't steer me wrong.

Outside of the Winters's house, I shuffled my feet, sweating and nauseous. I knocked and waited, cursing myself for thinking this was a good idea, when Bianca swung open the door.

Her eyes widened in surprise. "Hey."

She didn't open the door wide to allow me in but studied me and the gift bag in my hand.

It was Leo that saved me by yelling out from the dining room. "Hey, Court, you made it."

She looked from Leo to me with a wary grin, but motioned me in. "We were just about to eat. Do you like enchiladas?"

"Love them," I said with a wink.

Mrs. Winter, stood in the kitchen with Donnie by her side. They were setting dishes and silverware out and the smell of enchiladas and home and love was almost too much.

"Have a seat, Court," Mr. Winter called from the dining room table. "You want a beer, or I think we have some vodka if you prefer."

"A beer would be great," I said as I stressed over which chair I should sit in. Did they have specific chairs they all sat in?

Bianca pulled out a chair on the end and nodded to it. "You want another beer, Dad?"

He lifted his empty in answer and she left me at the table

while she moved to the fridge on the far wall of the kitchen.

"Happy birthday, sir," I said and handed him the gift bag. "I gotta admit, I had no idea what to get so I won't be offended if you want to return it. Receipt's in the bag."

"Call me, Glenn," he said as he took the bag. "And you didn't need to do this. We're just glad you could join us."

Bianca returned and placed a beer down in front of me and then moved to sit between me and her father, sliding his in front of him while she sat. She watched, looking a little nervous, as he pulled out the crystal platter and turned it over in his hands. She turned and shot me an astonished expression, telling me with a look that she noticed I'd picked something she'd liked. "Well, this is beautiful," he said as he sat the heavy platter down on the table. "Look at this Lucy. It looks just like the one my mom gave us for our wedding."

"The one Donnie broke," Bianca said with a smile and glanced over her shoulder where Donnie stood protectively near his mom.

Mrs. Winter looked out from the kitchen and an endearing look crossed her face. "Oh, it really does. How wonderful."

"Thank you, Court," Mr. Winter said while still admiring the crystal.

"You're welcome."

Bianca. Somehow, she never ceased to amaze me. And it was no wonder, really, that her family was just as amazing. Maybe I'd avoided other families because I'd been waiting for this one. They welcomed me in so completely, never making me feel like an outsider at all. They laughed and teased, we ate, we sang an awful rendition of Happy Birthday, we ate cake that looked like it had been frosted by one of the boys, but through it all I couldn't remember a time I'd smiled so much.

Bianca and Leo were washing and drying the dishes as I sat in the living room with Donnie and Glenn. I was actually sad the night was coming to an end and I would have to return to the quiet of my own apartment.

The Yankees were playing the Cardinals and Donnie shouted at the TV as St. Louis scored another run. I just grinned, only half-watching the game. My eyes drifted constantly to Bianca. I had so many things I wanted to say to her. At the bottom of the ninth, when it was clear the Yankees were going to lose, and Glenn was starting to yawn, I finally started to make my excuses.

"I should get going," I said as I stood. I shook Mr. Winter's hand, gave Donnie and Leo a small wave, and hugged Mrs. Winter so fiercely she yelped and giggled. "Thanks for having me. Those were the best enchiladas I've ever had." I wanted to tell her it was the best *night* I'd ever had. I was pretty sure she was responsible for this family unit that was so loyal and loving and I wanted her to know how much I admired her. A hug was the best I could give her, and I hoped she understood.

She placed a hand on my cheek and smiled. "Good to see you again, Court."

I pulled back and found Bianca standing at the door. "I'll walk you out."

The heat and humidity greeted us as we stepped out onto the sidewalk. Still, she wrapped her arms around herself like she was chilled.

"I'm sorry I didn't invite you," she said quietly. "I know family stuff is hard for you and I didn't want to make you uncomfortable."

I nodded in understanding. "You know, incredibly, I

wasn't. Your family is really great. Don't ever apologize for that or feel like you need to keep that part of yourself from me."

I wrapped my arms around her and she skirted hers around me and hugged me tightly. "Thank you for coming."

CHAPTER THIRTY-FOUR

Bianca

I STRETCHED AND yawned as I shut off my alarm. It was still dark outside, but I needed to get to work early to test my code one more time and then hopefully turn it in before the rest of the office got in. After taking off early Wednesday for my dad's birthday celebration, I'd had to work late last night to catch up. It had been worth the long night, but it'd meant I hadn't seen Court since Wednesday night. Fortunately, tonight was Leika's engagement party and the start of the weekend. I planned to steal as much of Court's time as he was willing to give me for the next three days.

His good morning text was already waiting for me, as it had been all week.

> *Court: Good morning beautiful girl. Knock 'em dead at work today!*

Pleased he'd remembered and had thought to mention it, I jumped out of bed and showered. With Court still on my mind as I looked for something to wear, I dug through the stack of clean laundry on the top of my dresser and pulled on a pair of lacy, black underwear and matching bra. I bit the inside of my cheek as his words came back to me.

Throw out the rules.

With a silent prayer I wouldn't regret it later, I snapped a picture of me in the frilly lingerie, face included, and sent it to Court.

His response was almost immediate and made me laugh out loud.

> **Court**: *I nearly choked on my oatmeal, 8B. That is seriously hot. Can I pick you up for Leika's engagement party?*
>
> **Me**: *I'll be waiting xoxo*

With our big assignments turned in, Robert, Jared, and I sat around mid-morning talking about our weekend plans while the boys tossed the nerf basketball back and forth. They'd stopped bothering to try and get me to play and I'd given up the pretense of joining in. Maybe there were some things at work I would never be able to fit in with the guys.

"Bianca," Mr. Ross's deep voice bellowed behind our pod and all three sets of eyes turned. As the director of engineering he had that sort of effect. Even if he wasn't speaking directly to you, you wanted to acknowledge him.

"Hi, Mr. Ross."

My podmates looked from him to me and back to him. He stood there holding a NYU coffee mug in hand looking crisp in his black dress pants and light blue button-down shirt. No tie, but he stood out among the sea of jeans and t-shirts.

"Great work on the intelligence library project."

"Thank you," I managed to respond without cowering or jumping up and down. He'd shocked me and both seemed like reasonable reactions.

He nodded to me and then briefly to Robert and Jared before disappearing as silently as he'd appeared.

When he was out of ear shot, Jared smirked and tossed the mini basketball in my direction. By some luck, I caught it gracefully.

I decided not to push my luck today and instead of taking the shot, passed it on to Robert. "You guys know of a good place to grab lunch nearby?"

"Just stick with us, Winters," Robert winked.

Score for the girly girl engineer.

The afternoon had been too crazy to think about the night ahead, but as soon as my bags were packed and I was headed home, the nerves and excitement started to build.

My phone buzzed.

Court: Be at your place in 15

Me: Gah! I'm not even there yet. I need time to get ready.

Court: You can entertain me with a fashion show... a naked one.

Me: No time for that. I have to get ready. Wait 15 and then leave.

Court: Fine, but I'm getting a naked fashion show before the end of the night.

My body shivered in anticipation. Stowing my phone in my purse, I hurried home.

I needed more time to obsess over every detail of my hair, dress, and makeup. I wanted to knock Court's socks off. Literally.

I was running through the jewelry options when I came up short outside of my parents' house. "Todd?"

"Hey, B." Todd stood from the front stoop, a bouquet of flowers in his hand.

"What are you doing here?"

He strode to where I was still frozen on the sidewalk and leaned in for a hug. "I'm in town for the weekend and wanted to surprise you. Tasha gave me your address."

I was going to kill Tasha. She'd probably thought she was doing me a favor, but she had the worst timing ever.

"I'm definitely surprised," I managed.

"Do you have plans? I thought I could take you to dinner?"

"Actually, I have a friend's engagement party tonight."

"Tomorrow?"

I shifted my weight from one foot to the other. My heart raced with worry and unease, but I felt compelled to give him closure. When I'd been desperate for his attention, all I'd really ever wanted was to have an answer. Yes or No – either way so I could have moved on.

"I'm sorry. I can't."

"The sort of guy?"

I nodded. "Yeah, but it's become more serious."

"I see. Are you happy?"

"I am. I really am. Hopelessly happy and in love."

Time apart had only made me realize how deep my feelings for Court were. I was madly in love with him, and

I realized the person I needed to tell was Court. Would he be there to catch me? Sure, he'd said he loved me, but could he really commit? I wasn't sure, but I was willing to risk it. No one free falls into true love, we leap of our own free will.

He studied me for a moment, but as if he'd seen that I wasn't faltering on my response he nodded. "Good, you deserve to be happy. I'm sorry for not seeing what was right in front of me for so long."

"Nah, don't be. We're good as friends." I smiled, hoping he could read my sincerity.

He nodded, the look on his face not completely sold on the idea.

"I should get going. I'm running so late already."

"Take care, Bianca," he said and dropped a kiss to my cheek.

I walked to the doorway and watched as he ambled down the sidewalk. Peace and contentment filled me and I smiled, feeling good about things falling in line. Those good feelings vanished when my eyes landed on Court, strolling down the sidewalk dressed in a classic black suit with a bouquet of red roses in his hands. He passed an oblivious Todd, but Court's face was hard and unreadable. I wanted to cry or disappear into a puddle on the hot sidewalk as each of his long strides brought him closer.

"Hey," he said gruffly, pulling at his tie.

"Let me explain. It's not what you think," I started, but he held up a hand.

"Just let me say something first."

I motioned for him to come inside and he did, handing me the roses and then hovering in the entryway.

"There are probably a million reasons why he's the better guy, but you can't be with him. He's better on paper, but I'm better for *you*." He ran a hand through his hair. "Do you remember the first time we met on the plane?"

"Of course."

"You asked me what it took for a woman to get my attention. Do you remember that?"

"Yes," I said, the trepidation clear in my voice.

"I think I knew the answer even then, but I just wasn't willing to accept that some woman I met on a plane could knock me on my ass with one look. It was you. You were what it took to get my attention. I took one look at you in your sparkly shoes and electric blue eyes and I fell for you. I didn't want to believe it was possible, but I think I've loved you from the minute I saw you. You were so sincere, honest, beautiful, and completely true to yourself. I told you to be something other than that and I'm sorry. I never should have let you do that. Not for some other guy and not for me. I love you. YOU, 8B."

He looked like he wanted to say more, but he didn't, and silence filled the house as I watched emotion and love distort his beautiful face.

"I love you, too."

His head snapped up and his eyes locked with mine. "You do?"

"Duh," I said and wrapped my arms around his neck. "Which is exactly what I just told Todd. He wished us well."

Court's eyebrows raised in disbelief. "You did?"

"I left out your name in case he's a secret spy sent by your father, but yeah. I don't want Todd or anyone else, just you. I'm sorry I didn't tell you sooner."

A cocky grin took over his face and he wrapped his arms around my waist and buried his face into my neck. "My little, 8B. All mine."

He pulled back, mischief and trouble written all over his face. "Have time for a naked fashion show?"

EPILOGUE

Court

I was sweating through my shirt, the jewelry box in my pocket starting to feel heavy. All the events leading up to this had been easy. Deciding when and how to propose, buying the ring, even planning out the things I wanted to say as I asked Bianca to marry me had come naturally.

In the six months that we'd been officially dating, I'd left no question about my intentions of marrying her and keeping her forever. But planning out your life with someone was a lot different than asking your girlfriend's father if he approved of you enough to allow you to take over his number one responsibility – taking care of his kid.

I didn't take that responsibility lightly. He hadn't taken it lightly either. All his children had grown up watching him love their mother unconditionally – in sickness and in health. He had provided for their family financially, and most importantly had been a steady and reliable fixture in their lives. Each of his kids loved him and looked up to him and he'd earned that.

I wasn't nervous about being that person for Bianca. I'd give anything for her. She'd blossomed in the short time I'd known her. Come into her own and found her way. And I loved her more every day. No matter who she decided to be or what changes life brought us. There was no version of her I wouldn't love.

But I was nervous her father wouldn't see all the things in me he needed in order to feel comfortable that I'd be able to provide and love his daughter for the rest of our lives. I was ready to make my case, though.

"Mr. Winters." I cornered him in the back yard. Bianca and her mother were at the store getting groceries for our Sunday dinner and the boys were lounged out in front of the TV inside.

"Court," he lowered the newspaper and smiled. "How many times do I have to tell you to call me Glenn?"

"Glenn," I said and took a seat across from him on the wicker patio furniture.

"Beautiful day out." He looked up to the blue sky as if he'd just noticed and folded the newspaper and sat it on the table. He leaned back and pulled his coat tighter around his midsection. The sun might have been shining bright, but the late winter temperatures were still brutal.

I nodded. I couldn't think of a single thing to say about the weather.

"I wanted to talk to you."

A flash of concern crossed his face, but it was gone quickly. "Of course. Everything okay?"

"Yes. Things are really great. Actually, I wanted to talk to you about Bianca. I know we've just been dating a short time, but I'd like your blessing to ask her to marry me." I pulled out the ring box and sat it on the table.

His eyes were glued to the box and every second of silence felt like an eternity.

"I love your daughter, sir. I'd do anything for her, for any of you. I didn't have a traditional family like this growing up, but I promise I'll do my best to give her everything she wants and needs. You may think it's crazy to propose this fast, but I've been as patient as I can. I was ready to propose six months ago."

I had other things I'd planned to say, but I stopped and waited for him to say something. Anything. If he had questions, I'd answer them. If he had concerns, I'd tell him how they weren't justified.

"I proposed to Lucy on our third date. I didn't have a ring, I hadn't asked her father – hell, I hadn't even thought it through. I just knew I needed her. Love makes people do crazy things, but you and Bianca... that's not crazy. She loves you. You've made her happier than I can ever remember her being. That's all I want for her and for you."

I let out a breath I hadn't realized I held. "Thank you. That means a lot."

Lucy called out from the house as she and Bianca returned, and Glenn and I stood. I tucked the ring back into my pocket and he placed a hand on my shoulder. "Welcome to the family, son."

He pulled me into a hug and I let him envelop me and found my arms moving up to embrace him back before I'd even thought about doing it. Family. I'd finally found my family.

This had always been part of the deal with Bianca. She held her family close and I'd known there was no way to be with her without loving them, too. And I did. They'd all become important to my life. Even Donnie, who had been the hardest to get to know, felt like family. But Mr. Winter had given me something I didn't realize I'd needed. He'd become the male role model, father-figure, I'd never had. I'd thought I'd outgrown the need for such a thing, but he continued to teach me things about family and love and I couldn't wait to see what was next.

Bianca

Things I'd learned about Court Adams:

1. He was smart. Like, really smart. He'd always teased me about my book smarts, but Court was a knowledgebase on every subject. Sports, Pop Culture, History, Arts – his brain was sexy.

2. His brain wasn't the only thing that was sexy. Okay, I already knew this, but my new favorite thing was lying in bed on Saturday mornings and exploring his body. Every hard line.

3. He was romantic. He sent me flowers to work every week and planned elaborate date nights showing me parts of the city I didn't even know existed.

4. He loved my family. I knew bringing him into my family would be hard on him, but he'd taken it in stride. He always showed up – birthdays, doctor appointments with my mom (he was a saint for this

alone), Donnie and Leo's school events, even Sunday dinners.

5. He loved me. He never left any room for me to question his feelings. He told me every day, he showed me in every touch, every look, and every word that came out of his beautiful mouth. His love was shown in ways I hadn't expected, too. He was adamant that I get to experience everything. When I'd suggested living together he'd told me no, that he wanted to wait until we were married. When I'd told him, I couldn't wait to get married and have kids, he'd told me there was plenty of time for all that and I should enjoy being young.

I mulled over all the amazing things about my boyfriend as I helped my mom wash the dishes from our Sunday dinner. The boys, dad, and Court were all outside on the patio. I could hear hushed whispers and laughter as I rinsed plates.

"What are they doing out there?" I asked my mom with a curious glance.

She just smiled. "Your father has some ideas on how to renovate the patio this spring. They're probably talking about that."

"Donnie and Leo are talking home improvement? I doubt it," I said as I finished the last dish.

"Grab the wine and let's join them." She pointed to the half-empty wine bottle Court had brought over for dinner.

I grabbed it and my wine glass and followed my mother outside. It was early February and the winter chill hung in the air. The fire pit was lit, and the propane heaters were going, but I still hunched my shoulders up as the wind whipped around the small enclosure.

The men stilled as they spotted us joining them and then my brothers and dad parted away from Court.

"What's going on out here?" I asked hesitantly, stepping toward Court.

No one said a thing and I turned a circle looking at all their faces. My mother had joined my father and she wore a giddy smile as my father wrapped an arm around her shoulders and drew her into his chest. Leo and Donnie had matching conspiratorial smirks like they were in on some big secret and happy to be privy to something I wasn't.

When I turned my gaze back to Court, he held a small red box in one hand and reached out his other to me.

I barely registered the sound of my mother whimpering over my own gasp. "Oh my God."

Leo appeared at my side, taking the wine and glass so my hands were free. With tears building in my eyes and my heart beating rapidly in my chest, I reached for Court. He smiled down at me with a cocky grin, but I felt the hint of nervousness in the firm grasp he had on my hand.

"I think you're probably getting tired of me telling you how much I love you and what you mean to me, but since I only plan to do this once in my lifetime you'll have to forgive my selfishness in doing this the way I want. And Bianca, I want to tell you I love you. I want to tell you now and tomorrow. In front of your family, our friends, and random strangers I pass on the street. I never thought that I'd have someone like you in my life. I didn't think I deserved it. Even now as I ask you to spend the rest of your life with me, I wonder if you'll be settling by saying yes. But I desperately want you to say yes and let me spend the rest of my life loving you the best way I know how. You told me once that I made you feel electric, but you got it all wrong. You're electric, 8B."

Everything you touch sparks and comes to life. That's what you did for me – you brought me to life and I want to spend what's left of that life with you. Will you marry me?"

I didn't pull my eyes away from Court as he got down on one knee and opened the jewelry box. I didn't look at the ring, I didn't look to my mother whose cries of joy rang out into the evening, or at Donnie and Leo who were snickering like school girls. I kept my eyes on Court's when I said yes because he was all that mattered. He breathed out a sigh of relief and stood and took my mouth with his. And it was there – voltage and current and *love*.

No more shuffling my feet, no more cursing the failed attempts. Current flowed from him to me and arced. An electric discharge that glowed. That was what Court and I had. Love framed in an electric blue glow.

THE END

Thank you for reading Electric Blue Love.
If you want more of Court and Bianca,
sign up to receive a bonus scene:
https://www.subscribepage.com/electricbluelovebonus

ACKNOWLEDGEMENTS

THERE ARE SO many people to thank for this book. First and foremost, to my author partner in crime, Ann. I had this little idea about writing a novella with these characters and she pushed me to make it a full-length novel. Thank you for seeing that these characters had more to say even before I did!

To Amy & Devyn for taking me in and giving me all your love and support.

To Jill for answering a million questions every time I get ready for a release. You're amazing!

To Jennifer for editing and Jena for another amazing cover and for dealing with my neurotic and indecisive design decisions.

Thank you to my awesome beta readers: Aisha, Brooke, Heather, Louise, Michelle, Mary, and Sara. To my critique partners Amanda & Iva. <3 Bonus thanks to Amy for content editing this first – your advice was so spot on and I really think it made this book so much stronger.

To my daughter, Audree, who is my number one fan and

most loyal cheerleader. My husband and son, my dad, my sister, and the many friends and family who support me not only on release day, but every day.

To my reader group – you guys are totally rad!

And as always, to my angel mother.

NEVER MISS
A THING

Sɪɢɴ ᴜᴘ ʜᴇʀᴇ to be included on Rebecca Jenshak's mailing list! You'll receive new release alerts, get access to bonus materials and exclusive giveaways, and hear about sales and freebies first!

https://www.subscribepage.com/rebeccajenshaknewsletter

ALSO BY
REBECCA JENSHAK

ABOUT THE AUTHOR

Rebecca Jenshak is a self-proclaimed margarita addict, college basketball fanatic, and Hallmark channel devotee. A Midwest native transplanted to the desert, she likes being outdoors (drinking on patios) and singing (in the shower) when she isn't writing books about hot guys and the girls who love them.

Made in the USA
Columbia, SC
07 July 2022

62879633R00183